Not a Chance in Hell

The Chances
Book 6

Emily E K Murdoch

ARE YOU SIGNED UP FOR DRAGONBLADE'S BLOG?

You'll get the latest news and information on exclusive giveaways, exclusive excerpts, coming releases, sales, free books, cover reveals and more.

Check out our complete list of authors, too!

No spam, no junk. That's a promise!

Sign Up Here

www.dragonbladepublishing.com

Dearest Reader;

Thank you for your support of a small press. At Dragonblade Publishing, we strive to bring you the highest quality Historical Romance from some of the best authors in the business. Without your support, there is no 'us', so we sincerely hope you adore these stories and find some new favorite authors along the way.

Happy Reading!

CEO, Dragonblade Publishing

Additional Dragonblade books by
Author Emily E K Murdoch

The Chances Series
A Fighting Chance (Book 1)
A Second Chance (Book 2)
An Outside Chance (Book 3)
Half a Chance (Book 4)
A Chance in a Million (Book 5)
Not a Chance in Hell (Book 6)
An Eye for the Chance (Book 7)

Dukes in Danger Series
Don't Judge a Duke by His Cover (Book 1)
Strike While the Duke is Hot (Book 2)
The Duke is Mightier than the Sword (Book 3)
A Duke in Time Saves Nine (Book 4)
Every Duke Has His Price (Book 5)
Put Your Best Duke Forward (Book 6)
Where There's a Duke, There's a Way (Book 7)
Curiosity Killed the Duke (Book 8)
Play With Dukes, Get Burned (Book 9)
The Best Things in Life are Dukes (Book 10)
A Duke a Day Keeps the Doctor Away (Book 11)
All Good Dukes Come to an End (Book 12)

Twelve Days of Christmas
Twelve Drummers Drumming
Eleven Pipers Piping
Ten Lords a Leaping
Nine Ladies Dancing
Eight Maids a Milking
Seven Swans a Swimming
Six Geese a Laying

Five Gold Rings
Four Calling Birds
Three French Hens
Two Turtle Doves
A Partridge in a Pear Tree

The De Petras Saga
The Misplaced Husband (Book 1)
The Impoverished Dowry (Book 2)
The Contrary Debutante (Book 3)
The Determined Mistress (Book 4)
The Convenient Engagement (Book 5)

The Governess Bureau Series
A Governess of Great Talents (Book 1)
A Governess of Discretion (Book 2)
A Governess of Many Languages (Book 3)
A Governess of Prodigious Skill (Book 4)
A Governess of Unusual Experience (Book 5)
A Governess of Wise Years (Book 6)
A Governess of No Fear (Novella)

Never The Bride Series
Always the Bridesmaid (Book 1)
Always the Chaperone (Book 2)
Always the Courtesan (Book 3)
Always the Best Friend (Book 4)
Always the Wallflower (Book 5)
Always the Bluestocking (Book 6)
Always the Rival (Book 7)
Always the Matchmaker (Book 8)
Always the Widow (Book 9)
Always the Rebel (Book 10)
Always the Mistress (Book 11)
Always the Second Choice (Book 12)
Always the Mistletoe (Novella)
Always the Reverend (Novella)

The Lyon's Den Series
Always the Lyon Tamer

Pirates of Britannia Series
Always the High Seas

De Wolfe Pack: The Series
Whirlwind with a Wolfe

Noble titles throughout English history have, at times, been more fluid than one might think. Women have inherited, men have been gifted titles by family or gained them through marriage, and royals frequently lavished titles or withdrew them as reward and punishment.

The elder Chance brothers in this series agreed to split the four titles in their family line during the Regency era, rather than the eldest holding all four. It is a decision that defines their brotherhood, and their very different personalities.

Now with the next generation, one Chance father has allowed his son to inherit his title before his own demise, echoing kings and queens who have abdicated their titles throughout history. Perhaps his brothers, the uncles of this next generation, will follow suit...

Get ready to meet a family that is more than happy to scandalize Society...

Chapter One

March 5, 1840

"THAT'S IT!" LILIANNA threw up her hands and suppressed a smile. "I'm not going!"

Various groans rang out in the large hall at her pronouncement—which she'd known would happen. But still. It was so much more amusing to toy with them.

"Lil, you promised—"

"I'm *never* going to get my chance to go to a ball and dance with a—!"

"I will make her. If we all try together, we can force her into the carriage. Take an arm—"

Expertly sidestepping her siblings' attempts to force her toward the door, Lilianna allowed a small chuckle to escape her lips.

Well, really. They were all so obsessed with her attending these balls. She knew why, of course, but there was no need for them to be so blatant about it.

A middle-aged genteel woman pushed forward carrying a giant, white feather in the air above her head like a dagger she was about to bring down on an unsuspecting person. She seemed unsurprised by the chaos unfolding around her. "Out of the w-way, I'm t-trying to—"

"Leave off, it's Mama," said Samuel, pulling Benjamin back.

Lilianna stuck her tongue out at her two brothers, which only encouraged Benjamin to launch forward and Samuel to steady his grip.

"Come on. Mama will get her out of the door," said the eldest of her brothers with a shake of his head and a smirk rather like Lilianna's own. "If anyone can, it's her."

He wasn't wrong, though Lilianna did not particularly wish to admit it. Florence Chance, Marchioness of Aylesbury, was one of the gentlest, kindest, and most compassionate people Lilianna had ever met. And Lady Aylesbury was Lilianna's mother. Most people would envy the daughter of such a lady.

And Lilianna did love her, obviously. But still, she was so… so… so placid.

Nothing like her eldest daughter at all.

"I don't want another feather, Mama," Lilianna said, dodging her mother's fussing attempts to continue her adornment.

"B-But everyone w-will…"

Their mother halted, her tongue tying itself in knots as it so often did, and her four children fell silent.

Lilianna watched, her affection for her mother always strongest when she was struggling to articulate her words. Fifty years of age, and she still found it astonishing that her aunts and other ladies' mothers spoke as clear as a bell.

Yet she wouldn't change Florence Chance for all the tea in China.

Her mother fixed her with a stern look, which was a surprise in and of itself. "Y-You must be perfect. You m-must always be p-perfect! Everyone w-will be looking their b-best. To catch a—"

"Husband," chorused both Lilianna's brothers and her sister, Frank.

Perfect. Yes, Lilianna was well aware what her family expected of her. Perfection. Well, she could be perfect.

Frank rolled her eyes, sticking her hands in the pockets of her trousers—trousers her father had only yesterday forbidden her to wear. "Honestly, Mama, we know! We know you want Lil to marry, we know how important it is that her marriage is to the right sort of man—"

"*Any* man would be the right sort, at this point," muttered Samuel.

Lilianna whacked him on the arm unceremoniously.

"Ouch! Damn, Lil, that hurt!"

Their mother's face drained of color. "D-Don't swear in front of—"

"Frank knows far better curses than I do, don't you, Frank?" Samuel grinned.

Lilianna sighed as she accepted the feather from her mother and listened to her sister squabbling with their brothers. Again. One would hardly know Frank—or Francesca, to those who wished to die a terrible death—was nineteen.

Really!

"It's evidently a good thing you're not coming with me, if you can't learn to behave like a lady," Lilianna said serenely, pulling on her pelisse.

Frank snorted. "What, you mean like you?" She stuck her tongue out, waggling it this time in a clear reference to Lilianna's rudeness.

Lilianna rolled her eyes. "I am the eldest daughter. I can do no wrong."

Which wasn't entirely true. In fact, the whole reason the family was so worked up tonight was because of her, was it not? Her inability—no, that wasn't quite the right word... Her *insistence* that she would not be marrying any of the hoi polloi who asked her.

Though it wasn't as though she had been inundated with offers. Just five.

Then again, one of the Miss Quintrells was the second-most popular lady and she had only received three. So perhaps Lilianna should have been happy with her handful.

"—b-be late, and then w-what will p-people—"

"I could not care less what people say, Mama," said Lilianna grandly, pulling on her gloves, perhaps more confidently than she felt.

You must be perfect.

Benjamin, with his dark hair and dark eyes already a great temptation for the ladies of Society, snorted. "Well, you should! It's our Chance name that you're ruining—"

"'*Ruining*'? By having standards?" Lilianna scoffed, adjusting her diamond necklace and glancing at herself in the looking glass hanging by the door.

It showed a tall, young lady with a straight, aquiline nose and gray eyes, which her mother had once said changed with the weather. Her figure was passably good, her complexion fair, and she knew how to dress for both. A compassionate modiste had assisted in styling her in gowns that accentuated rather than hid her curves, and in this light-gray silk gown, which was just a few inches too long for her—

"Lord Zouch is a perfectly good match," said Samuel.

"Lord Zouch is a bore, and a drunk, and he has a cousin who is far more charming," Lilianna said serenely, speaking over her brother without turning to look. "I'd sooner marry the younger than the elder."

"Then why don't you consider his br—"

"I'd rather marry neither of them. I keep telling you, Samuel, I see no need to merely marry because I can," Lilianna said sternly, turning to glare—to glare at them all. It was time they all heard this, though it was hardly the first time she was saying it. "I am a Chance. I have standards, expectations—"

Frank rolled her eyes. "We're *all* Chances."

Lilianna glared at her younger sister. "Then why don't *you* go and get married?"

"You know your sister cannot attend many Society functions until you yourself are married," said a new voice to the medley, calm and quiet and yet with a confidence that no one else in the family had. "You know that, Lil. Other families may feel otherwise, but that is one rule the Chances do not ignore."

She sighed as her father entered the hall.

Well, excellent. Now I am truly outnumbered.

Her father was a tall man with hair graying in parts, and a look of mischievousness that some people took for carelessness. They had the same fine fingers and the same ear for music, the same carefree spirit. But there was no one who cared for his family more than John Chance, Marquess of Aylesbury. And that meant marrying off his daughters.

"I don't suppose you are accompanying me this evening?" Lilianna said smoothly.

He wasn't. She could tell by the utter lack of care he and his valet had given to his attire. No Chance would consider attending one of Lady Romeril's balls with that cravat.

Her father smiled. "No, that is your mother's punishment this time."

Lilianna opened her mouth in mock outrage. "How dare you? I assure you, being in my company is a delight!"

"I see," said the Marquess of Aylesbury with a grin. "And how, exactly, have you delighted your siblings so far this evening?"

She looked around. Frank was looking irritable and mulish, her arms crossed. Samuel was still rubbing his arm where she had whacked him—with cause. But probably harder than she ought. Benjamin was looking around at them, but he seemed most concerned about their mother, who had pursued lips and was standing by the door, her fingers on the handle.

Lilianna sighed. "I just don't want a fuss, that's all."

Which was only half the truth. Being made a fuss of, that was wonderful. Being fussed *over*, that was her personal vexation.

And ever since she had reached her twenty-first birthday, there had been far more fussing about her prospects than delightedly fussing over her company.

A prickle of discomfort curled around her. And she wasn't *that* old. Not really.

"Cousin Maude is far older than I," she said quietly. "And she is unwed."

Her mother and father exchanged a look. It was a look that said, *I told you that she would bring this up.* The answering reply was something along the lines of, *I didn't say she wouldn't. I said we didn't want to have to argue about it.*

That was the lot of an eldest daughter. Eventually, Lilianna would be expected to go off and get married to some poor idiot who'd had the good sense to ask her, and then she would go off and be bored in his house instead of in her own, providing him with one baby after another at his request.

Was that all there was? Was that truly all life could offer?

"Cousin M-M-Maude is different," her mother said finally. "She doesn't have any sisters."

"Oh, don't worry about me," Frank said darkly. "I'm not allowed my own toolbox, so what does a ball matter to me?"

She was ignored.

"That is just the way Society is," their father said with a heavy sigh. "I cannot pretend to understand it, Lil."

"Well then, why not—"

He held up a hand. "But that is the way it is, and there's no arguing with me about it. I can't change it," he said fairly. Far too fairly, in Lilianna's opinion. "I never had sisters, so I cannot understand the whole thing."

"So why not let me—"

"I am telling you to go to that ball and make your mother proud," John Chance said quietly. "Is it really that difficult?"

Lilianna pursed her lips. *No, not difficult.* Not difficult, per se. She was outstanding in balls—dancing beautifully, conversing lightly, never letting any particular gentleman believe that he had monopolized her, but making every conversational and dance partner feel special.

It wasn't difficult. Just dull.

"No, Papa," she said quietly.

For the briefest of moments, her father placed a hand on her shoulder and grinned. "I know you can do this."

But do I want to? Lilianna wanted to cry. *Can you not all see just how repetitive this all is? London, Bath, the country, London, Bath, the country—round and round we go, seeing the same people, eating the same food. Do you not all want something… something else?*

"Now, I want you to promise me one thing," said her father sternly.

Lilianna stiffened as she saw her siblings stare over their father's shoulder. Promise? Promises were something that the Chances—at least, this branch of the family—took incredibly seriously. A promise was never requested without the expectation that it would, no matter what, be fulfilled.

"Promise?" she repeated warily.

Her father winked. "Don't get engaged the moment you enter the ball."

A laugh escaped her before she could stop it as Frank said, "Why on earth not? If she can finally find a man she likes…"

"Yes, well, that is rather the problem, isn't it?" quipped Samuel with a laugh. "First it was Lord Zouch—"

Benjamin cut him off. "She saw him off quickly enough."

Lilianna glared, but plainly, she was out of practice because her brothers continued.

"And then Lord Hastings," said Samuel.

"Then that earl, what was his name?" pondered Benjamin.

"I heard that Mr. Lennox had considered offering but was scared off."

"Then Lord Zouch *again*, poor fellow."

"There's one that we're missing, though," her eldest brother, Samuel, said pensively. "Who was it again? Began with a P…"

This time, it was her parents who chorused, "The Right Honorable Henry Ponsonby-Jentham!"

"Yes, that was it." Samuel grinned. "And you didn't fancy becoming the Right Honorable Lady Lilianna Ponsonby-Jentham?"

Lilianna grimaced. "That's not how that works."

"Our family is hardly conventional in that manner. You, too, could be a right honorable."

"I'll give you a *right honorable* in a—"

"And th-that means it's t-time to go," interrupted their mother with a smile.

Ever the peacemaker, Lilianna thought with a guilty twinge. And their mother so often had to be, at the moment.

The marquess cleared his throat. "Now, do I have your promise, Lil?"

For a moment, she hardly remembered what on earth her father was talking about. Then she laughed. "What, to not get engaged the moment I enter the ball? I think I can safely say, Papa, that I won't be getting engaged tonight at all."

All three of her siblings groaned.

"Will we ever be rid of her?" Samuel asked with a dramatic sigh.

It really was unfair of them all to put this pressure on her. Besides, two could play at that game. "Why doesn't Samuel have to marry?"

"Now, then, no delaying tactics," her brother said hastily with reddening cheeks as he stepped forward to open the door. "Out you go."

"Yes, I really do think, as Papa's heir—"

"Out, out, out!" Samuel said loudly.

"See if you can k-keep the others out of t-trouble for one evening," said Florence Chance sedately, kissing their father on the cheek.

Lilianna had to look away—the expression of devotion between her parents was so excruciating—so she heard instead of saw her father's response.

"Just so long as you know I'll be waiting for you when you get back…"

Stepping into the balmy night and almost tripping over her long hem—she really must ask Clarke to take it in—Lilianna attempted to scrub the recollection of what her father had said from her mind. *Well, really!* It was probably a good sign that her parents were still… well… affectionate. But that didn't mean that she wanted to hear the evidence!

The carriage was waiting, the horses stamping in the cold, evening air. A footman opened the door for her and she pulled a blanket over her knees as she settled on the seat.

Her mother joined her within a moment, cheeks pink and clearly delighted by her husband's affection.

Lilianna looked away. *Dear Lord.*

"You know, m-marriage is not s-so terrible."

That caught Lilianna's attention. It was rare that her mother ever attempted to truly persuade her eldest daughter to wed, for which Lilianna was grateful. So what had changed? Why was the whole family so determined to marry her off?

"I did not say marriage was terrible," Lilianna said quietly as the carriage launched forward and the sound of hooves echoed in the night air. "When it works, when the two people truly care for each other… I mean, look at you and Papa."

Her mother glowed with happiness, even in the gloom of the carriage. "M-Marrying for love—"

"I know, I know, it's incredibly rare." Lilianna huffed, turning from her mother to look out of the window. Nothing could be seen, the sun having set hours ago. "It's just… Well. All the Chances have married for love so far."

Which was terribly unusual, she knew. There simply weren't that many love matches made every Season, yet her father, and all three of her father's brothers—and now her cousin Thomas— had all wed the brides of their dreams. Nothing had halted their love stories, and that was all very well… but Lilianna had attended four Seasons now. Countless balls, dances, dinners, afternoon teas, picnics, rides, hunts. The sheer amount of croquet she had played meant she was probably qualified to *teach* the wretched pastime.

And yet not a single gentleman who had crossed her path had been worthy.

"Lady Romeril said—"

Lilianna groaned. "Lady Romeril is part of the past, Mama!

No one truly cares what she thinks."

Which wasn't completely true. Lady Romeril had been a... a doyenne of Society for as long as Lilianna could remember. She'd overheard her aunts once discussing with her mother whether or not Lady Romeril would continue to host her annual ball, and one of them had said that Lady Romeril had been hosting the ball for over forty years, and only death would end it. Perhaps not even then.

"Besides, Lady Romeril always has the most terrible guest list," she pointed out to her mother as the carriage lurched to one side, taking a corner at a high speed. "She always chooses the people she thinks will create the most scandal—"

"Th-That's not entirely... Well..."

"—and she tries to get people into... into awkward situations." Lilianna swallowed. "Not that she has ever maneuvered me into such a thing, naturally."

No one ever was going to find out about that. The audacity of Mr. Lister attempting to corner her in that drawing room, the very idea that she would even think of him as a potential suitor!

The man's black eye had caused a great amount of comment the next day, apparently. Lilianna had refrained from noting it.

"You are so b-beautiful, and—"

Lilianna snorted. "You *have* to say that. You're my mother."

"Lil."

Sighing heavily, Lilianna turned to her mother, who was beaming.

"I m-may have to say it," said Florence with a mischievous grin, rarely seen on the shy woman's face, "but I don't have to th-think it. And I do. Your b-beauty is more than skin deep. You are ch-charming."

Charming. Yes, that was what the Society pages had described her as when she had come out as a debutante. Charming.

It was just another word for *unusual*, and Lilianna knew it.

So, she had opinions. So, those opinions were rather lofty. She thought a lot of herself, her family, their position in the world—and why not? They were the Chances!

"No one wants a charming wife, Mama," Lilianna said softly.

Her mother frowned. "Of course they do."

"Anyone who has proposed to me so far has only done so because they want to marry into the Chance family—and do not attempt to tell me that it's not true," she said firmly. "Because it is."

The carriage rattled along the Bath streets, lights flashing past them now. When was it that the gas lamps had been put in on this part of town? Lilianna could hardly remember, but they had made a great difference to the way the place looked at night.

"F-Family name is, alas, s-still important…"

"Not for most people. Most people have no respect," Lilianna said sternly, as though it had been her mother who had been outrageously rude. "They treat me sometimes like I'm a nobody! The modern world has a great deal to offer us young ladies, but still—the cheek!"

She'd been refused a table at Don Saltero's Chelsea Coffee House only yesterday. Refused! A Chance! And she had given her name, making sure to enunciate it clearly, and the man had just looked blank and repeated the fact that no tables were available.

"I c-cannot pretend to understand this m-modern world of yours," said her mother quietly.

Lilianna sighed. "Before we know it, ladies will be gallivanting about without chaperones."

She still could not decide if she liked the idea or not. It was a change to the rules, the rules she had studied so hard and perfected over the years. It was outrageous that others could simply walk over them and pretend they did not matter.

But on the other hand, being able to attend gatherings without her mother or father or Clarke present, the freedom to walk wherever she wanted, visit any place she liked…

"I s-suppose I would then n-not have to venture out at n-night to k-keep you company."

And with that phrase, all the anger and bitterness in Lilianna drained away.

There was nothing Florence Chance hated more than venturing out in public, Lilianna knew—all her children did. She was a true wallflower, one who grew best at home.

And she was coming out here to help Lilianna find a husband. Her selfishness melted and only guilt was left behind.

"I know you don't want to be here, Mama."

"I d-didn't say—"

"And I will try to uphold the Chance name," Lilianna continued, feeling in a way as though she were promising something. "I will do my best to shine at this ball, and though I can't promise to allow Lady Romeril to maneuver me into a scandalous position—"

"Heaven f-forbid!"

"—I will…" Lilianna closed her eyes, took in a deep breath, and opened them again to see her mother suppressing a smile. "I will attempt to give every gentleman I encounter a fair opportunity to… impress me."

For want of a better word.

The carriage was slowing, drawing to a halt outside a building from which music and chatter emanated.

Her mother nodded. "G-Good. Let's go in, sh-shall we?"

Just be perfect.

Lilianna had no time to say anything else before the door nearest her was opened. Her mother frowned as she tugged on the skirt of her dress. One of the adornments on the silky material, a pearl broach with gold spikes, had caught between the carriage's cushions. "G-Go on," she said. "I'll be j-just a moment."

Stepping forward, Lilianna intended to descend in a rush of silks and feathers, emerging like a princess onto a royal stage, dazzling those who were also arriving at Lady Romeril's ball at the same time and amazing them with her elegance.

She didn't. The hem of her skirt got caught on the step, gravity suddenly lurching forward. The world was spinning and Lilianna was falling, falling… She was going to fall face-first on the pavement and disgrace the name of—

Strong hands. A steadiness, a balance in the world. Heat, and pressure around her.

Lilianna swallowed. She was horizontal, parallel to the ground, caught in the arms of—

A gentleman smiled down. He was the most handsome man she had ever seen: almost overpowering in his good looks, a roguish grin creasing the corners of his mouth and his eyes dancing dangerously.

"Well," the gentleman said, his voice honey and spices. "I suppose we will just have to get married, then."

Chapter Two

"**Y**OU ARE GOING to be late."

His butler's calm and collected voice was one of the few constants in the life of Arthur Nelson, Earl of Taernsby. Not that he was accustomed to that title yet.

"I am never late," said Arthur vaguely, sitting by his desk with his feet up beside the blotter.

Haslehaw cleared his throat, his strong chin elevated slightly in the air. "Lady Romeril was most insistent."

"Yes, I suppose she was," Arthur said sharply. "The woman cannot stay away from scandal and I suppose I would be an interesting catch for her. The rake who inherited an earldom."

Not that he considered himself a rake—quite the opposite. There was nothing rakish about bedding several women, one after another… Well. Perhaps he was a bit of a rake.

"I really do think it is time for you to leave, my lord," said the butler stiffly, his groomed, silver eyebrows arched just slightly. "I have had the carriage called around and—"

"I will go when I am ready, Haslehaw, and not before," said Arthur, his focus dropping to his letters. "That will be all."

The butler did not leave. In all honesty, Arthur had not expected him to. The man had been his brother's choice for butler and was very much his older brother's man even now, despite the most unfortunate accident.

Now Arthur had inherited title, lands, and apparently, the butler. Which made everything nice and awkward.

His gaze focused on the words before him and he groaned.

—never felt this way before and if you offered your hand in marriage, I would gladly accept—

Arthur cast it aside and picked up another one. This was from the youngest daughter of Sir Arnold Quintrell.

—heard the most strange rumor that you were not wishing to be wed, but I am sure you suggested—

Yes, he was sure he had *suggested*, Arthur considered with a wicked grin. But actually *said*—promised? Definitely not. His conquests were never given anything near such hope as that.

The rest of the letters were all the same. All written hastily, all on delicate paper with excellent penmanship—or rather, penwomanship—and all of them hoped he would come to call again. Privately. Without their fathers' knowledge.

Arthur sighed heavily as he collected all the letters from his previous lovers together. It was a shame they did not understand how fleeting his attentions were. Once sated, his appetites usually craved something of a different flavor.

After all, how could he be expected to eat from the same plate every night for the rest of his life?

"Burn these, would you?"

Haslehaw stepped forward with a frown. "His lordship—that is, the previous earl—kept his correspondence for at least three years."

"I am sure my brother did, but as he is dead and I am your lord now, I gave you an order," said Arthur tightly through gritted teeth.

He did not need to be reminded. He knew his brother was dead, the man who had been far better suited to this *earling about* than he was. The man everyone had liked and respected. Mostly.

"But how will you know how to reply?" His butler rapidly blinked.

Arthur sighed heavily. "I won't."

"But what reply will you send?"

"None."

Now both of Haslehaw's eyebrows were raised. "My lord, you will forgive me for saying so—"

"I suppose I will," said Arthur with a wry smile. "You know I am utterly dependent on you right now, Haslehaw. Being an earl is turning out to be a much more complicated business than I had imagined."

Not that he had ever given the role much thought. That had been his brother's burden to bear, and the two boys had grown apart as it had become more and more clear that Arthur's position as spare to the title meant that, to their father, his younger son may as well not have existed at all.

After all, Archibald had been here! He would marry, and have sons, and there would be no need to trouble the family with rehabilitating Arthur's dreadful reputation.

Until the accident.

"Look," Arthur said aloud, his thoughts meandering. "Who is the heir?"

His butler looked astonished. "I-I... I don't know what you mean, my lord."

"If I died, right now, through some sort of drunken orgy with a whole bedful of women," Arthur said calmly, enjoying the twisting discomfort that fluttered over the older man's face, "who would be the next person to step into this study and put his feet on the desk?"

Haslehaw swallowed. "No one."

Arthur waved a hand. "Come, come, now, I will not be offended. I know some lords probably find it difficult to accept that they will one day die and pass on the title to another, but there must be some distant cousin of whom I've never heard who—"

"There is no one, my lord, no other male in the Taernsby line," said the servant quietly. "Should you die, most unfortunately, and more unfortunately still before you have produced a male heir, the title would become extinct."

A cold shiver shot down Arthur's spine. "'Extinct'?"

It was inconceivable. There had been Earls of Taernsby ruining ladies and upsetting their neighbors for… well, hundreds of years. There was still debate about just when the earldom had been created, but the very latest date given was in the fourteenth century.

And he was about to be the last?

The butler spoke quietly. "I know his lordship, your brother, I mean, had given some thought to marriage."

"The bastard never got around to it, though," Arthur muttered. That would have made things far easier.

The butler cleared his throat. "Quite."

"Well, there's nothing for it then, is there?" Arthur said cheerfully. "I'll just have to marry—and soon, in case I die without the required heir and spare."

Haslehaw winced. "I would not quite put it like that…"

Probably not, thought Arthur ruefully, *but I'm not wrong*. This pile, the London townhouse, the morbid manor in Wiltshire where he had been born and raised—it all needed looking after. Preferably by servants, yes, but eventually, he would die and there had to be an heir.

And there was only one way to get one of those.

"I have to marry."

The butler blanched. "Tonight, my lord?"

"No, not tonight, don't be—" Arthur caught the man's eye and saw with astonishment the small smirk that denoted that the man had made a jest. "Good heavens. Well done, Haslehaw, you caught me completely unawares."

Haslehaw bowed. "Thank you, my lord."

"Right." Arthur blinked. *Now that was unexpected.* "So, I need to marry. I don't need to make a song and dance of it, do I? I mean, any woman will do. It doesn't actually matter who she is."

"I could not possibly comment, my lord," said the butler stiffly. He nodded to a servant standing just outside the door and a footman entered, holding out their master's greatcoat. "I wonder if there will be any eligible young ladies at Lady Romeril's ball. The ball you are late for."

Arthur had to give him credit for a conversation well-timed.

"I'll pick one at the ball and marry her," he said to Haslehaw five minutes later as the other servant helped the earl into his greatcoat by the front door. "Never fear!"

"Any woman will probably say *yes* to you, my lord," Haslehaw said quietly. "I have not heard that any woman has been able to say *no* to you."

Arthur grinned. "Damned straight."

So, he would select a bride at Lady Romeril's ball, marry her within the month, then they could get down to the important bit: creating heirs. He had a feeling he was going to like that bit.

"Yes, I'll just marry the first one who takes my fancy," he said aloud with a wink at the old man. Not any of the ladies who had written letters, though. He was bored of them already. "How hard can it be?"

As Arthur had expected, the ball was frivolous and packed. The sheer number of ladies on offer assaulted him, like stepping into a patisserie and not knowing how to stop engorging oneself.

Arthur exchanged a smile with a pretty, young thing who looked just right: quiet, innocent, flushing at the look of a man, so likely as not pliable. He took in those shapely arms. Potentially *very* pliable.

He had only taken two steps toward her, however, before a woman who looked suspiciously like the young lady's mother hurriedly stepped between them.

"My lord," the dour-faced woman said stiffly, bobbing a curtsey before shepherding away the wistful woman who had to have been her daughter.

Arthur halted in his steps and sighed. Well, if that was to be a sign of the things to come, perhaps it would be trickier than he'd thought to find a willing bride. But surely not every eligible woman here was accompanied by so sharp a mother…

Perhaps it would be easier to pick one off when they were entering the ball, rather than when already here. Yes, that was a good idea.

Arthur strode past the smoking room, one of the three card rooms that looked absolutely packed, and exchanged a wink with Lord Glenarm, a stout and flushed fellow who appeared bored to tears in the company of the lean and square-jawed Lord Zouch. Poor man. He couldn't help being so dull. Probably.

The cold, night air was refreshing and Arthur looked along the long street to catch a glimpse of those who were arriving. Lady Romeril only invited the very best, as ever, but there were always a few people who managed to find their way onto the guest list precisely because they would cause a stir.

Like himself, for example.

One carriage caught his eye. It was resplendent, unmistakably repainted recently and with feathered plumes on the horses' heads, which looked ridiculous.

It also, however, had a russet-and-gold crest painted on the doors.

Something jolted in Arthur's stomach as the memory of what that livery meant soared into his mind.

Of course. The Chance family.

Not a family he knew well. The Chances were far too prim and proper to have anything to do with the house of Taernsby. Especially not a reprobate like himself.

But there were several young ladies now of eligible age in that family, were there not?

Well, any one of them would do. It wouldn't make much difference which one it was. One lady was much the same as another.

Arthur watched with amusement as the footmen in Lady Romeril's livery hastened to the carriage. Evidently this was an eagerly anticipated arrival.

He moved quietly, his black, almost-midnight jacket making him invisible in the night air. Standing right beside the door, he waited to see which one would emerge. Not that he knew all their names, as there were far too many of them.

Would she be pretty? Would it matter?

Arthur made sure not to investigate that particular thought. He didn't have the luxury of hoping for a pretty one. A Chance bride with a Chance fortune and the Chance fertility would be more than enough.

The door opened. An elegant swish of skirts emerged.

Well, he liked what he saw so far. This was a woman with taste, the gray-pearl silver of the gown the height of fashion. And she—

She was stunning.

Arthur's chest heaved painfully as his pulse skipped a beat. Dear God, he hadn't known they made women like that anymore. Tall, and refined, and elegant, with a serious expression twisting her mouth and her eyes focused on—

She was falling.

Arthur did not think. He did not have to think. His instincts forced him forward before any of the waiting footmen seemed to notice that something was amiss.

Her gasp blossomed into the night air like a rose and Arthur caught her, his arms wrapping around her and pulling the Chance woman close to him.

And he kept her there. Somehow, time had ceased, stalling like a clock yet to be wound. Arthur looked down into the face that had so easily captivated him.

Saints alive, the woman must know how devastatingly arresting she is, mustn't she?

Her lips parted, her eyes wide, her cheeks flushed, and Arthur fought back the instinct to kiss her immediately and mark her as his own. This had to be done properly. At least, as properly as a rake from the Taernsby family could ever manage.

"Well," he said, ensuring his voice was pitched low, suggesting intimacy and connection from the start. "I suppose we will just have to get married, then."

It was not one of his best lines, but Arthur was rather proud of it, considering he'd had but a heartbeat to think.

She gazed up, lips still parted, and Arthur started to lower his head, welcoming the invitation. Oh, it would be sweet, indeed, to taste those plump—

A hand, a fist, a blazing shot of heat then pain.

"Dear God!"

Arthur almost dropped her, the surprise was so startling. For a moment, he could hardly understand what had happened, until he saw the woman shake her left hand. Her left fist.

The woman had—*punched him.*

"Release me, you dog!" she said sharply. "Unhand me at once!"

Unable to disobey her order, Arthur found himself righting her then stepping back. The sudden absence of her in his arms was painful, though arguably not as painful as the stinging mark on his cheek.

Heavens, she was going to leave a bruise. On *him*!

"Absolutely outrageous," the woman was muttering, smoothing her skirts with shaking hands. "Never expected anything so despicable."

Arthur stared, mouth open.

He couldn't help it. Well, he was hardly one of the best catches in the whole of the *ton*, but damnit, he came from a good family. Well, a good family that had fallen on hard times and even worse morals. But still. He was of the Taernsby line! He was a Nelson!

Moreover, he was good-looking. He knew it, had known it for years, ever since he had gone up to Cambridge and discovered that though his studies were dull, his provost's daughter had been far more interesting. And she had been interested in him. They all had been, all the ladies he'd encountered ever since. They liked his broad frame, the sharp edge of his cheekbones, the way he knew precisely what to say and how to touch…

But this woman—*this* woman, whom he had just rescued, for want of a better word, from a fate worse than death, for falling flat on one's face outside Lady Romeril's ball would undoubtedly end one's reputation… she had not flushed, or simpered, or even smiled.

The hussy had punched him in the face!

"I think perhaps you misheard me," Arthur heard himself saying, his voice still low and sweet and shadowy. "I said that I suppose we will just have to get married—"

"Absolutely not," the woman said sharply, taking a step away but not retreating.

Arthur stared, a frown creasing his forehead.

Well, that was rare. It was not often that he could be completely astonished. He had encountered most of what he considered possible in Society, and some of it more than once—but never before had a woman been so absolutely determined to reject him in every way possible!

He twisted his jaw, the ache in his cheek now throbbing up his temple. And the woman had a left hook that could have felled a lesser man.

Dear God, who is this woman?

"Lil?" Another woman, older and most definitely the younger's mother, was now emerging from the carriage. "Is anything am-miss?"

Ah, this must be Florence Chance. Arthur found himself relaxing, the tension that had sparked in his shoulder blades slowly receding. The shyest of the Chance matriarchs, from the little he had heard about them. It would not be too difficult to charm such a genteel lady.

"S-Step away from m-my daughter, or feel m-my wrath!" stammered the woman, stepping forward with her fists raised.

Arthur took a hasty step back. What on earth was going on? Wasn't the Chance family upstanding, respectable?

"I am quite all right, Mama. Please do not worry yourself," the young woman was saying.

"Lilianna, y-you almost fell!"

"But I did not fall, Mama, and I am quite well, I assure you."

Arthur stared, transfixed, at the exchange. Clearly, the mother, who though she must be nearing her fifties was still stunningly handsome, needed to be placated.

So this *was* Florence Chance, the Marchioness of Aylesbury? But wasn't she timid? At least, the gossip had always said so. Her manner of speech seemed to indicate she would be. So why was she acting as much a tigress as her daughter?

"This gentleman is just leaving," the woman who had to be Lady Lilianna Chance said coldly. "He has no further business with us."

And in that instant, something cracked open Arthur's heart and incited a flame he had never felt before.

He had never seen a woman more magnificent. More imperial, more imperious! She issued orders to a perfect stranger as though she had been obeyed all her life, and what was more, deserved to be.

Paired with a face like that, and a body he had felt pressed against his that had flared heat through his loins…

Arthur grinned. *Well, what do you know?* It wasn't falling in love, certainly, but it was more than lust. And that was all he needed. "Lady Lilianna, I think you should reconsider my proposal."

He had expected her to smile. He had expected her to flush. He had expected her to at the very least be polite.

Lady Lilianna snorted. "'Proposal'? Don't make me laugh, sir. Your arrogance does not suit you."

Some of his confidence melted into irritation. "You are very sure of yourself, aren't you, Lady Lil—"

"And you are very presumptuous, whoever you are, to address me before we have been introduced." Lady Lilianna looked him up and down with a blatant review. "And perhaps even then."

Arthur's mouth fell open. The ego of the woman! Could she not see that he was one of the most handsome men in the *ton*?

Perhaps it was too dark out here. Yes, that had to be it. Well, it did not matter. As soon as she was inside and saw the man she was treating so abominably, perhaps she would change her tune.

"You do not interest me. Go away," said Lady Lilianna carelessly, slipping a hand into the crook of her mother's arm and walking away.

Walking away. From him.

The entire world faded into the background. There was only him and Lady Lilianna Chance. The woman he would marry, come what may.

Almost stumbling over his own feet this time, Arthur hastened after them. He must have been standing there dumbstruck for quite a while, for when he entered the atrium of Lady Romeril's home, the two Chance women had already been divested of their pelisses and entered the ballroom.

Arthur grinned to himself. All the better. They would be able to see him clearly there, and he could turn on the charm and get Lady Lilianna Chance underneath him in three hours. Perhaps two, if he was lucky. There had to be copious bedchambers here.

He would ensure to be caught, scandal would abound, and they would be announcing their betrothal before the week was over.

"If you are following me in some pathetic attempt to attract my attention, please know that I am addressing you out of pity and nothing else."

Arthur's words caught in his throat.

Lady Lilianna was looking at him like…

Like he was nothing. Like he did not belong there. Like there was nothing more irritating to her than his presence.

And the fire that had always forced Arthur forward, always ensured he was in the center of the trouble and victorious in every fight, spurred him to speak. "Lady Lilianna, you appear to be under the misapprehension that I—"

"I honestly do not care," she said lightly, giving her mother what appeared to be a warning look. "Please go away and bother someone else."

Arthur stepped forward, stepped closer—far too close.

As Lady Aylesbury gasped in horror, Lady Lilianna merely

held his gaze. "You are bold, sir."

"I *am* bold. Because I know what I want," Arthur said quietly, fully conscious the entre ballroom was staring at them now. *Well, let them look.* They could all say that they were there when the Earl of Taernsby and his future countess first met. "And I want you, Lady Lilianna. Now. Marry me."

She snorted. It was not a very nice snort, and it was not the sort of response any man wanted to a proposal. Especially now he had done so, from his count, three times.

"You may be bold, yes, but I know what I am worth," said Lady Lilianna. Instead of lowering her voice and trying to keep their conversation private, as so many other women would, she had instead raised it.

Well, two could play that game.

"Oh, really?" Arthur arched a brow and leaned forward. Gasps rang out around them. "And what is that?"

"More than a random stranger who does not have the manners to wait for an introduction," she shot back.

Delight warmed Arthur's torso. *Oh, this woman.* He was going to enjoy bedding her. "In that case, I am elated to inform you that I am an earl."

A flicker of doubt in her eyes, a softening of her shoulders. Lady Lilianna had let go of her mother now and had squared up to him, but she suddenly seemed conscious that she was standing almost nose to nose with a complete stranger.

Not for long.

"The Earl," Arthur said grandly, "of Taernsby!"

He did not receive the reaction he'd expected.

Lady Lilianna laughed. *Laughed.* At him. Loudly, and in public. At Lady Romeril's ball.

"Taernsby? So you're a Nelson. Not a very impressive family, nothing to the Chances. Yes, the Nelsons, I've heard of you. That would make you the notorious rake," she said dismissively. "Such a shame. You were almost starting to interest me."

His heart sank. "But—"

"I said before and I shall say it again, and I really don't expect to have to say it a third time," Lady Lilianna said serenely, as though she declined proposals from earls every day of the week. "I know what I am worth, my lord, and you… you are not it."

She swept away, her mother sending him an ice-cold look before following after her.

It took Arthur a few heartbeats and a jagged breath wrenched from his lungs to realize the marquess's daughter was not coming back.

Lady Lilianna Chance, the first woman he had ever met to match him in wits and sarcasm, was… gone.

Whispers were echoing around the ballroom, growing louder as more and more people started to discuss the scene they had just witnessed.

Arthur ensured to hold his head high. Well, first point to Lady Lilianna, he had to admit—but it would be the last.

He would have her.

Chapter Three

March 6, 1840

I T WAS, ALL in all, not a night to remember.

Lilianna groaned as her maid pinned up the last of her curls. "What a night."

"I am sorry to hear that you did not have a good evening yesterday, my lady," said Clarke placidly.

Just three years older than herself, Clarke had been a stalwart guide through the complexities of Society when Lilianna had first come out, and she would be lost without her.

Her talent for hair would certainly look better, though.

"Have you... erm... read that pamphlet I gave you, Clarke?"

Her maid's bright eyes brightened in the looking glass reflection. "Oh, yes! I had no idea that there were so many modern ways to style a lady's hair nowadays! The maid who taught me was quite adamant a lady's hair should be just so."

Lilianna's shoulders slumped. Her previous lady's maid, who'd taught Clarke, had been decrepit, indeed. Even Clarke's own mousy, brown hairstyle would have better suited a grandmother. "And you haven't tried one of the newer styles today because...?"

"Well, I can't have you be my first attempt, can I now?" said her maid fairly, as though it were obvious. "I'm going to have to practice."

"Practice. On whom?"

Who precisely was going to be subjected to the learning attempts of Clarke was never discussed. At that moment, Lilianna's bedchamber door burst open and her sister yelled with something akin to mirth, "You've got to see it!"

Clarke dropped a pin and Lilianna tutted at her wayward sister. "Frank, honestly, you could knock."

"I said, *you've got to see it*, and I said so advisedly," said Frank, her shoulders shaking with laughter. There was a pencil stuck in her hair and ink smudges all over her fingers—fingers, Lilianna saw with a sigh, that were leaving marks all over her bedchamber door. "Now!"

Lilianna waved away her maid and rose to her feet, shaking her head ruefully. When Frank got something in her head there was absolutely no way to encourage her to think of anything else. The conversation had to be had, the design looked at, and a sufficient amount of praise given. Then, and only then, would Frank be able to talk on any other topic.

What was it to be today? A blueprint for a library? An engine designed to put out fires? Lilianna had been most impressed by her design for drying one's hair swiftly but had been immediately put off it when she'd realized one's entire head had to be placed in the thing.

When Frank had started talking about "prototypes" and "test subjects," Lilianna had been careful to avoid her eye.

"It's the most absurd thing I have ever seen," Frank was saying, her ink-splattered hands grabbing Lilianna's as she dragged her along the landing to the head of the staircase. "I don't know how you did it!"

"*I* did it?" Lilianna said, amused. "But I haven't done any… anything."

Words failed her as her sister pulled her down the staircase. When they were only halfway, it became clear what Frank had been talking about.

Roses. Roses, everywhere. Not a bunch of roses, or a bouquet of roses, though Lilianna wondered if that was how the effect was created.

No, this was *festoons* of roses. Roses covering every inch of the floor of the hall. Roses in vases everywhere. Red, and white, and yellow. Some were neatly budded and some were already in full bloom. The scent was overwhelming, the sensation giddy, and Lilianna almost tripped over the last few steps as she and Frank descended.

What on earth?

"I can't believe it," she breathed.

Frank giggled. "Believe it!"

"I suppose this is all your doing," said Samuel as he stepped out of the breakfast room and gingerly attempted to make his way through the maze of roses. His foot knocked a vase and it fell over, spilling flowers and water across the marble. "Oh, damn."

"I won't have that tone from you. You're seven and twenty and you know better," said their father, emerging from the library with a grin. "And speaking of knowing better, what on earth have you done to some poor young man, Lil?"

Lilianna flushed. "I haven't—I haven't done anything!"

Nothing that would require a response like this! Good lord, there must have been no other roses left in the whole of Bath.

A memory prickled at the back of her mind.

"I am bold. Because I know what I want. And I want you, Lady Lilianna. Now. Marry me."

She pushed it aside hurriedly. No, the irritating Earl of Taernsby would not have done anything so foolish. The man was a terrible flirt, yes, but from what she'd heard of his exploits, he was more in the deflowering business than the flower business.

"Frank, to whom have you been speaking?" Lilianna asked, turning on her sister.

Frank snorted. "I'm not even officially out, Lil. Whom do you think I've been talking to?"

Lilianna turned back to the flowers, her mind hardly able to take in their sheer number. Roses—everywhere. It was like something out of a dream. Like a page from a romantic novel.

This did not happen in real life, did it?

"I-I am v-very impressed, Lil," her mother said, emerging from the library and looking disheveled.

Disheveled?

Lilianna caught her father's glance at his wife and flinched. Did they have to be so obvious?

Then her mind caught up with her. "'Impressed'?"

"W-Well, you m-must have done s-something right," her mother said, gesturing at the sheer number of roses. "Wh-Why else would all th-this b-be here?"

"Morning, all. I thought I'd call on you and see if—heavens above!"

Lilianna whirled around, dreading the thought that someone from outside the family would find her here, surrounded by roses—but it was only Evelyn, her perennially paint-splattered cousin with her dark hair plaited and encircling her head like a coronet.

"Morning, Cousin," Evelyn said with a dry laugh, pecking her on the cheek and looking about her in wonder. "Who's the lucky man?"

"He's not *lucky*," Lilianna snapped. "I mean—"

"Poor sod, he's probably bankrupted himself," said Samuel conversationally, sitting on the stairs to avoid the roses. "And for *you!*"

Lilianna stuck her tongue out as Frank said, "Aha!"

"'Aha'?" Lilianna repeated, turning to her. "What do you mean, 'aha'?"

"I mean, aha, I've found the note!"

"This is the beginning of the end," her father was saying casually to her mother. "I never expected any gentleman to be this extravagant. I never was!"

"Yes, I kn-now," her mother teased with a grin.

Lilianna tried to take in a deep breath, but her lungs weren't working. This was all too overwhelming, all too much! This number of roses, it was obscene. It was nonsense. No sane man would have done such a thing.

"What does the note say?" her cousin asked eagerly, stepping forward.

Lilianna reached for the note, but it was too late. Frank had already opened it, grinning as her focus settled on the words before her.

"Oh, my!"

"Frank, give it to me," said Lilianna.

"I was the one who found it," said her younger sister immediately, their childhood rivalry returning as though it had been yesterday. "Finders keepers!"

"It's addressed to me, though, isn't it?" Lilianna persisted, unable to reach her sister because of the sheer plethora of vases around her feet. "Give it here."

"Read it out!" called their brother from the stairs.

It was all most irritating, and the worst of it was that Lilianna could hardly ignore the utter number of roses. It was like ignoring the sky. It was *there*.

"'My dearest Lilianna,'" Frank began.

"A promising start," muttered Cousin Evelyn with a wink.

"Frank, give it to me," said Lilianna through gritted teeth.

"'My dearest Lilianna, I was heartbroken we could not resolve our differences last night,'" Frank continued to read aloud, to much guffawing from their brother. "'I hope that this small token of my affection—'"

"'Small'?" muttered their father.

"'Affection'?" repeated Lilianna in amazement. Who on earth could have deluded himself so utterly to think that she would welcome this? Last night, she had spoken to no one of consequence. No one who... She swallowed.

Frank narrowed her eyes at the interruption. "'I hope that this small token of my affection will right any wrongs I may have accidentally committed,'" said Frank in a loud voice. "'Your very own, Taernsby.'"

Taernsby.

Lilianna's cheeks were burning as her family's laughter rang out around them.

"D-Dear me, I knew you h-had m-m-made an impression," said her mother gleefully. "Well d-done!"

Well done? How could her mother congratulate her on this—this spectacle? Had she not last night also seemed offended on her behalf? How quickly that man had managed to earn the marchioness's favor.

Perfection, that was what Lilianna had been expected to deliver: but this was surely far beyond anything a perfect daughter would be presumed to live up to?

"It's a joke!" And not a particularly amusing one, either, but Lilianna had to say it—it had to be true. Why else would the foolish man do something so… so…

"Oh, I don't know, he sounds smitten to me," teased Frank, a gleam in her eye. "Have you finally met your match, dear sister?"

"Not a chance in hell," Lilianna snapped, heat scalding her face.

"I think you like him," said Samuel with a grin. "Do you like him, Lil?"

"She doesn't *like* him, she loves him!" crowed Benjamin.

"Who?" said Cousin Evelyn bemused. "I still don't really understand who on earth this man is. The name sounds familiar, but…"

"He's a nobody!" Lilianna said sharply.

The hall quietened. Both of her parents were looking at her with that irritating knowing look that she hated, and Samuel was still grinning. Frank looked… well, more curious than anything else, and poor Cousin Evelyn was looking around her in bewilderment, as though she might be able to decipher the truth of who this man was from the copious flowers he had sent.

Lilianna tried to calm herself, but it was a mistake. Her nostrils filled with the overwhelming scent of the roses, piles of them, making her head spin and her temples ache.

This was outrageous. This was too much!

This had to be stopped.

"He's a rake," she snapped coldly. "A scoundrel, a seducer of ladies—"

"*Lilianna!*" her father chided.

"—who doesn't care a fig about what happens to them after he is done with them," said Lilianna, ignoring her father's exclamation. A door opened and shut behind her, but what did that matter? It was probably just Benjamin returning from whatever nonsense he had gotten up to. "The man is an utter joke, and so is this. I wouldn't expect anything more impressive from him, and this is not that impressive at all!"

"Lil," said her mother quietly.

"Honestly, Mama, you saw him! What an arrogant, igno-rant—"

"Lil," murmured Frank, even quieter than a whisper.

But Lilianna would not listen. Surely, her mother had seen just how ridiculously this Lord Taernsby, this *fool*, had acted at Lady Romeril's ball? And Frank, she hadn't even met him. She couldn't know what a rogue he was!

"I think I can quite definitively state that I have absolutely no interest in seeing this Taernsby fellow again," said Lilianna in a clear voice that rang out around the hall, roses and all. "And if he were here, I would tell him just the same thing!"

"Well," said a smug voice just behind her. "I suppose that saves you from having to repeat yourself."

Lilianna froze.

No. No, surely not. She had dreamt that voice, or she was so tired from the late night yesterday and she was imagining that it sounded just like…

Turning slowly on her feet, careful not to move them too much in case she knocked over one of the many vases littering the floor, Lilianna saw—

The Earl of Taernsby.

A curse that would have gotten her scolded by her father crept into her mouth, but Lilianna pursed her lips and prevented its escape.

Frank was not so controlled. "How the hell did he—"

"*Frank!*"

Lilianna tried to smile at the sudden outrage in both her parents' voices. She could always rely on Frank to distract her family. Not that she wanted a distraction right now. She wanted to escape.

He was far more handsome than she remembered, and she had been taken by his looks then. In the light of day, however, the Earl of Taernsby was devastatingly impressive. Far too alike one of the marble busts in the British Museum, he was tall, taller than her, dressed in that ruffled yet fashionable way that was starting to become a trend in the nobler set, and he had a smile on his face that told her two things.

First, that he had overheard almost all, if not all, of her speech… Fine, *tirade* against him.

Second, that he was delighted by it.

The latter irritated her far more than the former, and while the chatter behind her rose as her parents berated Frank for her rudeness, and Samuel attempted to intervene, Lilianna said in a low voice, "You have some nerve coming here."

She had intended her words to be low, and vicious, and they were.

Lord Taernsby, however, merely inclined his head. "Good morning to you, Lady Lilianna."

"Don't talk to me," she said curtly. "I have no interest in hearing what you have to say."

"I think you do. I think you are intrigued by me now," said Lord Taernsby, stepping forward.

Lilianna attempted to step back. A vase crashed to the floor, roses flying everywhere, water soaking her feet.

"There's no escape from me, Lady Lilianna," said Lord Taernsby quietly, his serious eyes fixed on hers. For some reason, she could not look away. "I thought the roses would get your attention—"

"They are more an inconvenience than a delight," she hissed.

"—and I have given you some time to think over my proposal."

For a moment, Lilianna just stared, uncomprehending.

And then she began to laugh.

Oh, he is ridiculous. He did not honestly think his pathetic attempt at humor last night, which had merely vexed her, not amused, had been tantamount to a proposal?

But as her laughter died away, echoing horribly in the hall as her family's argument behind her increased in volume, Lilianna was disconcerted to see that the man before her was not laughing.

He was no longer smiling. Instead, he was looking at her like… like…

Lilianna swallowed. *Well.* No one had ever looked at her like that before. As though she were a delicacy on a plate he was ready to eat. As though she were removing her clothes slowly and suggestively. As though they were alone together, and it was their wedding night, and he was about to…

"And you can stop that," she hissed, stepping forward in an attempt to show him just how serious he was.

The Earl of Taernsby was unmoved. "Stop what?"

"Looking at me like—like *that!*" Lilianna said, jabbing her finger against his chest.

It had been a clever idea. She probably could not get away with punching the man in the jaw again, and besides, her hand was still sore from when she had done so last night.

But Lord Taernsby was faster than she had expected. He grasped her finger, then her hand, holding it close to him, forcing her palm to splay against him, her fingers struggling against his hold.

"Let me—"

"Go?" he finished, raising a sardonic eyebrow. "But then you wouldn't be touching me, Lady Lilianna. And I know how much you enjoy being close to me. Feeling my embrace. Why else would you throw yourself into my arms?"

Lilianna gasped. The intimacy with which he had spoken, his low voice, so low that none of her family could hear just how informal he was being…

And he was right, damn him. At least, about enjoying being close to him. A thrill roared through her as her hand was captured by his own. It was intoxicating being possessed in this way. No man had ever touched her like this. No man had ever been so bold as to touch her outside of a dance, and then, only chastely.

About one thing, however, he could not be more wrong.

"I-I did not throw myself into your arms."

"Didn't you?" Lord Taernsby's gaze flickered to her lips, and he wetted his own before he looked again into her eyes. Lilianna's stomach lurched. "What a shame. I was hoping it was your way of indicating that you were ready."

Oh, this heat—how is it so hot in here? "'Ready'?"

"To be mine." His voice had lowered, but that did not matter. He had somehow pulled her close. "Are you ready now to admit it, Lilianna?"

Lilianna tried to breathe, but it was getting increasingly difficult. "M-My title is *Lady* Lilianna."

"I know it is, to the rest of the world," Lord Taernsby said possessively, and somehow his other hand was reaching for her free one. "But to me—"

"—and that's that," said a voice from a long way away, a voice she knew. "That's Frank dealt with. Now, Lilianna—Lil?"

Lilianna blinked. That was her father's voice.

Wrenching her hand from Lord Taernsby's grasp and hoping to goodness neither her father nor her mother nor, heaven forbid, her sister or cousin had heard the nonsense the man had spouted, she attempted to draw herself up.

It was difficult, when one's legs were about to give way.

"Lord Taernsby was just leaving," she said calmly. At least, that was what she had intended. As it turned out, her voice had quavered somewhat.

The Earl of Taernsby gave her a wicked grin.

"*Right now,*" Lilianna added, her voice stronger now. "The poor man made a mistake."

"'Mistake'?" repeated her father behind her. His voice sounded bewildered. "What, did he intend to send you a hundred roses, not a thousand?"

"Lilianna," the wretched man said in a low voice.

Lilianna attempted to ignore the way that Lord Taernsby's tone thrummed through her body, vibrating in a way that was most delicious and certainly never to be repeated. "No, Papa. Lord Taernsby intended to send one hundred flowers to each of his ten current pursuits," she said sweetly. "Unfortunately, all of them were delivered here, but I am sure we can send them back."

"You should be careful, Lilianna," Lord Taernsby said quietly, stepping closer to her once more and making her lungs tighten. "If you intend to play this game with me, I can assure you, you will lose. I have seduced more women than you have ever met."

"So go seduce, then!" she shot back.

The gentleman's lip quirked. "I'm doing it right now."

It was most unfair of her lungs to fail her right at this moment. Lilianna gasped, staring, eyes wide and mind spinning.

The arrogance! The cheek! And saying such a thing right in front of my parents, too!

"Go away," she eventually said in a jagged voice.

Lord Taernsby raised an eyebrow. "Attempting to increase my ardor by putting off the inevitable?"

"Inevitable"? "Ardor"?

It was a miracle that Lilianna was still standing—it truly was. Her knees were quivering, her whole body suddenly aware of every part of her skin, and this man—this irritating man…

Lilianna swallowed. "Don't be ridiculous," she said curtly. "I thought merely to relieve you of any further embarrassment."

"Oh, I wouldn't worry about that," Lord Taernsby said, stepping around her. "I don't embarrass easily."

And neither do I, Lilianna thought wildly as she watched the man approach her parents, bowing low and speaking quietly to them. *At least, I didn't. Not until you.*

She hated how much of an effect the man had on her. Hated how he could look at her and make her quiver. Hated his reflexes, so much faster than her own, able to manipulate her body to be close to him without so much as an apology.

And most of all she hated, *hated*, how her body responded to him. How she wanted him to touch her, wanted him to be close.

Her mother laughed.

And that was it. Lilianna could put up with a lot—thanks to Lord Zouch, she already had—but she was not going to permit this joke of an earl to impress her mother.

"All right, that's it!" she said firmly, striding forward and ignoring all the vases of roses that she knocked over in her path. "I have had quite enough of this!"

"Lilianna—"

"Lil!"

She ignored her sister, father, and cousin. Her mother merely stood there, mouth agog, as Lilianna grasped the collar of the Earl of Taernsby and started to walk.

Dragging him backward behind her.

"Christ, what—"

"Lilianna, put him down!"

She ignored her brother's laughing remark. She ignored Lord Taernsby's splutters, his muttered curses as he tried to twist out of her grip, the way his feet slipped on the wet, marble floor as he desperately tried to keep up with her rapid pace.

Not until a footman had opened the front door and Lilianna had thrust the unwelcome man down the steps did she take another breath.

"I hope this makes my feelings on the matter perfectly clear," she said sweetly, relishing the way Lord Taernsby straightened up with red cheeks and blazing eyes. "I have no wish to see you again, I don't care what you think or what you want to say, and you have mortified me for the last time."

Lord Taernsby's expression twisted into one of wolfish delight. "I've mortified you, have I? Well, that's a start."

Casting a prayer up to the high heavens for patience with this cretin, Lilianna snapped, "You are a rake, doing all this to please yourself and give yourself airs."

"That's not what—"

"I know your reputation and it does not impress. You can't, you *won't*, seduce me, I have no interest in being abandoned after being bedded, and I don't want to see you again," Lilianna said sharply. "To think you thought a *Chance* would fall so low. That my father and uncles and brothers and cousins would allow you to pursue such a scandal with me. The arrogance."

For a moment, Lord Taernsby's face fell. "That's not what I—"

Whatever else he was going to say, Lilianna never knew. She stepped inside and indicated for the footman to slam the door in his face, which the manservant seemed to relish the chance to do. Lilianna brushed her hands together as though she had just dropped a most disgusting thing outside a window and turned.

To see her family all staring.

"What?" she snapped in a most unladylike tone.

Frank grinned. "So. Who's your friend?"

Chapter Four

March 10, 1840

H E'D PROMISED HIMSELF that he would never walk down here. But then, Arthur had promised himself a lot of things.

The carpet was more frayed than he remembered. Arthur's foot almost caught on the edge when he turned a corner, but that wasn't why his pulse was beating so frantically in his ears.

They're all here.

Arthur heaved a sigh as he started to walk slowly along the portrait gallery. It had been a pleasant enough idea. He had no idea which Earl of Taernsby had first thought of it, but the family legend went that it had been long before any royal family or ducal line had had the thought to collect such artwork.

Heaven forbid the idea that a Nelson wasn't original.

The family line, generation to generation, each earl painted in his own fashions in his own style. Arthur paused for a moment beside a Tudor-era-looking earl, his lacey ruff surrounding his neck as he held a globe in one hand and a book in the other. The man had Arthur's nose. It was quite disconcerting.

He moved on, lingering at some paintings longer than others. Each earl held the objects he felt most encapsulated his time as the earl. For some, keys. For others, compasses, architectural tools. Those were the ones who had built wings onto the manor. One of them held the lead to a pair of hunting dogs. Only one was painted beside his wife.

Tension scratched at Arthur's temples as he progressed down the line, the fashions becoming more and more familiar. There was a headache building at the base of his skull by the time he reached one wearing breeches and stockings, a powdered wig on his head.

His grandfather.

To his right, his father. Arthur peered into the painting, wondering if he would spot anything new. But no, there was his father, just as he had always been. A little stern, a little defiant, but no real harm in him.

And there…

Arthur swallowed as he stood before the painting of his brother. Archibald.

He'd spent a great deal of time worrying about what he should have been holding, Arthur could remember.

"It's got to define me for an age!"

The words came echoing back into Arthur's mind as though they had only been spoken yesterday. The odd thing was, it had only been a year ago.

Four weeks after the paint had dried and the new Earl of Taernsby's painting had been added to those of his forefathers, the earl in question had been dead. There'd then been a new, new Earl of Taernsby.

Arthur's stomach lurched as he took another step to the right. There. That gap on the long corridor wall. That was where he would go.

He stood there for a moment, gazing back the way he had come. From this angle, he could not exactly see the details of each painting he had passed, but the shimmer of their gold-gilt frames was enough to give a sense of just how many there were.

And then him.

He would not let the line die out.

He was alone now. Oh, in a way, he had always been alone, his older brother treated by the world like a king and Arthur himself just… there. Their mother had died shortly after Arthur's birth, and their nannies and tutors had been cold, old biddies and bores, the lot of them. But even as the sole object of their father's affection, Archibald had always attempted to ensure that Arthur had been included. That he had still been considered family, as much as he could be.

And now Arthur was completely alone. Just him against the world.

He would not be the last Taernsby.

"I promise you that, Archibald," Arthur said quietly, as though the old rotter could hear him. He glanced back at his brother's portrait. The young man stared out, unseeing, unknowing what was to occur in just a few short months. "I will marry. I will bear heirs. I will not let the line die out."

"Ahem."

The clearing of the throat was quiet, but in the utter silence of the portrait gallery, it rather felt as though someone had let a gun off.

Arthur jumped, then cursed his own foolishness.

What, did you think you were going to be shot too?

"I do apologize for the interruption, my lord," said Haslehaw awkwardly.

Arthur winced. *My lord.* He still was not used to that. He always looked around for his father instinctively when he heard that phrase.

"Please do not concern yourself, Haslehaw, I was just..." *Just what? Just walking up and down morbidly, thinking of death and the end of your line?* "Just thinking."

"Indeed, my lord," said the butler, gaining a little of his own equilibrium. "I would not have disturbed you, naturally, but there is a... a visitor for you. One I could not send away."

Now that was different. "I was not aware it was a butler's duty to turn away his master's guests."

Haslehaw shuffled his feet and glared at the carpet. "This one, my lord, I am sure is unwelcome. But then I thought, perhaps you do things differently to my previous lord. Perhaps you delight in the visits of street urchins with nothing better to do than infringe upon a lord's time and charity."

Arthur grinned. "Ah, now that's a guest I am very much looking forward to meeting."

It was worth it, just for the look on his butler's face. The gaping expression only became more horrified when the two men descended the stairs, then descended the servants' staircase when the butler indicated the way.

Haslehaw bristled. "I won't have that—that *thing* above stairs!"

It had been a good few years since Arthur had been downstairs in the servants' quarters of the Bath townhouse. It was smaller than he remembered. The kitchen was bustling, too many people attempting to work in a space that appeared designed for one. Cook was shouting orders as footmen and maids rushed about, and what Arthur presumed was a scullery maid was hastily picking things up and moving them about without, as far as he could see, any real purpose.

In the middle of the chaos was a large, oak kitchen table. Sitting at the table, elbows leaning on it and leaving dirty marks wherever they were placed, was—

"I thought you said it was an urchin?" muttered Arthur as he smiled at the little girl.

The butler shrugged. "I do apologize, my lord. Is there a feminine equivalent of urchin?"

Though it was on the top of Arthur's tongue to curse his butler to high heaven for making him feel the fool, he didn't bother. The man was clearly exhausted, attempting to acclimatize to a person like him. An earl like him.

"This—this *thing* has forced its way in here and is demanding food!"

Arthur took a swift step back. The wiry-haired Cook, her mobcap askew, had limped forward with a rolling pin in one hand and what appeared to be either a very fancy pastry knife, or a torture implement designed for the nostrils.

"What am I supposed to do with it, eh?" Cook glared.

Arthur swallowed. *Well, the answer feels obvious.* "Feed it?"

Cook's glare did not waver, but the direction of her gaze did. It fell on Haslehaw, standing just behind Arthur.

Arthur did not see precisely what his oldest servant did in those few heartbeats, but Cook lowered her rolling pin, stuffed the torture device into a pocket of her apron, and muttered something that could have been, "Waste of good food."

Still, it appeared that Arthur's tenuous grip on power remained. A bowl of stew was dropped in front of the urchin along with a spoon that had seen better days. The child pulled the bowl close and, ignoring the spoon, picked it up and started pouring the food down her throat.

"Careful now. You'll get hiccups," said Arthur with a broad grin, sitting opposite the scrap of a child.

And she truly was a scrap. Nothing of her at all. How old could she be—eight? Nine? Perhaps older but half-starved half her life.

"You should get yourself to St. Thomas's," he said quietly. "I hear they feed their children well."

The girl snorted. "There's never enough room there, sir."

The words were said swiftly so she could return to the business at hand: putting as much of the stew in the bowl into her belly as she could manage.

Arthur waited this time, rather than attempt to talk with her. Only when the girl had licked the bowl thoroughly and looked up with just a hint of stew on her nose did he try again.

"I told you that you could only return if you had information," Arthur said pointedly. "And so far, you've only informed me about St. Thomas's."

The girl grinned. "How much is it worth?"

Haslehaw gasped. "The cheek!"

"Oh, she knows how desperately I need the information, that's all," said Arthur with a laugh. "Good for you, chit. Here."

Plunging his hand into his waistcoat pocket, Arthur pulled

out a handful of coins. The girl's eyes widened.

"Yes, please!"

"I don't think you'll have enough information for all of this, even for me," he said dryly. "Look. Here's half a crown, and that's before you've told me anything."

The girl snatched at the coin, but her eyes never left the pile of sovereigns, crowns, shillings, and pennies still resting in his palm.

"If you want more," Arthur said slowly, "I'll need more information. The better the information, the better the coins."

The girl nodded, her quick eyes flickering to him. "I've followed her now a few days and I can tell you almost anything you like about her. What do you want to know?"

Arthur hesitated.

What did he want to know? Everything, but that wasn't exactly a helpful directive. *Anything that would help me woo the precocious Lady Lilianna Chance into my bed*, which wasn't the sort of thing one could say to an urchin, especially not to a girl.

"What do you think I should know?" he returned quietly.

The girl's face grew pink. "If you want to court the lady, milord, I'd say… where she goes and who with and what she do there and favorite flowers and the like. Wouldn't you?"

She was a marvel. Arthur returned her smile. "Something like that, yes."

"The lady likes her routine," said the urchin happily. "Goes to the same places almost every day. She likes Milsom Street the best, and then she always…"

And the details poured out of her. *Really*, thought Arthur as he made a mental note of everything the child said, *the government should look into this.* No one noticed a child, did they? And their minds were like sponges, taking in everything they saw. They were goldmines.

"—and she don't like roses," the girl finished.

Arthur's smile evaporated. "She doesn't?"

Blast. It could have worked so well. *What woman doesn't like roses, for pity's sake?*

"How do you know that?" he added, frowning slightly. "It doesn't seem to be the sort of thing you could just pick up walking past her."

The urchin stuck out her chin. "I tell you why, because she was walking along with a friend or sister or cousin or something, and she was going on about how some idiot—"

"Yes, well, thank you," Arthur interrupted hastily.

He decidedly ignored the pinched lips and overall look of mirth on his butler's face. Well, the man had to have some enjoyment in life, didn't he?

"I don't know what she do like, though," the girl said, frowning. "She hasn't mentioned anything else."

Well, that was no matter. There were only so many flowers a woman liked.

"Haslehaw," Arthur said, turning to him. "Send an order up to the florist, will you? A thousand delphiniums."

There were stifled gasps about the kitchen. Well, if he was going to make an impression…

"Better make that two thousand," he said thoughtfully. "Or three—I leave it up to your discretion, Haslehaw."

The butler looked as though he were experiencing a sudden migraine. "My… My lord, the cost!"

"Oh, figs to the cost," said Arthur, standing up and brushing a few pastry flakes from his shoulder. How had they gotten there? "I can't hang around and argue with you. I'm off to Milsom Street."

The girl's eyebrows grew severe. "Oi!"

"Oh, yes, whatever you say," Arthur said absentmindedly, handing over the entire handful of coins to the startled child. "There you go. Keep an eye on her, would you?" he added to the staff. He tried to ignore the muttering.

The urchin blinked. "How much will you give me next time?"

Arthur cuffed the girl about the ear before remembering her gender. "Damn, I do apologize."

"I'm not a *lady*," said the girl with a crinkled nose, as though to be a lady was a most unfortunate thing. "Can I have more stew?"

"No," grumbled the Cook behind Arthur.

"Yes," said Arthur vaguely, his mind already in Milsom Street. "Have as much as you want."

Milsom Street wasn't that far from the Taernsby townhouse. In truth, there were few places in Bath far from Milsom Street. The place was all a bustle, the bright sunshine and the sultry air welcoming out all those who had come to Bath for the Society, and all those who had come for its restorative waters.

The pavements were packed.

"Oh, sorry," said Arthur helplessly as he accidentally knocked into a woman whose parcels went flying. He stepped back hastily but only succeeded on stepping on the toes of a gentleman. "My apologies!"

It was crowded. How he was supposed to find Lady Lilianna Chance in this, he had no idea…

"And I told him it was absolutely ridiculous," came a genteel voice with an edge of steel. "I mean, a waltz! Was he mad?"

Arthur grinned. Ah, there she was—fortune had smiled upon him. And he had the perfect excuse.

"See you tomorrow," Lady Lilianna said to her companion, a young woman with very similar brows to her and a smiling expression. "Don't do anything I wouldn't do, Evelyn."

"You'll be all right on your own? You don't want a ride, at least? I know I promised your mama I would accompany you, since we turned away your maid as chaperone."

"Don't worry. You go home and rest. It's not a long walk. I shall be perfectly safe."

"Very well. I won't tell your mama if you don't tell mine."

"I'm no tattler. Besides, with my bonnet adjusted just so, no one of the *ton* ought to recognize me."

Oh, she was sure of all that, was she? That she was to wander around alone, unremarked, unaccompanied? Arthur was quite certain he was what chaperones had been designed for.

The other woman said something else that Arthur didn't catch and the two women laughed before Evelyn, whoever she was, departed.

Leaving Lady Lilianna alone.

Reminding himself that he was now one of the most eligible bachelors in the *ton*, and that ladies had been throwing themselves at him all week, Arthur stepped forward. Lady Lilianna was walking slowly along, a basket on her arm, and it was not difficult at all to nudge her elbow with his own.

She turned around to see who had bumped into her. "Excuse you, I—oh, hell."

Arthur grinned. "Goodness, hello! What a surprise!"

"Go away, you poor man," Lady Lilianna said wearily before turning and walking away.

Arthur almost halted in his tracks. That was not the way it was supposed to go. She was supposed to flutter her eyelashes, blush at the sudden contact between their bodies, invite him to walk her home and—

Damn, she was getting away.

He had to put more speed into his pace to catch up to her, and when he did so, Lady Lilianna rolled her eyes.

"Do you have no concept of being unwelcome?"

"If I ever am, I shall let you know what it feels like," Arthur said cheerfully. "And may I say how pleasant it is today?"

"I dare say you will, but I wish you wouldn't," said Lady Lilianna calmly. "Good day."

The woman was infuriating enough to drive a saint to drink. That was surely why all this fire was pouring through his veins and he simply *had* to keep talking to her.

Lady Lilianna had turned a corner and departed from Milsom Street onto the quieter Green Street. Arthur followed her, relieved he would not have to be fighting his way along the pavement to keep alongside her.

Not that he was particularly welcome to do so, of course.

"You know, I think fate is conspiring to push us together," Arthur said conversationally, ignoring the snort of derision from his unwilling conversational partner. "Here we are, running into each other, you without a chaperone in sight—"

She pinked a little at that but seemed eager not to acknowledge her faux pas. "Don't be daft, man. It isn't fate conspiring to push us together—it's *you!*"

Her color was high and it did nothing but heighten the perfect symmetry of her mouth. Arthur swallowed, trying not to stare. He almost tripped over a stone on the pavement in doing so.

When he looked back up at Lady Lilianna, her mouth was quirked in a smile. "Do you honestly think I don't know?"

"How beautiful you are?" Arthur said swiftly, always ready to step into an opening. "I am not sure. When was the last time anyone told you—"

"Really? That tired, old line? I have such low hopes for you, my lord, yet still you manage to disappoint," Lady Lilianna said wryly. "Honestly, man, I *know!*"

Whatever it was she knew, Arthur was completely lost. She'd said the two words as though they were obvious, and the slight lift of her brow suggested she was waiting for him to reply.

Arthur wet his lips. *Well, damn.* It was unpleasant to the extreme to be on the back foot like this. How did every other gentleman manage it? "I… I don't—"

"Kay is the sister of our stableboy, you dolt," said Lady Lilianna with a laugh as she halted, turning to look at him, hand resting on her basket. "You think I don't know you're having me followed by a little girl? You think she isn't telling me absolutely everything—well done on the handful of coins, by the way. It was almost a sovereign, all told. She's delighted."

Arthur opened his mouth and absolutely nothing came out.

Hell's bells, she knew all this time? She knew. The girl had told her—naturally, the girl had told her, why wouldn't she? There was no reason for her not to attempt to gain money from both sides. He should have thought of that.

A sensation started trickling down his spine, pouring through his body, that was new. It was hot, and sticky, and uncomfortable, like sitting through a heatwave in the blaze of the midday sun in your mourning suit.

It took Arthur a few moments to realize what the devil it was. *Embarrassment.*

"I... I feel stupid," he found himself saying in a low voice.

Lady Lilianna smirked, those delicate lips coming together in a delicious line. "And so you should."

Irritation fueled by the embarrassment flared through him. "There is no cause to be so arrogant."

"I don't have time for your nonsense, I'm afraid," Lady Lilianna said dismissively. "I'm busy."

"'Busy'?" Arthur chuckled darkly, shaking his head. "You're standing here talking to me, as I knew you wished to! Why would you say that you're busy?"

"I'm actually standing here because I have an appointment," said Lady Lilianna silkily. "Ah, here he is."

Arthur swung round to face the incomer. Whatever gentleman was attempting to have his way with Lady Lilianna Chance, he had another—

The words he was about to shout, whatever they were, died in his mouth. The man approaching them was at least double their age, perhaps older, wearing clothes that had seen better days. So had the man. He was quite evidently a man without a home.

Arthur swallowed. His father had always ensured he never spoke to what every previous earl but one had called "the undeserving poor." They were dirty. They were criminals. They were—

Bowing to Lady Lilianna?

"Good afternoon, Mr. Creighton," the genteel woman said politely as she curtseyed.

It was impossible not to stare. *Just what is going on?*

"I haven't forgotten your favorite, Mr. Creighton," Lady Lilianna said with a wry expression. "I know I did last time, and I apologize."

"Oh, fine ladies such as y'self can't be expected to remember little, old me."

"Do not sell yourself short, Mr. Creighton. You are not little and you are certainly not old," she said with a chuckle.

Arthur stared in confusion between the two of them. So... So one of the most beautiful and infuriating women in the world... fed the homeless?

"—and that pie there is for your wife, Mr. Creighton. Do give her my best wishes," Lady Lilianna said, pointing at something in the basket.

Mr. Creighton was beaming. "Oh, she'll be so pleased that you remembered, Lady Lilianna. Why, she always said..."

Arthur could not help but stare. This was not the sort of activity a young lady got up to, and most certainly not alone, and yet here she was, doing it. No big charity gala, no beaming for the newspapers as she cut a ribbon. No, Lady Lilianna Chance was doing something real. Something important.

He watched as the man bowed again, receiving a curtsey from the noblewoman, then departed, holding his head significantly higher than it had been when he had arrived.

"You're still here," said Lady Lilianna quietly, raising herself up and staring boldly.

And all the clever lines, the impressive flirting, it all vanished the moment he caught her gaze. "I want to know you better."

"Get in line," Lady Lilianna said with a wry laugh. "Half the *ton* knows I am eligible, and my dowry—"

"I don't care about dowries or eligibility or any of that rot," Arthur said urgently, taking a step toward her, almost brushing his hand against hers. *Dear God, so close...* "I care about *you*."

She stared, eyes wide and lips parted. Her breath blossomed across his face and Arthur longed to have it on his neck, his own breathing life into her as he pressed a hedonistic kiss on her lips.

"I…" Lady Lilianna whispered.

A jolt roared through Arthur and he willed himself to lean forward, to close the gap and kiss the dratted woman.

Show her, don't tell her. Show her just what delights you could offer. Show her what being the Countess of Taernsby could be.

"You care about me?" Lady Lilianna murmured.

Arthur nodded, wishing to goodness his boldness was not failing him. Why wasn't he kissing her?

She smiled, and this time, it was a genuine smile, perhaps the first he had seen from her. "But you don't know me, my lord. You don't know me at all. You desire a dream, and when you wake up, you'll be left… with me."

Just as he leaned forward, pushed beyond all endurance and aching to know how she tasted, Lady Lilianna Chance stepped back.

Arthur blinked. She must have stepped down a side street, for she was gone.

Chapter Five

March 16, 1840

"Y OU LIKE HIM."

"I like no one."

"You have to admit, the delphiniums were beautiful."

Yes, they had been. Lilianna was not going to admit it out loud, as that was a slippery slope when it came to one's sister, but still. They had been beautiful. And decadent. And overwhelming—was the man just made of money? Did he have nothing better to do than spend it on such frivolities?

"I hope Mama sent some to Uncle William and Aunt Alice," she said quietly, turning a page of the book she was pretending to read.

Frank snorted. She was seated on the other side of the library at the table, two large mathematics books open before her. "From the sound of it, Mama has been sending them to everyone. The whole of Bath has some of your flowers."

"They're not *my* flowers," Lilianna said with a twist in her stomach.

Her sister snorted again and did not turn around. "They were sent to you, weren't they?"

They had. It was not something that Lilianna could deny, even if she wanted to.

"By that admirer of yours."

"He's not my *admirer.*"

"Even if you don't like him, you can't pretend the Earl of Taernsby is not an admirer," Frank said, her voice drifting off into vagueness as she turned a page. "Honestly, Samuel has left this volume in a very bad state of repair."

"I don't think he ever expected to look at it again," said Lilianna with a wry look. "That man left mathematics behind as soon as he could."

"I don't understand why, it's so elegant," said Frank, scribbling some notes in that notebook she always had with her. "Elegant like those delphiniums."

"Frank—"

"Did you know that Fibonacci's mathematical sequence can be found in flowers?" Frank's voice rose in volume as her excitement grew. She turned, pushing strands of hair that had fallen from her simple bun behind her ear. "Is it not incredible? I was speaking to Aunt Dodo, and she said—"

"As the family's other mathematician, I can assure you Aunt Dodo will participate in this conversation far better than I will," said Lilianna dryly. "Than I am."

Sometimes you had to put your sister back in her place.

"Shouldn't you be practicing the pianoforte?"

Lilianna groaned. "You know I hate that thing. I can play it only passably. Why can't Mama let it go?"

"She wants us to be perfect ladies," Frank said with a snort. "Perfect."

Perfect. Not gallivanting with gentlemen with terrible reputations and even worse expectations.

Frank sighed and turned back to her books. "There's no need to get in a snit with me because your gentleman caller—"

"He is not *my gentleman.*"

"—hasn't sent any more flowers," finished Frank, flourishing a pencil across her notebook, then underlining whatever she had written several times. Or crossing something out. It was impossible to tell.

Lilianna sighed. "I don't know why you keep teasing me

about him. I have absolutely no interest in the fool. Whatever his name is."

It was a lie, and not a very good one. There was something… something strangely tantalizing about a man who just wouldn't stay down when he was pushed. So long as he never pushed her too far—which, she had to admit, he hadn't done. Yet. Nothing she said appeared to make any difference to the bounder. He just kept… pursuing her.

The man simply wouldn't give up. It was a strangely attractive quality.

Not that she was attracted to him. Not at all.

"Just admit you're intrigued by a man who sees past your snobbery and seems to like you," said Frank quietly from the other side of the room.

"*Snobbery!*" said Lilianna hotly, dropping her book down the side of the armchair and preparing herself for a fight. "I'll have you know—"

"A letter for you, Lady Lilianna," said a voice.

Lilianna looked round. "You really must make more of a noise when you come into the room, Humphreys."

Their dour-faced butler nodded. "Yes, Lady Lilianna."

Frank grinned. "Yes, in case you overhear Lil speaking about her future betrothed."

Lilianna scowled. "A letter, Humphreys?"

She tried desperately to concentrate on the servant before her, but her mind was still swirling with her sister's words.

"Just admit you're intrigued by a man who sees past your snobbery and seems to like you."

What on earth had her sister meant by it? She wasn't a snob. A snob thought they were better than they were. She was marvelous. It was impossible for a Chance to be a snob.

A delicate clearing of the butler's throat brought her back to the present. He was standing before her, a letter on a silver platter.

"Right, yes, a letter," she said, taking the proffered missive and glancing at it.

The handwriting was unfamiliar. That was not unusual; handwriting was so varied even within a singular person. Why, sometimes she could hardly make out Frank's handwriting at all.

Not that that was saying much. The girl hardly ever used a pen; it was all pencil at the moment.

"Aren't you going to open it?"

Lilianna blinked. Her sister, and their butler, were staring curiously at the letter in her hands.

Drawing herself up as imperiously as she could manage, Lilianna nodded her dismissal to the servant and waited for the door to close behind him before looking at the letter once more.

"Why don't you want Humphreys to know what the letter says?" Frank asked curiously.

Shooting a glare at her sister, Lilianna pointed out, "I don't particularly want *you* to know what it says, either."

Her sister frowned. "Why are you so precious about a letter when you don't even know if it contains anything interesting?"

Because I hope it does, Lilianna did not say. *I hope it's from…*

Not that she was going to defile her mouth by uttering his name. Most definitely not. And the likelihood of the Earl of Taernsby sending her a letter was remote. They weren't engaged! They were hardly acquainted. Now that she came to think about it, Lilianna wasn't even sure if they had been introduced. Technically.

"And you are very presumptuous, whoever you are, to address me before we have been introduced. And perhaps even then."

A smile slipped across her face.

"You're thinking about him again."

"No, I'm not," snapped Lilianna. "Go back to your mathematics, Frank."

Frank smirked. "Go on. Open it."

There didn't appear to be much else to do. After all, one could not simply sit looking at a letter, hoping it would reveal its contents to you through osmosis.

The seal was a swirly T. Lilianna broke it into fragments before unfolding the letter.

Dear Lady Lilianna Chance,

I hope this letter finds you well. In the cause of getting to know you better, furthering my justification of my pursuit of you, I invite you to take a stroll with me around the Fish Pond lake. I will be there at two o'clock in the afternoon and look forward to your company.

Yours most faithfully,
Taernsby

Postscript: Wear blue. You look fantastic in blue.

Lilianna did not require a looking glass to feel heat burning in her cheeks. She probably looked a fright—but what else could she do?

Fantastic in blue, indeed. Did the idiot not know she looked marvelous in every color?

"Was he very rude?"

"Very," said Lilianna quietly. And then, "Not that it was from the person you think."

"Whatever you say, Lil." Frank grinned. "Goodness, an admirer. It's been what, five minutes since you had a new one?"

If Lilianna had not been so concerned to keep the full details of the letter to herself, she would have thrown it at her sister. As it was…

"I feel in need of fresh air," she said aloud. Not that she would go *there*. No, there were plenty of places in Bath where she could take the air and stretch her legs. A constitutional would be most advantageous, especially after luncheon.

Frank raised an eyebrow. "Do you, indeed? Shall I tell Mama you need a chaperone? Of course, we always need them, but in particular when meeting with a gentleman who—ouch!" She was too busy rubbing her sore arm to finish that thought.

Lilianna strode out of the room. It took five minutes to track down their mother, and another five to convince her to loan Lilianna the requested garment.

"B-But you have a p-perfectly good one yourself."

"I know," said Lilianna, smiling sweetly. "But yours has that beautiful lace around the collar and cuffs. It will go so nicely with my bonnet."

Her mother arched an eyebrow but said no more. And so it was that about twenty minutes after receiving Lord Taernsby's letter, Lilianna strode down the steps of her Bath home in the brightest scarlet pelisse anyone had ever seen, Clarke a few steps behind her, the lady's maid looking a bit green, Lilianna had to admit.

"My lady, I'm not sure I should be out for a walk just now," said Clarke, clutching her stomach.

"Nonsense," Lilianna said. "Fresh air will do you good." Besides, she would not give Lord Taernsby the satisfaction of her arriving without a chaperone this time.

Nor the opportunity of stepping too close to her.

She gulped.

Lilianna's smile remained buoyant even as her spirits fluttered.

What on earth was she doing? She hated the man! No, hatred was too strong a word: she disliked the man. She did not think of him at all. She couldn't stop thinking of him.

Treacherous mind, it was always doing what she didn't want.

The Fish Pond was almost deserted. Lilianna's shoulders sagged, just a little. Part of her had hoped it would be bustling, and she could take some time observing this Earl of Taernsby to see what he was like.

Though perhaps that would have been easier without the bright-red pelisse.

"My lady, you must excuse me." Clarke swallowed and rubbed her stomach. "I need only be gone a moment."

"Yes, of course. I'll wait. I'm sorry I dragged you out here." Lilianna winced as she watched her lady's maid rush off to the nearest bench to rest upon, though she knew it was quite some distance away. She also knew her maid well enough to know when her courses were bothering her.

She was a fool for coming here, for insisting on Clarke instead of her mother to act as her companion, that deep, dark part of her no doubt counting on her maid to be more lenient than her parent.

Still, despite her promise to stay put, she found her feet wandering, her eyes looking to and fro.

The moment she turned the corner and the Fish Pond lake came into view, someone called her name.

A very handsome, very irritating someone.

"I knew you wouldn't be able to resist, Lady Lilianna," said the Earl of Taernsby with a knowing look.

Lilianna held her head high as she stalked past him. *The cheek!* She was... curious, that was all. Could a woman not have some curiosity!

"I have no idea what you mean," she said stiffly.

"And I see you have come alone," he added. "Did you sneak out from behind your mother's skirts to meet with me?"

She swallowed. She had no retort to that. She had not intended to come alone. "Good day."

She continued to walk past him, a spring breeze tugging at her curls. Part of her was disappointed. If he had said nothing, or merely smiled, or bowed and thanked her for coming—well, maybe then she would have deigned to spend time with him. Five minutes. Maybe ten, if he were fortunate. As it was—

"Oh!" Lilianna gasped.

It was difficult not to. Some brigand had taken a hold of her sleeve!

"I told you to wear blue." Lord Taernsby's voice was low and intimate and suggestive all at once.

Heat blossomed in Lilianna as she tugged her sleeve away. Some of the lace ripped.

Botheration. She would have to apologize to her mother.

"And here I am, wearing red," she shot back. "Would you rather have me at home wearing blue?"

The twinkle in Lord Taernsby's eye was far too knowing. "You chose to defy me."

"You can't defy someone you never had any intention to obey," Lilianna said, her pulse racing.

Why was this man so infuriating? How did he manage to say just the right thing to vex her?

Because she *was* vexed. Not intrigued. Not interested. Not hoping in any way that he would get as close to her as he had before, breathing her air, pressing himself against her...

Lilianna swallowed. *Most definitely not.*

"Why have you taken so against me, Lilianna?"

"Because—Because of things like that!" she said hotly, trying to keep her voice low. It would not do for any of the other people meandering about the Fish Pond to overhear what, admittedly, sounded like a lovers' tiff. Not that it was. "Because of the way you speak to me. It's—"

"Frighteningly intimate, isn't it?" Lord Taernsby whispered.

Lilianna took a hasty step back. How precisely he had managed to—to creep up on her like that, she had no idea. The trickster!

"I take against anyone who presumes an intimacy with me that they have not earned," she said sharply. Her fingers were tingling. With cold. Presumably.

Lord Taernsby was smiling. *Smiling! At me!* "And just how does one go about earning such intimacy?"

"You couldn't—you can't," she said hastily. Lord, the last thing she needed to do was give him hope! "You are..."

Handsome. And charming. And rakish. With a terrible reputation of your own and a lowly reputation from your family.

You're nothing like the sort of man whom I would wish to pay his address to me.

Lilianna swallowed. The words would be so easy to say, yet they did not come. They soared around her mind and made it impossible to think of anything else.

"You are not worthy of a Chance," she said finally.

The smile on the Earl of Taernsby's lips disappeared. "And what makes you so self-righteous as to think that?"

"My family is noble, and respected, and—"

"Oh, and you think the Taernsby name nothing of much import?"

Lilianna allowed the imperious look that she had perfected over the years to keep riffraff like this man away from her to shadow her expression. "Not much, no."

There it was—the flaring nostrils, the flattened lip that indicated the flicker of anger she had hoped to inspire. Now all she had to do was laugh at him in the next two minutes, and he would be so mortified and irritated that he would stride away and never speak to her again.

She had done this before. Countless times. The few men on whom it had not worked had ended up proposing to her and finding themselves distinctly disappointed.

So why did Lilianna feel disappointment that this... this whatever it was, was already over?

Lord Taernsby grinned. "You can't frighten me that easily."

Lilianna hissed with an intake of breath. *He is impossible!* "You are so... so... *so*—"

"Yes, I get that a lot," he said easily, eyes flicking up and down her as though he were measuring her for a new gown. "And you are *so* too, Lilianna. Very so."

"*Lady* Lilianna," she snapped.

"Lady Lilianna," Lord Taernsby replied in a mocking tone. "Why does anyone like anyone? Where does attraction come from?"

Attraction. It was not the sort of word one bandied about in public! It was bad enough she was standing here with him, without a chaperone in sight.

Lilianna glanced around them and saw with relief that the Fish Pond's shores were mostly devoid of people. Very few, in fact, and no one currently close enough to see them. The only people she could see appeared to be leaving.

She swallowed. "So you *are* attracted to me."

"The feeling is entirely mutual."

It was impossible not to snort at that. *"My lord!"*

"Oh, don't you 'my lord' me. I think we are both old enough to speak the truth when we find it." Lord Taernsby raised an eyebrow, which had a devastatingly wicked effect on the fine features of his face. "Or were the Chance ladies not taught to be honest?"

Hatred, or something very like it, flared. "How dare you?"

"I dare because I wish to have a direct conversation with you, Lady Lilianna Chance, and at every opportunity you make it impossible," said Lord Taernsby sharply. "Have I asked you to marry me today?"

"I—what?" Lilianna felt wrong-footed, as though the whole world was upended whenever she was in this man's presence.

How did he do it? Make it impossible for her to find her center, to understand what the world was doing? Why was there so little equilibrium in her soul whenever he crossed her path?

Or, she supposed, in this case when *she* crossed *his* path. But no matter. The point was—

"Is your silence acquiescence?"

Lilianna blinked, confused for a moment, then shook her head in horror. "No! No, absolutely not! I will not marry you, my lord!"

"You will not marry me today, to be sure. We would need a few weeks to get everything prepared." Lord Taernsby had an impish grin on his face. "So how about the first of April?"

"Never," shot back Lilianna succinctly. "I don't understand why you would think I'd agree to... to..."

"Perhaps you don't know me just as much as I don't know you," Lord Taernsby said quietly, stalling her words. "Perhaps I want to reveal myself, just as I want you to be revealed. To know you."

Lilianna swallowed the myriad of questions that arose from such a ridiculous statement. The man was wholly mad—that was the only explanation. Why else would he... Why would he be so... so...

So forward.

"And so I ask again, why have you taken against me?"

Because you're everything that I can't understand, Lilianna wanted to scream. Not that it would have been very ladylike. *Because people like you upset the order of things, and I have my life perfectly ordered, thank you very much.*

"I may as well ask why *you* are so *taken* with *me*," she said, hoping her desperation to change the topic of conversation did not show in her—

"You are so desperate to change the conversation," said Lord in a musing tone. "Why?"

This was a mistake. She should have known coming here had been a mistake—she had thought so instinctively and she should have listened to that instinct. She should turn around right now, walk away, find Clarke, and ensure never to accept an invitation to anywhere that also had the Earl of Taernsby on the guest list.

But her curiosity would not let her depart.

What was this man's interest? Why was he here—why was *she* here?

What was there between them, already, and quite against her wishes, that had brought her out here to speak with such a rotter?

"You won't answer the question, then," she said softly, unwillingly meeting his gaze and feeling heat boil in her stomach. "You have no reason for your interest in me. I am just another of a long line of women whom you wish to woo, bed, and then abandon."

A twist of his jaw, a throb in his temple, yet the Earl of Taernsby did not speak. She watched him, waiting, lungs tightening as she waited for an answer, any answer.

No answer came.

Lilianna sighed. "How very disappointing."

She turned away. There was nothing else for her here, no reason to stay. The afternoon was drawing on and the sun offered little warmth at this time of year.

And she would have stridden off, head held high, if it had not been for the mud. That was the trouble with standing beside a lake for so long. Without her noticing, Lilianna's feet were now slipping in mud—mud that would not provide her with a steady hold for much longer.

"Arrgh!"

It was most unladylike of her to produce such a sound, yet what else could she utter? It was the perfectly normal response of a woman who had slipped suddenly in squelching mud, careering toward the muddy ground, only to be caught—

To be caught.

Lilianna blinked up into the face of a gentleman she was starting to know a little too well. He was looking down, a hint of a smile on his lips, his eyes possessively raking over her.

But it wasn't his eyes that were the problem. It was his hands. The Earl of Taernsby's hands. One was around her waist, holding her parallel to the ground, evidently refusing to let her up for some unknown reason of his. And the other...

Heat burned Lilianna's cheeks. The other was clasping her— her buttock!

"Unhand me," she snarled.

Or at least, she had intended to snarl. Unfortunately, the phrase came out as a whimper, which was most definitely not what she had intended. Most irritating it was too.

For some reason, her gasp made Lord Taernsby grin. "We have got to stop meeting like this."

His voice was a growl, a jagged tone wrenching something deep into her.

Lilianna wetted her lips in preparation for a response and for some reason, he groaned. The man actually groaned! And his hand was still on her behind!

"I think you owe me a kiss now, Lilianna," Lord Taernsby

murmured.

"L-Lady Lilianna," she spluttered, hoping to goodness no one could see them. Walking alongside him in a public park, she might feign innocence—her chaperone was somewhere nearby. But to be caught in this compromising position? Why, it was a scandal!

The Earl of Taernsby grinned wickedly, his grip tightening. "That wasn't a no."

"You have not a chance in hell," Lilianna whispered.

She was going to say more. She was going to point out how utterly ridiculous it was to presume that he could kiss her—her, Lady Lilianna Chance! And in public too!

She ought to point out that gentlemen did not go around kissing ladies in public. As far as her experience went, gentlemen did not go around kissing ladies to whom they were not engaged. She certainly had not had a single kiss bestowed on her, and quite right too. The last thing she was going to permit was such an assault on her dignity!

The speech was impressive, but it was not needed. Not when Lord Taernsby lowered his lips to hers and pressed upon them a chaste kiss…

The kiss did not remain chaste for long. When Lilianna gasped in shock and surprise at the sudden intrusion, then whimpered at the delicate pleasure that tingled down her mouth and into her core, Lord Taernsby took advantage of her parted lips and deepened the kiss.

His tongue—his tongue was in her mouth!

Lilianna struggled, her hands splaying against his chest, but her efforts swiftly ceased as the aforementioned tongue caressed her own.

Oh, what sensation was this? What trembling overcame her body? How did every inch of her respond in need, clutching at Lord Taernsby now instead of attempting to push him away? Why did a moan erupt in her throat, swiftly swallowed by his tantalizing kisses that possessed her utterly, showed her, without words, precisely what he wanted from her?

When the Earl of Taernsby finally released her, standing her upright and taking a step back in the squelching mud, Lilianna could do nothing for a moment but raise a hand to her lips.

He had kissed her. She'd had her first kiss.

"That," Lord Taernsby said in a ragged voice. "*That* is why I am interested in you."

And all the heat that had flooded her body disappeared, ice coldness replacing it.

Lilianna swallowed. "So that is all. You want my body."

"I want to possess you, to show you what it is to be adored," Lord Taernsby said in a low voice, reaching out for her.

This time, when she turned and marched away, Lilianna was very careful where she placed her feet. It would certainly not do to fall into a man's arms again. Not now she knew where that sort of thing could lead.

Chapter Six

March 17, 1840

THE CLOBBERING ON his bedchamber door should have been his first clue. The second clue, which followed swiftly after, was the shouting.

"Arthur Nelson, you come out here right now!"

The voice seemed very certain that Arthur was going to obey, and indeed there were harmonics in the tone that forced his spine to bend and made him sit up in bed.

Arthur looked around himself groggily, his pulse racing. Yes, he was in his own bed. That should have been a good sign, shouldn't it? And no, there didn't seem to be anyone else with him in here. Which was good. Wasn't it?

Who could be so angry at—Arthur groaned as he looked at the traveling carriage clock by his head. *Seven o'clock in the morning?*

"I'm warning you," said the severe voice of a woman unimpressed on the other side of his bedchamber door. "I'm coming in there if you're not coming out!"

Head still hazed with sleep, hardly knowing what to do against such a barrage this early in the morning, Arthur clutched his bedsheets.

The woman surely didn't think she was going to—
Crash!

The bedchamber door slammed open and Arthur jumped,

startled at the sudden noise. Standing there, outlined in the light of the candelabra she was holding, was…

Arthur relaxed and rubbed his tired eyes. "God's teeth, you alarmed me."

"Good," snapped the well-dressed woman, striding into the bedchamber and slamming a candelabra on the bedside table. A little wax overrun and made a stain that Haslehaw was surely going to complain about. "What on earth do you think you've been doing?"

Looking blearily up, Arthur attempted a smile. "Sleeping?"

His cousin brushed a lock of her raven hair from her dark eyes and glowered. "Arthur Nelson, I swear—"

"Yes, yes, you are very furious for a reason that I am sure will become apparent soon, and I am certain is totally rational," said Arthur with a wry grin, some of his brain finally getting itself in gear. "Will you do the honor of breakfasting with me?"

Olive brightened up. "Don't mind if I do."

"In about an hour." Arthur yawned, turning away and burying his face back into his pillow.

He deserved the whack on the shoulder, and he received several.

"You are wholeheartedly lazy and completely incorrigible and—"

"So exactly the same as when you last saw me, then?" Arthur muttered into his pillow with a grin.

It was all too easy to wind up his cousin. Thank goodness she had gone off and gotten married a few years ago. It had mellowed her out considerably and taken her several miles away at any given time.

Not that he wasn't happy to see her, of course. She was Olive. She was his favorite cousin. She was his only cousin.

Whack!

It was just that she was best enjoyed, most of the time, from a distance.

"I will see you in the breakfast room in twenty minutes," said

Olive sharply, pulling at the bell pull beside his bed and sniffing. "Twenty minutes, Arthur!"

It was more like thirty, in truth, but Arthur thought he could hardly be blamed. It was half the time he had suggested.

"You know you are bringing even more disrepute onto the family," his cousin said airily, as though they were continuing a conversation. She was buttering toast—or rather, adding a small amount of toast to a slab of butter. "It really is too bad of you, Arthur. Lady Lilianna Chance, of all people!"

Arthur sighed heavily as he sat and poured himself a coffee. Haslehaw had tried to insist that a footman do it, but no one did it right. "I truly care about her, you know."

Olive snorted. "You hardly know her."

The words stung, though perhaps more than his cousin could have imagined. She could not know, after all, that the same accusation had so recently been flung at him from Lady Lilianna's own lips.

"In fact, I know a great deal about her," Arthur countered. "She doesn't like roses, or, as it turns out, delphiniums. Who doesn't like delphiniums?"

His cousin's mouth was full of butter and toast, so she shrugged.

"She likes routine. Craves it, as far as I can make out. Any change to that routine makes her anxious, it… it makes her brows pucker here." Arthur gestured on his own face, smiling as he recalled her look of annoyance. "And she purposefully irritates me."

That scarlet pelisse. She truly is a minx.

Arthur grew lost in the memory of that afternoon. The way she had marched up to him, the ferocity of her words, the way she had never pulled away, not really, from that kiss. Oh, that kiss…

Someone sipped tea very noisily indeed.

Arthur jumped.

His cousin grinned. "Are you telling me that after all those lovers I am not supposed to know about—"

"Olive!"

"Oh, you should have heard how my father talked about you." Olive chuckled. "He always said that his older brother would have been very proud of you—"

There was a determined bit of grit in his eye, Arthur decided, and that was why it was watering so.

"—but you're telling me that you have actually found someone whom you like? That you like, Arthur, not just someone you want to… you know."

His cousin was flushing, which was most odd, considering she was a married woman, and had surely… you know.

Now *Arthur* was flushing. It was not a good idea to consider the fact that your younger and only cousin was no longer innocent.

Besides, her accusation about liking someone was completely wrong. So inaccurate, in fact, that it was laughable. Laughable!

"I don't like her," Arthur said roughly, pulling the stack of toast toward him and wondering if he could ask Cook to rustle up some bacon. "I need a wife to beget some heirs."

"Did you just say 'beget'? Who says 'beget' anymore?" Olive said with a scrunched nose.

Arthur sighed. "My point is, without heirs, there is no Earldom of Taernsby. I need heirs. I need a wife. I want *her*."

Want her so badly I would consider actually getting to know her. Want her so badly that she is seeping into my dreams, making it difficult to concentrate.

His cousin sighed. "Well, there's nothing for it, then. I shall have to invite her to tea."

Arthur blinked. "To tea?"

"Do you think she would accept an invitation from the Countess of Barlow? She does not know this is *your* residence specifically, I take it?"

To tea? What on earth is she talking about?

"I can talk to her, find out more about her. Find out what she is looking for in a man, you see?" His cousin was watching him carefully.

Why, precisely, Arthur had no idea.

Olive sighed again. "You always were dense. Are you forgetting what we used to do when my Mama and Papa or your Papa had guests and we wanted to know what they were talking about?"

Slowly, a grin crept over Arthur's face. "You wouldn't."

His cousin's expression was resolute. "I got married, Arthur. I didn't change that much."

It was a bad idea. That hadn't stopped him, and having Olive on his side truly made everything easier. Now Arthur came to think about it, he could hardly recall how he had managed to get Haslehaw and Cook to do what he wanted before her visit.

"No, over there," his sister said carefully, examining the positioning of the screen with an expert eye, as though she frequently orchestrated plots of this nature. "There."

Arthur snorted. "You truly think this will work?"

"I know it will," she said serenely. "Now, get back there and be quiet. I know it's an order you loathe, but I expect you to follow it."

"Yes, yes, yes," muttered Arthur with a grin as he disappeared.

He felt a fool. For twenty minutes, he sat there on a stool, hidden by the large, ornate Japanese screen. He amused himself for a while by looking at the elegant swirling patterns, the clever embroidery of the clouds, the figures who seemed so different, their clothes so colorful, their hairstyles unique.

Then he started to wonder whether Olive was having him on, whether Lilianna was actually invited at all, and whether this was all just one big jest to the countess.

Arthur was almost about to give up and come out from behind the screen, telling his cousin that she hadn't won this time, when the door to the drawing room opened.

"—pleasant to make your acquaintance last autumn in London," his cousin was saying, her voice growing closer and then a tad farther away. The sound of someone, perhaps two people, sitting on a sofa. "I've only just arrived in Bath and wished to renew our acquaintance. Are you sure your lady's maid won't join us?"

A nerve throbbed at Arthur's temple.

"She often prefers to take her tea with the staff. May I say I was honored to receive your note, Lady Barlow," came Lilianna's voice, sharp, aloof, yet friendly. Arthur's breath stilled at the sound. "Believing you were out of town for the whole of the spring, I did not wish to presume to send an invitation myself. I was not sure of your address in town."

"And yet here we are," said Arthur's cousin warmly. "Tea."

Arthur tried to shift silently on the stool upon which he was sitting as the sound of footfalls was accompanied by the clink of a tea tray.

She was here. She was here.

And somehow, that knowledge excited him, thrilled him in a way he did not understand.

It was ridiculous. He could not even see the woman.

"Tell me, what do you think of the crop of gentlemen this Season?"

Arthur froze. *Oh, come on, Olive—is she going to be that blatant?*

"I haven't ventured out into the harvest," came Lilianna's dry voice. "I've yet to see much maturity in the growth."

A smirk replaced the sensation of fear across Arthur's face as his cousin's laughter rang out around the drawing room. Honestly, Lady Lilianna was so… so clever. So dry, so refreshingly direct.

"Besides, what would I do with such a crop, place them in my barns?" Lilianna continued, mirth audible in her tone. "I'm not looking for enough grapes to make a vat of wine. I just want one perfect vintage."

Arthur sighed, then shook his head at his own stupidity. Honestly, was he truly going to let himself get carried away by a farming metaphor? It was foolish. Silly. Outrageous.

Somehow, she had made it… perfect.

"I believe you were fortunate in your own year of choice, Lady Barlow," Lilianna continued. "I congratulate you."

"Yes, he's a dear, to tell the truth," said Olive with a chuckle. "And you are correct. It is so hard to tell precisely whether or not a vine has grown into something suitable."

"The grapes on the vine can be… misleading," Lilianna countered.

And that was when Arthur could take it no longer. It was beguiling, having her so close and yet her not even knowing he was there.

Well, that can be remedied incredibly quickly.

"My Lady Lilianna," he said smoothly in his most charming voice as he rose from the stool and stepped out from behind the screen.

Olive groaned and placed her head into her hands. She appeared to be so embarrassed, she was actually glowing pink, but Arthur was not watching her. His attention was affixed on the other woman in the room, the one with her teacup halfway to her gaping mouth, staring at him with unmitigated horror.

He had hoped for delight, but any strong reaction at this point would do.

"May I make a suggestion?" Arthur said lightly, standing before them and wondering why on earth he was puffing out his chest in such a manner. "If you are concerned about the ripeness of the grape, why not have a taste?"

Olive groaned again and red splattered Lilianna's cheeks.

Yet she did not look away.

Yes, this was wonderful! Exhilaration roared through Arthur as she looked boldly at him, refusing to be cowed either by his sudden appearance or the devastatingly insolent way he had spoken to her.

She is more than a match for me, Arthur thought with delight. No other woman had managed to resist such an onslaught, and yet she had not run, had she?

Was she remembering the last time they had been together? Was she thinking of… that kiss?

"My, my," Lady Lilianna said distantly placing her teacup back on its saucer and the saucer on the table before her. "A distressed vine. Best we cut it off at the root, save it suffering."

This time, his cousin snorted a laugh. Arthur glanced at her with what he hoped was a silencing expression, but it only made Olive laugh more.

"In fact, I am not sure we should grow this vine again, are you, Lady Barlow?" said Lady Lilianna, turning to her hostess.

Arthur watched as his cousin struggled to retain her poise.

"Oh, I don't know," said his cousin mischievously, shooting him a knowing look. "Scolding him for his impertinence never seems to work for me."

"Very helpful," Arthur snapped.

He should not have spoken that way to her, but it was most provoking. This was supposed to be a grand entrance, an opportunity to turn Lady Lilianna pink and quivering at the reminder that the last time they were together, his lips had been on hers.

Not a time for his cousin and the woman he wanted to bed to laugh at him!

"I think you owe me a kiss now, Lilianna."

"L-Lady Lilianna."

"That wasn't a no."

"You have not a chance in hell."

Arthur cleared his throat, trying to both remove the memory of the kiss and remind the woman before him that he had kissed her, and quite thoroughly too.

Somehow, it appeared to work. Lilianna's gaze dropped, her cheeks flushing—and that wasn't the only part of her that was warming. Arthur watched with delight as heat spread like a tide across her décolletage. Oh, how he longed to touch that warmth, to feel it sizzle against his own skin…

"What were you doing behind that screen?" Lilianna asked accusingly.

Arthur swallowed. He hadn't exactly considered how he would explain his sudden presence to her, and now he was forced to consider it, he was rather discomforted by the idea of telling the truth. He was not a liar.

So, where did that leave him?

"I was sitting on a stool," he said helpfully, stepping forward and seating himself beside Lady Lilianna on the sofa.

His boldness was not rewarded. Without so much as a word, Lilianna rose, took three steps, and sat beside his cousin.

Irritation curled around his torso. Well, that was most annoying. Now instead of sitting beside the woman he would greatly love to undress and bury himself inside, he was having to look at her. Look at her sat beside his cousin.

Why on earth had he allowed Olive to convince him into this?

"A stool," Lady Lilianna repeated dryly.

There it was again, that—well, arrogance, for want of a better word. Arthur did not understand it. She was the daughter of a marquess, yes, but he was an earl. Did they not have a similar footing on which to converse?

She was staring like she had discovered him on the bottom of her shoe and was considering how to scrape him off without doing any damage to the sole.

And then—there it was. A flicker, just a heartbeat of a moment. Unguarded, Lady Lilianna had met his gaze and it was fire and heat and need and longing and that kiss was surely just as top of mind for her as it was for him.

Arthur grinned. Lady Lilianna looked away.

"Lady Lilianna, you are acquainted with my cousin?" said Olive.

"Your—Your cousin?" Lilianna's pert nose rose in the air.

"Yes, well, my husband's and my townhouse is undergoing a bit of a… renovation at the moment. This is my cousin's place.

Other than my mother, he's my only family, worse luck."

"I see," said Lilianna, her gaze still not finding Arthur's again. "Most excellent of you to lend it to your cousin for entertaining this morning, my lord. I wager this must be quite an inconvenience for you. So much so, you could not bring yourself to rise from your stool in order to pay proper respect to a guest at her arrival."

Arthur tried to hide the smirk threatening to stretch across his face.

"You know, when we were children, we were made to sit on a stool and think about what we'd done whenever we had been naughty," said Olive conversationally.

"Indeed?" Lady Lilianna said, the coldness having seeped right back into her tone. "How intriguing. So, my lord, what had you done that was so naughty that your cousin had required you to sit on a stool?"

She was looking not quite at him, but instead just over his right shoulder. What was she afraid of, Arthur wondered. Did she realize just how much she wanted him? Was she attempting to ignore the blatant attraction that they shared?

Just how far could he push her into discomfort?

"It's not, perhaps, the topic of conversation for elegant young ladies," Arthur said, arching a knowing smile across his lips. "I wouldn't wish to shock you."

"I don't think I can be shocked by your behavior any longer," said his cousin with a challenging air. "Go on, then. Tell us. Tell Lady Lilianna and me just what you have done."

Arthur swallowed.

Hell's bells, he wasn't a fool. He couldn't actually tell them—he would be dragged by wild horses before he admitted some of his personal enjoyments to his own cousin!

And Lady Lilianna…

Arthur had never concerned himself about saving his innocence. For the men in his year at Cambridge, losing one's innocence as soon as possible was far more important. It made a man of you, moved you from the realm of boyhood to the status of manhood.

The idea that he would wish to keep it for a particular woman, one he would meet in the future but had no idea whom she would be, would have felt outlandish.

And now?

Arthur cleared his throat. "I-I… I couldn't possibly—"

"What are you afraid of, my lord?" Lady Lilianna said suddenly, an impudent air in her tone. "Do you think you will offend me?"

Damn, woman. "Not offend, no."

"Then you think I will be scandalized."

She has absolutely no idea, does she? No idea at all. "Perhaps."

Lady Lilianna nodded sagely. "You wish to impress me."

Arthur almost bit his tongue. Were ladies permitted to be so direct? He was certain it wasn't allowed. "You know damned well—"

"Arthur!"

"—damned well," persisted Arthur, ignoring his cousin's cry of outrage, "that I wish to marry you!"

Any other woman would have gasped, perhaps clasped a hand to her chest. Others would have laughed, giggled, fluttered their eyelashes, blushed prettily, and told him to stop saying such things while inviting him with every ounce of their souls to continue.

Lady Lilianna did none of these things.

She did, however, lean forward with an intrigued look in her eye. "So you keep saying."

"Yes, and it's a little galling, to tell the truth, to have to repeat myself," said Arthur hotly, trying to keep his temper under control and failing miserably.

How did she have such an effect on him? How did she do it, this strange intoxication that dulled his sense and heightened his senses?

"You expected to charm me at first sight, I suppose," Lady

Lilianna said, her lip quirking. "Expected me to throw myself at you, to accept you immediately in the hope that you would actually follow through on the wedding."

"I would—I will," Arthur began, but he was almost instantaneously cut off.

"And yet you have a reputation, my lord, you must know that. How many ladies have you bedded this year alone?"

Arthur opened his mouth, attempted to calculate, realized he couldn't remember, and closed it again.

"You won't tell me."

"You wouldn't want to hear it." His voice was hoarse and he hated this, hated the power she had over him. He had never known this before.

"You are popular with the ladies, yet you are not popular with *this* lady," said Lady Lilianna, now clearly entertained. There was a glint of mischief in her eyes, making them all the more devastatingly attractive.

Arthur shifted in his seat. These trousers would have to be let out, they were far too small.

Oh. Oh, of course. He was hard again. Damned woman!

"Popularity with you, it seems, is a far harder prize," he said softly.

She evidently had not expected softness. Lady Lilianna blinked, clearly ready for a fight but not finding one.

"And yes, charming women has never been a particular challenge for me," said Arthur, leaning forward to mirror her, his trousers becoming tighter with every inch they grew closer. "And none of them ever interested me as you do. You, Lady Lilianna. I proposed marriage to you and I will keep on doing so until you—"

"Give up?"

Arthur allowed a wicked smile to crease his lips. "Give in. Surrender."

They sat there, not touching, just staring at each other. It shouldn't have been erotic, but it was. Arthur's pulse quickened, his breathing ratcheting up, and all he wanted to do was close the gap and taste those lips again, glory in the connection they started by the Fish Pond and would not be complete until he had her in his bed.

Even Olive could not object if he—

Damn. Olive!

Arthur's eyes widened as his head jerked to the side, to where his cousin was seated. To where his cousin *had been* seated.

He blinked. There was no one seated beside Lady Lilianna.

"She left a while ago," said Lady Lilianna quietly. Her breath blossomed on his cheek, they were so close. "You did not notice?"

"I don't notice anything when I'm with you." Arthur had not intended to say the words, but they were true. How could anyone?

When he looked back, Lady Lilianna was flushing. "You do speak such nonsense, my lord."

"I wish you would call me 'Taernsby.' Or 'Arthur.'"

"I am sure you do," she said, a feisty spark returning. "But I am afraid I will not—and I must be going. My *chaperone* awaits in the kitchens."

She stood up gracefully and Arthur shot up, picking up a cushion in haste to hold before him. Christ, if he didn't calm down soon, he was going to have a real problem on his hands.

Lady Lilianna raised an eyebrow at the odd way he was holding the cushion. "Well, it has been… I will not say a pleasure—"

"I could give you some," Arthur said in a low voice.

God, how he wished he could tempt her. But if Lady Lilianna had been easily tempted, some other man would have tasted of her before now. The thought was abhorrent. Arthur pushed it firmly from his mind.

Lady Lilianna leaned forward. She was going to murmur something in his ear. As she leaned, placing a hand on his arm, a jolt of need throbbed in Arthur's manhood.

"I doubt it," she whispered sweetly.

And then she was gone, striding out of his drawing room, leaving Arthur all alone.

For a heartbeat, he just stood there. Then he slowly, very carefully, lowered himself to lie on the sofa face-down. Then he shouted a few casual obscenities into the cushion.

When he looked up, Olive was standing by the sofa with her arms crossed and a frown on her face.

"'Renovation'?"

"I may have asked the staff to rearrange some furniture."

He didn't respond.

"And?" she said lightly. "How did it go?"

Arthur looked up, despair and frustration his only emotions.

"That well?"

Without replying, he turned his face back into the cushion and groaned.

Chapter Seven

March 19, 1840

"Now b-behave—"

"I know how to behave at a card party, Mama," said Lilianna dismissively as the three of them stepped into the Daltons' upper sitting room, where the evening card party was taking place. "It's Samuel you have to worry about."

He smirked. "Lil, I would never cause trouble."

"There he is, arguing with his sister in public," Lilianna said with a grin, nudging her brother. "Utterly incorrigible."

Their mother sighed. "I sh-should have asked your f-father to accompany us."

"Never fear. We won't let you down, Mama," Lilianna's brother said resolutely, helping himself to three glasses of wine from the platter of a passing footman and handing them around. "We shall be the pinnacle of… the pinnacle of… what shall we be the pinnacle of, Lil?"

"Propriety," she said with a wry smile. "I think that's the word you're looking for."

As befit the Chances. They were, after all, the most prestigious guests at this card party, as far as she could tell. There were the Glenarms, the Zouches, though thank goodness without their eldest son, and the Quintrells were here too. She'd heard tell the Braedons had been invited and it would have been lovely to see them again, but Lilianna could not be sorry that they were absent. There was only one person her roving eye was attempting to find.

Her shoulders slumped as she realized he was not there.

"—and p-please don't lose too m-much—"

"As if I would lose a hand of cards, Mama!" Samuel said beside her.

Lilianna barely listened. She was not here to see *him*, she told herself determinedly. She did not want to see him at all. Did not miss him at all—the very idea! No. Definitely not. *Not at all.*

"—won't you, Lilianna?"

"Whatever you say, Mama," she said swiftly, without waiting to see what the request had been. Her mother hated Society and had agreed to chaperone Lilianna before Samuel had also agreed to attend. The least she owed her mother was obedience.

Her brother was staring. "I thought you hated whist, Lil."

Ah. Well, that was why you should heed the conversation going on around you and not just blindly agree to whatever it was your mother wanted.

Lilianna smiled weakly at the older, dimpled woman who had at some point joined their trio. "Oh, Lady Dalton, how lovely to see you. Whist, was it?"

Ignoring her brother's snorts of laughter, Lilianna swept through the large room to a table with two empty chairs. The two gentlemen beamed at the approaching pair of ladies.

"Lady Lilianna," one of them said, rising to pull out Lilianna's chair.

Well, it was not much of a hardship, Lilianna supposed graciously as she accepted her cards. She would sit here for twenty minutes or so, endure whist, a game that had to have been created purposefully to annoy, then return to her mother. Whist could be endured if there was sufficient flattery involved.

For five minutes or so, she lost herself in the game. There was not much else to entertain in the place, after all. Lord Dalton had secured a trio of musicians, but other than that, it was the card tables and the company. There wasn't much to inspire a mention in the scandal sheets in either direction.

"And that's a trick!"

Lilianna smiled vaguely at the oval-faced young man who looked so pleased with himself. "So it is."

Her focus drifted around the room. Was there to be any excitement? There did not appear to be any guests of note, though there was a great deal of chatter over there in the corner…

And there he was.

Her whole body thrummed with anticipation. She had been unable to eke out the guest list from Lady Dalton, but she'd hoped, presumed, that the Earl of Taernsby would be here. And he was.

And he looked…

Lilianna swallowed. It was not appropriate for young ladies to be conscious of just how handsome a man was, and so she attempted not to be. Unfortunately, there was very limited control she could exert over her fluttering pulse and the tingles of heat flowing over her body.

Because her eyes could not look away from the tall, handsome man who laughed so charmingly on the other side of the room. Lilianna's eyes meandered lazily over the broad shoulders, examined the nape of his neck, noticed the way his crown curled.

Lord Taernsby laughed again and his merriment was a melody Lilianna wanted to hear again. It was most infuriating, but there it was.

It was pleasant to see him there. It was—

"Lady Lilianna," said a distant voice.

Lilianna blinked. She was still seated at the card table and judging by the way her companions were all staring, it was her turn.

Oh, dear.

"Right, two shillings," she said hastily, throwing down two coins and immediately returning her attention to Lord Taernsby.

He was no longer alone.

But he wasn't alone before, was he? Lilianna's mind whirled as the game around her continued. He had been laughing, so there must have been someone *with whom* he'd been laughing.

As Lilianna's attention moved to his companion, her blood ran cold.

A woman.

And not just *a* woman—that might have been bearable. This woman was beautiful. Stunning. Exquisite. By the delicate jade beading on her gown and the matching jade handle of her fan, it was evident she was a wealthy woman. By the way she tilted her head and giggled, her gaze feeding hungrily on the Earl of Taernsby, she was a woman on the hunt.

Lilianna watched Lord Taernsby lean close to the woman. He murmured something delectable in her ear.

"Lady Lilianna!"

It was only after she had thrown down the cards and stood up, her chair tipping over behind her, that Lilianna realized she had done so. She blinked hazily for a moment at her fellow card players, whose mouths were open and whose lips were making remarks of shock and astonishment.

"But the game—"

"What has happened? Where is she going?"

Lilianna neither heeded them nor replied to them. She was too busy being furious.

How dare he? How dare he?! Flatter her, kiss her, listen to her talk behind a screen like he was a complete imbecile… and flirt with another woman? Court *her*, whoever she was, perhaps?

No. Absolutely not.

She had never felt rage like this before, never felt pain like this before. She had perhaps never cared like this before, a thought Lilianna swiftly pushed away just as she had pushed away from the table.

She had to speak to him.

All thought of propriety was gone. All concern about what people would say, what the world would see, what people would think—it was all immaterial. She had to speak to him.

"—and then I told him," the woman was saying flirtatiously, casting looks up at Lord Taernsby that were unsubtle in their meaning, "I was only smiling at him because—oh."

"Lilianna!" Taernsby growled in pain.

Lilianna ignored him. It was easy to, when the rage of jealousy was still pouring through her veins, forcing her forward.

She'd grabbed him by the collar and began dragging him away from his new friend, continuing to ignore his muttered complaints. What did it matter? She needed answers. She deserved them. And she wasn't going to ask the questions she needed answering in front of that—that woman!

Lilianna finally released him when she had sufficiently dragged him to the other side of the room. It was quiet here, almost empty. Near the corner was a large potted plant and she pulled him behind it.

There. Still in public and therefore respectable, yet hidden enough to have a private conversation. As long as they kept their voices down.

"What the devil are you doing?"

"I think *I* should be the one asking questions, thank you!" she fired back in a hiss, glaring. "And keep your voice down."

"*Me*! Keep *my* voice down?" Taernsby's eyes were wide, his expression astonished.

Lilianna drew herself up and increased the ferocity of her glare. "Yes."

She was panting. When had that happened? She had not noticed. All she had been focused on had been getting that woman away. Or rather, him away from that woman.

Glancing over her shoulder, she saw to her satisfaction that the woman had drifted away. She was now surrounded by a trio of gentlemen who were making her laugh just as Taernsby had.

Lilianna turned back to him. "Taernsby, you—"

"Oh, is that what you're calling me now, is it?" He grinned. "Very intimate, I like it."

Tempted to swear under her breath just like Benjamin so often did, Lilianna squared her shoulders and glared. "How dare you?!"

Taernsby blinked. "How—How dare I?"

"Yes, how dare you?" Lilianna hissed, trying her best to keep her voice low and a smile on her face. It would not do for anyone to presume that they were sharing something ridiculous.

Like a lovers' tiff.

"Remind me, who was it who dragged whom over here?" he asked with a raised eyebrow.

"That isn't the point," Lilianna said dismissively, ignoring the way that such an expression warmed her. "I can't believe you. You were just standing there and—and doing it!"

Taernsby frowned. "I have no idea what you mean."

"Talking to her—laughing with her, flirting with her, whoever she is!" said Lilianna sharply. "I cannot believe you would do that!"

Her words hung between them for a moment.

She had expected him to glare, perhaps, or hang his head in shame. An apology would have been suitable, given the circumstances, and she would accept it graciously, making absolutely sure he would never do it again.

"You're jealous," said Taernsby, a delighted expression slipping over his face.

The room must suddenly have gained an influx of people. That was the only explanation for why heat poured through Lilianna's body, pink rising from her décolletage and surely covering her entire face.

"What? No, I'm not," she denied automatically.

"You are. You're jealous." The tall earl looked down at her with savoring eyes. "Lilianna—"

"*Lady* Lilianna," she corrected sharply.

Her correction did not appear to matter. "Lilianna," Taernsby said quietly, giving her name a timbre of seduction and intimacy that made her shiver. "You can attempt to berate me all you wish—"

"I will!"

"—but all you will do is convince me that you like me," he finished with a wicked look in his eye. "You do, don't you?"

"Nonsense," Lilianna said cuttingly.

How outrageous for him to even think such a thing, much less say it aloud! Like him? *Like him?* She could hardly stand the sight of him—but if she was going to have to suffer through it, she refused to do so while seeing him butter up another woman!

When Lilianna looked up warily, Taernsby was grinning.

"Why are you so upset then, Lilianna?"

"I told you before. It's *you*. How you act. Not me."

"Don't you think we're a little past that?" His voice was soft, alluring, tempting Lilianna to step closer to hear him. She only just managed to stop herself.

She swallowed—hard. "I just don't think you should be—"

"Paying any woman attention, other than you."

Lilianna frowned, her hands clenching into fists by her side. *Oh, he is so aggravating!* "That is not what I said."

"But it's what you thought," Taernsby countered. "Isn't it? Tell the truth, Lilianna. You aren't the sort of person to lie. Tell me. Why did seeing me speak to Lady Marjorie upset you so much?"

Her breath was short, her shoulders tight, and this was all wrong. The idiot man was supposed to just apologize and walk away, speaking to neither herself nor this Lady Marjorie ever again. But instead, she was here, talking to him, *needing* to talk to him, longing for the conversation to be prolonged.

Something wasn't right. Was she sick? Coming down with a fever, perhaps?

Lilianna gasped as Taernsby took a step closer to her, mere inches away now.

"Tell me what's got you so riled up."

The following words slipped from her mouth before she could stop them—but then, he had told her to tell the truth. "You are supposed to be courting *me*," Lilianna whispered, looking up into his eyes as a jolt passed through her stomach. "Not her. Not anyone else."

There was a look of triumph in his eyes, but it passed swiftly, leaving only something akin to understanding in its wake.

"You have been remarkably consistent in wishing me not to be courting you, Lilianna," Taernsby pointed out.

It was most unfair of him to do so. Lilianna could not deny it. How many times had he asked her to marry him now? Four? Five?

And each time she had rebuffed him, and reasonably so. The man was a rake, the Earl of Taernsby, a Nelson, whose family name did not offer much in the way of respectability. If she had known the Countess of Barlow was his relation, she would have refused to meet her for tea. She would not have fallen victim to their little trap.

She was a Chance. There was no possibility of her and him, of the two of them… No. It was not possible.

"You said you didn't like it," Taernsby continued, his voice low, persistent. "Except for that kiss, obviously."

Lilianna's cheeks burned. She had to stop him speaking. She could not hear about that kiss without thinking about… about how good it had felt. About how she had been unable to stop thinking about it since it had happened.

She had to stop him. "Taernsby—"

"Oh, I do like it when you call me that," said the earl in a whisper that had the harmonics of a growl. "Yes, I definitely like it."

Lilianna sighed with exasperation. "My lord, then."

"Are you truly that contrary?" he challenged her.

She looked up into his eyes and saw cunning, and cleverness, and smiled. "Yes. So, my lord—"

"You know, if you're not going to be nice to me, then I may as well walk away and find Lady Marjorie again," Taernsby pointed out easily with a shrug. "Is that what you want, Lilianna?"

Oh, it was all so frustrating! There was such heat within her, clouding her judgment, frustrating her mind into confusion, that she could not think what to say.

No, that was not what she wanted. Couldn't he see? Had she not been plain enough? There needed to be an understanding between them, though of what variety and nature, she could not fathom.

What I really want, Lilianna thought ominously, *is not to have him. Is for no one to have him.*

Yes, that was it. She did not want him, but she certainly did not want any other woman getting notions of having him to herself. That would be unsupportable.

What was the term for that?

"You know, anyone would think that you like me," Taernsby said lazily.

Lilianna's temper sparked up once more. "I most definitely do not!"

He examined her closely, his attention making her thighs tingle. When he spoke, it was in a low, melodious voice that made Lilianna want to do terrible things. "Then why are your hands on my chest?"

Her gasp was lost in his low chuckle. Lilianna looked down, horrified to discover that she had at some point, goodness knew when, splayed both palms against the Earl of Taernsby's chest.

He was warm. Very warm. She could feel his heat pouring through his clothes, layers of linen and cotton insufficient to keep his warmth away.

Unheeded, a low moan gushed from her throat.

It happened so quickly, she barely knew what he was doing. Taernsby grabbed her hands, grasping them tightly, then pushed them away.

Lilianna blinked, his absence, the lack of his touch suddenly cold. "Why did you—"

"Why did *you*?" Taernsby said quietly, his words urgent.

"God, woman, you blow hot and cold. I can't keep up with you. Do you want me?"

"N-No."

"Then you don't want anyone else to have me?" he shot back.

Lilianna swallowed, panic filling her mind.

What did she want? Why couldn't she stay away from this irritating man? Why was he making it so difficult? What was it drawing her here, making her focus on him to the detriment of everything, of everyone else?

It was akin to losing control and she did not like it. Her mind spun whenever she was in his damned presence and she couldn't explain it. There was no rational explanation.

She swallowed again and this time noticed how Taernsby's gaze followed the bob of her throat.

Lilianna smiled. But it wasn't all one way, was it? No, she had some sort of control or influence or something over him. She just did not understand what it was.

"Look at all the other ladies who are in attendance here tonight, Lilianna."

Lilianna almost shied away from the sudden connection, but she couldn't. That would require breathing, and apparently, she did not do that anymore.

The suddenness of his movement had shocked her, but not any less than what Taernsby had moved to do. He was standing behind her now, his right shoulder pressed into hers, and she could drink him in. Oh, this was too much. Too close, too intimate.

"Look at them," Taernsby repeated quietly.

She should have told him to leave her alone—should have stepped away, forced him to be reasonable. Perhaps tried to force *herself* to be reasonable.

Yet it was not possible. She was locked in the moment, unable to step away, unwilling to. This intimacy, this closeness, it was far too much.

Yet somehow not enough.

Lilianna obeyed, luxuriating in being ordered about in a way she had never celebrated before. She hated being ordered about—so why did this feel so delicious?

"You see them?"

"I… I see them." She gasped, just about finding enough air to speak.

Taernsby's voice was a breeze against her neck and it made her toes tingle. "Every single one of these ladies could be with me. They could be receiving my smiles, my laughter, my jokes. I could be standing this close to them, teasing them—"

Lilianna's gasp caught in her throat. Oh, she never wanted it to end.

"—yet here I am with you." Taernsby's voice became, just for a moment, a low chuckle. "And the thanks that I get for that? Very little."

Lilianna exhaled. "You don't want an easy conquest."

It was both the right and the wrong thing to say. Suddenly, his hips had angled against her buttocks and Lilianna could hardly think. The intensity of the touch was too much, and she wanted it again. And again. And again—

"You're right." Taernsby stepped back.

Lilianna almost put a hand out to the wall to prevent herself from falling.

What on earth was happening to her? What was he *doing* to her? It was ridiculous, it was wonderful, it was awful, it was utterly unacceptable.

After blinking a few times to ensure her vision wasn't going to disappear, Lilianna turned. Taernsby was leaning against the wall with that damned eyebrow raised.

He must have known how good he looked when he did that, didn't he?

Taernsby grinned, as though he could hear her thoughts. Was she that transparent? Were her thoughts etched across her face?

"So, you like me," he said conversationally.

"I do not," Lilianna said swiftly.

"I don't know why you're bothering to hide it," Taernsby said with a shrug. "I mean, you can lie to yourself—"

"I am not lying to myself!"

"—you can lie to me—"

Infuriating man. Did he think that everything he spouted was going to be agreed with—would be listened to? "I am not lying to you!"

"—but you can't lie to them," he said softly.

"And what's more—them?" Lilianna halted.

Somehow, she had stepped forward and was pointing a finger against Taernsby's chest, her nose a mere inch from his own as she glared, desperate to prove him wrong.

Because he *was* wrong. There was absolutely no possibility that she liked him. Him? With his arrogant manners and his presumptuous proposals and his devilishly kissable lips?

Wait a moment, that isn't right.

Taernsby was grinning. "Them," he repeated with a nod.

Slowly, Lilianna turned on her heels. Because she was in such close proximity to the most irksome man she had ever met when she did so, her shoulder rubbed into his and she almost curled into him.

Oh, no.

She stumbled away, trying to pretend to the entirety of the Daltons' card party, who were staring at the pair of them, that she had not been just pushing the Earl of Taernsby up against a wall and leaning so close to him that the merest breeze would have had them kissing.

Oh, no, oh, no, oh—

"You like me," came the quiet, confident whisper of a rogue. "And if you don't, you have certainly just given the whole card party that impression."

Lilianna swallowed, her cheeks burning as she took in people's expressions. Shock, confusion, in a few quarters delight at her potential societal downfall. In one corner stood her mother, whose mouth was open, and Samuel, who looked like he was stifling laughter.

She whirled on her feet. "You did this on purpose!"

Taernsby was grinning. "I can't say that I know what you mean."

"Yes, you do!" Lilianna could hardly speak, she was so mortified.

He raised both hands in surrender. "I was merely minding my own business when a beautiful lady dragged me over here."

"You—You flirted with that woman on purpose. You knew I would—"

"Would what?"

"Would care!" It didn't matter that she was honest now; the disaster was almost over. "Would bring you aside and argue with you and you, you'd get me all… all…"

Taernsby licked his lips. Lilianna tried not to notice. "Riled up?"

"Yes!"

His smile was now wolfish, hungry, eager, and *desperate for her*. "And is it working?"

It was a miracle she could speak and walk away at the same time. "No."

Chapter Eight

March 23, 1840

THE HAMMERING ON the door was most irritating, and worst of all, it did not appear to be ceasing.

"Haslehaw?" Arthur poked his head out of his study door and peered about the hallway.

It was the butler's job to answer the door. He did not have to have been born and raised to inherit an earldom to know that—it was how it had always been. For his father, and his brother, and he had presumed also for him.

So why was this incessant knocking continuing?

"Haslehaw?" Arthur repeated the name but louder this time, wincing as a particularly hard knock hammered on the door.

Really, it was most provoking. Whoever needed to see him that badly? Irritatingly, he could not ignore it, his study being right at the front of the house.

"Is anyone going to answer that door?"

There was not only no answer to the door, but no answer to his question.

Sighing heavily and rubbing his brow with tiredness—who knew that being an earl required so much paperwork?—Arthur strode across the hall and wrenched open the door. "What do you—Lilianna."

The woman—alone, again, the devious minx—glared up from the step, a fury the likes of which he had never seen before painted across her face.

If it hadn't been so arousing, Arthur would have grinned. *She's here.*

"You!" she snapped, painfully obviously less delighted to see him than he was to see her. "You!"

Ah. His attempt to soothe the beautiful beast had not gone to plan, then.

"Why don't we have this conversation inside?" he suggested hastily, glancing along the street.

Yes, as expected, there were plenty of people wandering the streets of Bath at this hour, and all of them were about to gain front-row seats of the spectacle that was himself attempting to court Lady Lilianna Chance. Without a chaperone in sight. The brim of her bonnet hung low over her face, as if an attempt to disguise herself had been made, but he doubted there were many who would look this way and not realize exactly who she was. He certainly would recognize her at a glance.

It isn't going badly, exactly, thought Arthur feverishly as she continued to berate him at the top of her lungs. Could a thing be described as going badly if it wasn't going at all?

"—the cheek. I thought even *you* would not lower yourself to—"

And it had started to finally go well. At least, that was what he had thought upon returning home from the Daltons' card party. How could he think otherwise? The way she had nearly pinned him against the wall, it had been enough to require half an hour sitting in a freezing-cold bath before going to bed.

"—could not have believed you would deign to—"

And now she was standing by his front door, shouting at him. Arthur blinked, centering himself and allowing his instincts to take over.

That was what he needed. Less thought, more action.

"Come here," he said, grabbing her arm.

He should have known that was a mistake.

"How dare you lay a hand on me?!"

"As far as I can remember, the last person to lay a hand on *me* was *you!*" Arthur pointed out, pulling her forward.

He was stronger than her, much stronger. Trying not to think about how delicate she was, how desperate he was to protect someone like her, even from herself, Arthur dragged her a few feet into the hall then slammed the door behind them.

As though summoned by the presence of a lack of work, Haslehaw appeared. "Did I hear someone knocking at the door?"

Lilianna ignored the butler entirely. "How dare you abduct me?"

Arthur rolled his eyes. "I haven't abducted you, I've—well, I've dragged you into my house."

"Against my will!"

"Ah, will the lady be staying for tea?" asked Haslehaw brightly.

Arthur pinched the bridge of his nose and wondered what he had done to deserve this. Well, actually, now he thought about it, the bedding of Lady Kimberton had been particularly dastardly… and he had made vague sorts of promises to Miss Halifax—or had that been her sister? In the dark, it could have been either.

Fine. Fine, he might deserve this. *Damn it.*

"Release me forthwith, you beast!"

"Not until you tell me what you are yelling about," Arthur snapped.

"I think Cook has some cake somewhere," said the butler quietly.

"And another thing!" Lilianna said sharply, clearly preparing herself for another verbal onslaught. "I have never… never seen…"

Arthur stared. For some reason, the woman's tongue appeared to have halted. Her eyes were wide and she was staring around herself in complete wonder.

What is going on?

"My lord?"

Well, at least that was one problem that he could solve. "Haslehaw?" Arthur said sweetly. "Go away."

By now the older man was growing accustomed to his rudeness. And to his master being alone with unchaperoned women. The servant hardly batted an eyelid as he bowed. "Of course, my lord."

"There." Arthur heaved, shaking his head slightly and turning back to the first problem. His first problem. His woman. No, that quite yet. "Now, what were you shouting about?"

It looked like his words could not quite reach her. Lilianna's lips had parted, and as they were now alone, Arthur permitted himself to look at them. Cherub lips, pink and wet from all her shouting. Desperately crying out to him to be kissed. Really, it was a shame that they had been unkissed for so long.

That was, assuming that Lady Lilianna Chance had not been kissing anyone else in the meantime.

Fiery rage flared and was hastily dampened. Arthur could not permit himself to lose control, or lose focus. He had to try to get somewhere with this hoyden.

"It's… It's beautiful."

Arthur blinked. "I am?"

Her expression sharpened and she scoffed as she threw a hand to gesture around the room. "Not you, you dolt. Last time, I left hastily, and I never had a chance to look around outside the drawing room. I didn't notice… this."

This. This?

Arthur looked around him, searching for the beautiful whatever-it-was that Lilianna was looking at. Her rapt expression suggested it was something truly delightful, but for the life of him, he could not spot what it was.

He glanced at her, stomach lurching at the expression of wonder. It was such… Not innocence. That wasn't the right word. At least, *she* was innocent, but the look wasn't.

It was… desire. Not for a man, but for pretty things.

Arthur attempted to look around through her eyes. What could she have been looking at?

Well, the stained glass windows around the front door certainly made the light magical in here. And the lantern light at the top, yes, that was unusual. Perhaps it was the marble; the blue threaded with white and gold was scarce, his great-grandfather had gone to a great deal of trouble to find that. Or perhaps it was the painting. The paintings. Most of the Rubenses were in the country house, of course, but there were sufficient here to ensure that guests and visitors knew of the estate's wealth.

Arthur tilted his head. Was that it? Pretty architecture, nice paintings? "You like it?"

He had not intended his voice to be so low, but somehow, speaking any louder would break the magic of the moment.

Lilianna nodded, her eyes still wide.

A smile crept across Arthur's face and he had intended it to be teasing, but when he spoke he was astonished to hear the genuineness in his voice. "It could all be yours, you know, Lilianna."

Whether it was what he said or how he'd said it, the moment was broken.

Lilianna shook her head, as though ridding her ears of water. Then her attention fell on him and it sharpened. "What does this mean?" she snapped, as though she had not just lost herself in a reverie for several minutes.

Arthur stared. "What does what mean?"

Her frown was so beautiful, he wondered how he managed not to kiss her. "Don't be so obtuse."

"Well, pardon me for being berated in my own home about something that I don't understand!" he said, unable to prevent himself from laughing. "Honestly, Lilianna, what are you implying?"

"Don't call me that," she snapped.

Arthur's mischievous nature sparked, and before he could stop himself, he returned, "Whatever you say, Countess."

Lilianna had been about to say something, but puzzlement appeared to overcome her. "Countess? That's my aunt. *I* am not a countess!"

"Not yet," said Arthur boldly. "Give it time."

He allowed the hunger he felt for her to rise in his expression. Just for a moment. A heartbeat of unrestrained desire, of lust pouring through his eyes and—

Lilianna took a hasty step backward, her cheeks scarlet. "Y-You can't look at me like that."

"I can look at you any way I wish," Arthur said quietly, silently rejoicing at the immense effect his passion had riled in her. "It's touching that I shouldn't be doing."

He saw the movement, even if she didn't feel it. Her fingers, they twitched. Twitched away from? Or *toward*?

Lilianna looked away at her reticule, which she opened with fumbling fingers. God, he loved to see the evidence of the effect he was having on her. Why was she fighting it? Why couldn't she just accept that he was ready to marry her within days, if they could manage the license?

"This," she said curtly. "This."

She'd taken a piece of paper from her reticule. Arthur recognized it immediately.

"You don't like my letter?"

Lilianna proffered it to him, but Arthur refused to take it. "I sent that to you. You are the intended recipient."

"I am returning it to sender," she snapped. "I don't—I didn't expect—you can't send me a letter!"

"I know we're not engaged, but whose fault is that?"

She ignored him. "And you can't send me a letter like… like this!" Lilianna said, her cheeks so red, Arthur rather wondered whether they weren't burning.

"A letter like this."

Well, he probably should not have sent it. It was an intense thing to do with a mistress, and Lilianna was certainly no man's mistress.

In a flash, an image appeared in Arthur's mind that he could not immediately quell. Lady Lilianna Chance, but not as she was standing here before him. No, this Lilianna was naked. Her imagined swells and curves had a very real effect on his body and Arthur grimaced, trying to control the lust that threatened to overtake him.

"Taernsby?"

Arthur swallowed. "I like it when you call me that."

"Oh, hell," muttered Lilianna, dropping her gaze. It lifted again almost immediately. "I suppose I am one of several women to receive such… such obscenities?"

"You think I would do such a thing?" Arthur had not intended his voice to be so broken, so cracked, but the accusation had stung far more than he had expected.

His pain must have been obvious. Lilianna hesitated, her hand holding the letter lowering to her side. "I… I just… I thought—"

"You thought I could write these words to anyone but yourself?" Arthur snatched the letter from her unresisting hand and unfolded it, hardly knowing what he was doing. "'Dear Lilianna—'"

"Don't read it!"

"'It has been several hours since I have last seen you, and each one has been more painful than the last,'" he continued doggedly, lowering his voice but refusing to halt. Lilianna's eyes did not leave him as he spoke. "'Your beauty is beyond any other woman's and I will be desolate if you do not accept me—'"

"Taernsby."

"'—as your husband,'" Arthur read aloud, his pulse throbbing in his ears as he approached the part he knew she was most mortified by. The part he could hardly believe he had committed to writing. "'Because as your husband, I will give you such pleas—'"

"Don't."

And he halted.

He was panting as though he'd run a mile, his fists itching as though he needed to fight his way through a brawl, and he wanted—

He wanted her. Arthur wanted Lilianna to listen to him, to actually believe him when he read aloud what he had written at some godawful time in the morning.

Her eyes were closed. Her beautiful eyes were hidden from him and to Arthur's horror, he saw he had gone too far.

Oh, hell. This courting thing is harder than it looks.

"Why are you doing this?" Lilianna spoke quietly as she opened her eyes, brilliant with unshed tears. "I don't—I don't understand. No man has ever—"

"Just because no man has told you of his desire," Arthur returned just as quietly, "that does not mean he has not felt it. And what I feel for you…"

"You don't know me. Why is this happening? What do you want?"

He shrugged as nonchalantly as he could, though discomfort rested. Why was he like this? Why not be honest with her? Why pursue a woman who so clearly did not wish to be pursued?

But revealing that would be revealing a part of himself. The portcullis came back down. "Is it too much to presume that someone is attracted to you?"

Arthur had expected her to retreat another step, but this time, Lilianna stood her ground.

"Attracted to my b-body."

"Attracted to *you*," he amended.

Lilianna shook her head. "Attracted to the Chance name, perhaps."

"Is it too much to think that someone would want you for you? Would kiss you for you?"

His words echoed around the marble hall and so too did her gasp.

She was thinking about the kiss. *Their* kiss. Arthur could see it in her eyes, the soft, molten look that he had only seen once before on Lady Lilianna Chance's expression. He had presumed the kiss would be sufficient, make her see, feel how much he wanted her—but all it appeared to have done was cloud the issue.

He could do more.

Arthur swallowed, his jaw tightening. If she were just some woman he desired, he would have done more by now. Pinned her to a sofa or a wall and kissed all the way down those perfect breasts and nestled his face between her thighs and—

But this wasn't just some woman. This was Lilianna. Hang the Chance name, she could have been from any family well-bred enough to be a Nelson bride.

She was Lilianna. And he would not touch her, not to convince her to accept him. Arthur may not have liked the thought, but he could not deny it.

He wanted her to say *yes* to him, not to what his fingers or tongue could do.

"Lilianna," he whispered.

"I don't know what you want," she said suddenly, her shoulders slumping, a true vulnerability coming over her that was almost painful to see. "What do you want, Taernsby?"

Arthur stared. What did he want? He wanted… He wanted her. He wanted to possess her, own her, keep her with him every day for stolen intimacy and every night for slow, luxurious pleasure-giving.

He wanted to know she was his. For her to know that, for the world to know that no one could even look at her without his permission.

And that scared him. That possessiveness, that need to own her, where had it come from?

What would it make him do?

There was only one way to combat it, and though bile rose in his throat at the mere thought, Arthur forced himself to speak. "Come with me. I… I want to show you something."

He did not grab hold of her this time. This was a conversation she had to come to willingly. If there was any sort of coercion, it would be tainted somehow. Ruined.

And so he turned on his heels and started to walk toward the staircase.

For a moment, only his steps echoed on the marble. Then, as he placed his foot on the first step, a second pair joined him.

"Where are we going?" Lilianna said stiffly as she walked beside him up the staircase. "If—If this is a ruse just to get me in your bedchamber—"

"Who says I would need a bedchamber?" Arthur returned. "A man can ruin a woman anywhere, if he knows what he's doing."

It was the wrong thing to say—too rough, too coarse. She was all softness and smooth, like silk that had been left out in the sun.

God damn, but he needed to get a grip on himself.

No, not that sort of grip…

"Here," he said aloud. "Gallery."

It appeared his brain was only permitting him to say single-word sentences at the moment, and perhaps that was all to the good. He did not appear to have made much progress with his longwinded speeches, after all.

Lilianna looked curiously along the long corridor. "A portrait gallery?"

Arthur nodded, hating how swiftly she was able to undo him. Perhaps that was why he wanted her. Possessing her would mean that she could not possess him. "Nelsons. Earls. Taernsby."

His foolish mono-word sentences aside, Lilianna appeared to understand. She started to walk down the long gallery, still dressed for the outdoors—bonnet, pelisse, and all, as if ready to escape at any moment. She paused at some paintings more than others, though he could not see any particular rhyme or reason for her choices.

By the time Arthur and his guest had reached his grandfather, his pulse was painfully quick. Surely, a man's heart should not have been beating like this? It wasn't natural.

"He looks very like you," she said about the next portrait.

"I suppose I look like *him*," Arthur said shortly. "My father."

"Your father…" Lilianna said, her voice trailing off as she

looked between him and the painting.

Try as he might, he could not help but wonder what she was thinking. The family had always said that he was the runt of the litter. More like his mother than his father, that was what his grandfather had said.

"More's the pity."

He'd hated that when a child, but as Arthur had grown, his mother's softness and gentleness had felt more and more like weakness. Her death when he had been small made her fainter still, memories of her vague, undefined. Yet every time he had peered in a looking glass he had seen her there, looking back at him through his features.

"You truly see my father in me?"

The question slipped out like a foolish schoolboy. Arthur cursed himself silently for the weakness. *You're here to impress her, you dolt, not ask inane questions.*

"I think so," said Lilianna quietly, examining him closely. "Similar eyes, similar mouth… but there's a kindness in you that I don't see in him."

Arthur's mouth went dry.

Dear God, she was perceptive. Or at least, he hoped she was. It was perhaps the nicest thing anyone had ever said to him.

"So this must be your brother."

Arthur nodded. Better that than risking his tongue when he was feeling like such a dullard.

Lilianna examined the painting closely. "He looks young."

"He was." Arthur had not considered that he would be speaking about Archibald, but with his painting there, there was no avoiding it. No avoiding him. "A good man."

"You say that as though you are not sure," she said softly.

Damn this woman's perception. "No man is all good."

"No man is all bad, either," she countered, turning back to the painting.

"Then you've never met a truly bad man," Arthur muttered, half to himself. His attention flickered, just for a moment, to the portrait of his grandfather.

Lilianna took another step to the right. "And this is where you will be, I suppose."

"I suppose so," he said wryly. "I have to select a portrait artist soon, apparently, so that he can begin."

"And the rest of the wall…" Lilianna's voice trailed away again, but this time, she raised a questioning eyebrow.

Arthur took a deep breath. *This is why you invited her up here in the first place*, he reminded himself. And this was hardly a fresh, new conversation in the world of their families. It was dynasty. It was the core of nobility. It was to be expected.

Perhaps not discussed in such a blatant way, but…

"I need an heir."

The words sounded rather bald when spoken like that, but Arthur did not permit his gaze to depart from her own.

"Everyone needs an heir," she said softly.

He chuckled ruefully. "And I suppose I am not the first gentleman to state that, although I apologize for the directness. I need an heir, Lilianna."

They stood there, mere feet apart, his words between them.

Understanding dawned in Lilianna's eyes. "I see. And you'll marry any woman who will take you, to get yourself an heir as quickly as possible."

"No, I chose you," Arthur said quietly.

It felt… vulnerable, this conversation. Exposing. He was hardly revealing anything truly terrible about himself, but in a strange way, he felt painfully bare.

"Why?"

There was only one way to answer that. "Why do you think?"

She had not expected that. Her half-step back and quirk of a smile was swiftly overcome by surprise at his directness. Arthur waited, forcing himself not to hold his breath. There was nothing left to do now but wait.

"Because… Because I am a Chance," Lilianna said, holding

herself up straight as she always did whenever she thought of her family. It was one of the first things he had noticed about her. "I am part of one of the most respected, the most coveted—"

"And that's it, is it?" Arthur interrupted. "You think I wish to marry your name."

A flicker of uncertainty. "Well, what else would draw you to me?"

"You have what, a thousand cousins?"

Lilianna's brow furrowed. "Twelve. Why?"

"And how many of them daughters?" Arthur continued. She knew where he was going with this, didn't she?

It appeared not. "Seven, including my sister and me." She frowned.

"I could have offered marriage to any of them, but it was you I asked. You were the one who threw herself into my arms—"

"I *fell!*" Lilianna said hotly.

Dear God, he loved it when she was riled. "It makes no difference to me. I chose you, Lilianna. You told me there was not a chance in hell, but here you are, standing in my townhouse, looking at my portrait gallery. Looking at the line of paintings where one day, your son—*our* son—could be painted."

Arthur's gasp caught in his throat. That had probably been too far.

Dots pinked in her cheeks. When Lilianna finally spoke, it was more a whisper. "You… You want to marry me? Truly?"

And there it was. He would have her. It was only a matter of time.

Arthur shrugged with what he knew was a charming grin. "Maybe. If you ask me nicely."

Chapter Nine

March 27, 1840

L ILIANNA LOOKED AT the invitation in her lap and bit her lip.
The carriage tilted to one side as it rattled along, closer and closer to their destination. A destination that she was still not entirely sure was a good idea.

"S-Stop biting your lip."

"I wasn't," Lilianna said swiftly. She looked up and met her mother's eye. "Not much."

Florence Chance grinned. "So I see."

The whole thing would have been so much easier, of course, if she could parse her feelings for the man who had sent the invitation in her lap, but that appeared to be impossible. Try as she might, Lilianna only managed to get herself into knots whenever she thought about him.

Worse, when she considered the conundrum at night, she grew warm all over, heat peaking between her legs, where a dull ache made it most difficult to fall asleep.

She blamed him for that, too.

The Earl of Taernsby. He was wonderful, and arrogant, and irritating. And he was a Nelson, not a particularly noble house. He was wealthy, yes, but not spectacularly wealthy. Well-bred, but not truly noble, not like the Chances were. He was, among the gentility… average.

A memory sparked in Lilianna's mind: of the way he had

pulled her into his hallway and for a moment she had thought he had been about to ravish her and *she had wanted him to.*

Lilianna cleared her throat as the carriage wended on its way. Perhaps not *that* average.

And it was not like she had ever been pursued by a man like... Well, like this. Lord Zouch had been uncouth and ill-mannered, Lord Hastings had been ignorant and naïve, and the less said about the Right Honorable Henry Ponsonby-Jentham, the better.

Taernsby was quite different. Different from any man she had ever met.

The carriage slowed and eventually came to a stop.

Lilianna swallowed. "We're here."

Her mother raised an eyebrow. "So I see. S-Sit still."

Lilianna obeyed, closing her eyes as the Marchioness of Aylesbury leaned forward and adjusted one of the curls near her temple. "You don't have to worry, Mama, the wind will mess it regardless."

"But w-when you get out of the c-carriage, you should at least m-make an effort," said her mother sternly. "I w-want you to be p-perfect."

The carriage door opened as Lilianna nodded, a twisting pain in her stomach.

Perfect. Yes, she had to be perfect, and that meant finding the perfect husband.

So what did she think she was doing, accepting invitations from *him?*

"Finally," said a voice accompanied by a hand offering to help her down. "I thought you'd never get here."

Heat seared across her body, but Lilianna did not have time to collect herself. There was no time to think, no time to even consider. Her mother was gesturing to get out of the carriage but that would put her right in the arms of—

Not the arms. Definitely not.

Lilianna rolled back her shoulders and tried to calm herself. It was a concert. That was all. There would be plenty of people there, and they would not all be staring.

Probably. How much gossip had emerged from the Daltons' card party, anyway? She had never thought to ask her mother, and yet now Lilianna could not comprehend how she had failed to inquire.

"Mama," she said hastily, "how much—"

"Out," her mother said firmly, giving her that glare that said in no uncertain terms that stammer or no stammer, she would be having words with her if she did not obey.

Lilianna sighed, but then a perfect daughter did what she was told.

The Earl of Taernsby's hand was still proffered in the open carriage doorway. She took it.

Thank goodness for her gloves. As Lilianna stepped out into the cool, evening air, the scorching heat from Taernsby's fingers were only just mediated by the soft fabric of her gloves. If she had not been wearing them…

"You're here," he said as Lilianna wrenched away her hand and tried to pretend she had not been burned. "You came."

Lilianna flushed. "I… That is to say, we accepted your invitation, did we not?"

And the only reason she had accepted it was because it had been addressed to both of them, the earl doing something properly for a change. Without her mother here, Lilianna would have felt quite exposed. *With* her here…

Well. A grin flickered across her face. The last time Florence Chance had seen Lord Taernsby, she had threatened him to a duel, as far as Lilianna could remember. She may have been shy, but there was no one more protective of her daughters than the Marchioness of Aylesbury.

Cheered by this thought, Lilianna turned to help her mother from the carriage—only to discover that at some point during her reverie, Taernsby had managed to do so before her, the footman off to the side and allowing the earl to perform his duties.

Lilianna slipped her hand through her mother's arm hastily. "Shall we go inside? My mother—"

"*My* mother always recommended this box, so I selected it with both her and you in mind, my lady," Taernsby was saying in a low voice to Lilianna's mother. "It was always her hope that I would only share it with the most discerning of ladies."

Oh, what rot!

Lilianna almost said the words aloud but bit down on them before they escaped. Taernsby had somehow taken her mother's free arm and placed it upon his, and he was guiding them into the concert hall and past numerous people who were staring at them.

All that guff about his mother—well, really! Lilianna knew what he was up to, naturally. It was blindingly obvious! Charm the mother in an attempt to win over the daughter.

If the strategy weren't so tired, she would have been irritated.

Lord Zouch had tried that, and so had the Mr. Ponsonby-Jentham. Neither of them had gained much ground with her mother.

Society expected the Marchioness of Aylesbury to be weak, just because she was shy. *Well*, Lilianna thought triumphantly as they stood in a short queue waiting for their tickets to be checked by a man in red livery, *Taernsby is going to get rather a surprise.* Her mother would never—

"Oh, you are w-witty, m-my lord." Chuckling, Florence Chance tapped the man on the arm as Lilianna stared in mortified astonishment. "Quite unlike the other rakes m-my daughter has—"

"*Mama!*"

"—attracted," her mother said sagely, turning from her daughter and dropping her arm. "What d-did you think I was going to s-say, Lil?"

Lilianna flushed. *Nothing I could say in company.*

"It does not surprise me that your daughter has gained so many suitors, my lady, after taking after you so clearly," Taernsby said smoothly, his charm radiating on the both of them, but the full blast directed at her mother. "It must be a great delight to you, to have your beauty reflected in Lady Lilianna."

Oh, for goodness's sake.

Her mother giggled.

Lilianna sighed heavily. *Well, that is it, then.* She had been relieved that her mother had been included in the invitation because she had been so certain that the great and nervous Marchioness of Aylesbury would be an adequate buffer between Lilianna and the earl.

"—too kind! T-Tell me about your m-mother. I only had the p-pleasure of her company once, in Y-York, a long time ago. I was sorry to read of her passing."

"Oh, York! What a splendid place York is, I wish I spent more time there," said Taernsby genially.

Lilianna stared. She was standing just behind her mother now, out of her eyeline, and so could stare unashamedly at the spectacle her mother was making of herself. Laughing at his words? Asking about his mother? What on earth?

He was charming her mother.

Irritation crawled through her bones. The cheek of the man. Charming her mother, as though that were a surefire way to get her to like him!

Lilianna made sure to glare at the man over her mother's shoulder. If he could see just how infuriated she was by his antics, how absolutely outrageous she thought his behavior…

Her mother was chattering away quite happily. "—n-never heard B-Beethoven in concert. I'm v-very much l-l-looking forward to it."

Taernsby caught Lilianna's eye. Despite the very obvious displeasure that she had ensured was splashed across her face, he grinned.

"Mothers love me," he mouthed. Then he winked.

Oh, it was enough to draw lightning down from the heavens! Lilianna deepened her scowl to the darkest she could manage, but all it appeared to do to the man as they stepped forward and

Taernsby showed his tickets to the footman was amuse him!

Amuse him! Her, amusing *him*!

"Mothers love me."

The three words gave a jolt to her stomach as they moved up the staircase toward the boxes. What on earth did he mean by that? Mothers. Mothers, plural.

"And yes, charming women has never been a particular challenge for me. And none of them ever interested me as you do."

Lilianna swallowed. Well, she had never presumed that the Earl of Taernsby was a saint, not with his reputation. And it was perfectly normal in Society, much as she did not like it, for a gentleman to enter into a marriage with a great deal more experience in… in those matters, than his wife.

Still. The idea of Taernsby being with other women, seducing them, kissing them as he had kissed her…

"I said, don't you think, Lil?" her mother asked her.

Lilianna blinked. "How—How did we get here?"

It was a foolish thing to say and she regretted it instantly, but there appeared to be no way of taking it back.

They were standing in a box. Four seats in resplendent red velvet were there, angled slightly to the right so that each guest would face the stage, where a gaggle of musicians appeared to be squabbling over sheet music.

She had no memory of walking here, so lost had she become in her thoughts.

"I mean," she said, clearing her throat, "how did you secure such a box, Taernsby?"

Her mother pinked. *"L-Lilianna!"*

"My lord," Lilianna added guiltily.

His grin only increased her self-ire.

When had she started to think of the annoying man as Taernsby, rather than Lord Taernsby? It had happened so gradually, Lilianna could hardly recall.

Well, that would have to go. There was no possibility of her falling into that habit again.

"Taernsby—I mean, my lord," Lilianna said, hating herself and her own foolishness. "I shall sit here."

"Oh, no, you must sit here," he said, striding forward and placing his hand on the back of a chair. "I think you will prefer the acoustics."

Lilianna almost rolled her eyes. *Prefer the acoustics, indeed!*

It could not be more plain what the brigand was up to. The four seats were angled to the right, toward the stage—so the leftmost seat was almost completely out of sight of the one on the very right… where Taernsby was currently placing her mother, gracing her knuckles with a kiss as he did so.

Her stomach tightened. And so that way, he would sit between them… and her mother would not be able to see much of what they were doing.

Not that they would be doing anything. Obviously. *Oh, this man!*

"S-Sit, Lil," her mother chided softly. "I believe th-they will start s-soon."

Taernsby stood by the chair he had allotted her with a hand outstretched and an eyebrow raised in challenge.

Oh, what was the use? She should never have accepted the invitation, that was her trouble. But it had been so… so formal. So unlike the letter he had previously sent.

Lilianna's cheeks burned as she sat, the memory of that letter heating her from within. That a man could write such things, could *think* such things, and then set them down in pen and ink. Could send her that letter, knowing she would read all the things he wanted to do to her…

"Do you like Beethoven, Lady Lilianna?"

She started and turned to glare at Taernsby, who was seated beside her. "What, you can address me appropriately now?"

"I told you that mothers love me, and I spoke the truth," he said lightly with a seemingly well-practiced air of levity. "You think they would continue to love me if I did not speak to their daughters with respect?"

"And will you *treat* me with respect?" she shot back, trying to keep her voice down. A few ladies seated in a row just below them looked up curiously.

Taernsby grinned. "You think I have treated you with anything else, in our entire acquaintance?"

Lilianna swallowed what she wanted to say, which was that she had never been treated with such disrespect in her life. Respectful gentlemen did not go around kissing ladies beside lakes!

The trouble was, that was not the sort of thing one could say to an earl at a concern with one's mother present.

"Mama?" Lilianna said uncertainly.

"Oh, don't m-mind me, Lil," said her mother happily as she settled herself in her new seat—farther away from them, leaving an empty seat between herself and the earl. "I th-think I shall h-hear far better from here."

"But…"

Her words trailed away as she saw her mother's smile. *Oh, bother it all.* He was right. Mothers did love him.

"Oh look, there's Lady Romeril," said Taernsby, leaning forward and pointing at the row right in front of the stage. "And goodness, look who is with her!"

Lilianna's mother craned forward to look.

"Now, are you going to behave?" Taernsby said in a low voice as he leaned toward Lilianna.

That was when she knew she was most definitely in trouble. No man deserved to smell like that. Like… like heat. Like the radiating heat from red bricks after they'd been sitting in the midday sun for hours. Like touching them would not only scald, but burn, burn a scar into you that would remind you forever just what you had touched.

Her breath hitched in her throat. "*Me*, behave?"

"Yes, *you*," said Taernsby with a wicked grin. "I've brought you all this way—"

"It was *our* carriage that brought us here, actually."

"—and I have sufficiently distracted your mother, and that means that we have what we so desperately need."

Lilianna wetted her lips. "'Need'?"

His eyes had flickered to her lips at the small movement but returned to her eyes as he nodded. "Time."

Time.

Oh, there wasn't enough time in the world to understand this man. Strong and controlled and uncontrolled at different passing moments in any given minute, Lilianna could not understand what he wanted. He said he wanted her, he said he wanted heirs—but why her? Why not any other woman? He seemed to not need her dowry—and he already had a title of his own, so marrying the daughter of a marquess would not necessarily raise his status.

"Time to better understand each other," Taernsby said quietly as the conductor strode out and gentle applause started to ripple through the cavernous space. "Time for you to understand me, and me to understand you."

The chatter about the place was dying down as the conductor tapped his baton on the music stand before him, but Lilianna could not concentrate on that. She could barely concentrate on getting enough air into her lungs. "'Understand'?"

It was more a whimper than a word, and she hated her weakness for it.

The music started.

It was beautiful, and it was played brilliantly. Never before had she heard Beethoven played so exquisitely. Perhaps if she had been with anyone else, she would have cared more.

But Lilianna was concentrating on keeping enough air in her lungs not to faint away while sitting a mere two inches away from a man who seemed able to set her skin ablaze with a single look.

Taernsby smiled. "Can you accept that I'm courting you now?"

Lilianna tried to think.

Courting. That was what he called it, though she was almost certain that the kissing was supposed to happen *after* the courting. After the engagement. For some, after the wedding.

Not for gentlemen, of course. But for ladies like her, this was all wrong. It was the wrong way around.

"I think you owe me a kiss now, Lilianna."

"L-Lady Lilianna."

"That wasn't a no."

"You have not a chance in hell."

Lilianna raked her gaze over him and Taernsby accepted it, not turning away or flushing at her investigatory expression.

What sort of man was this, who could so easily charm mothers and yet had never wed? He wanted an heir, yes, but he could offer matrimony to anyone. She had said *no*, declined his offer of marriage countless times. And he was still here.

Still looking at her as though he wanted to rip all her clothes off and—

"Fine," she muttered.

Taernsby grinned. "Is *that* how you'd like to acquiesce to my courtship, Lil?"

"Don't call me that," she said sharply in a quiet voice. "Only my family calls me that."

"Fine," he said in a mocking, teasing tone. "My countess."

A shiver rushed up her spine. It truly was most unfair of him to speak like that. Like they shared secrets. Like this was merely an evening of entertainment for them before they returned to their home. Their bed.

And then she gasped.

It was a small miracle that a gasp was the only reaction she had to such an unexpected gesture. Before she could understand why he had done it, or even consider what it must look like if her mother looked over at them, Taernsby had done the unthinkable.

He had taken her hand in his own.

Lilianna immediately tugged hers away—at least, she tried to. The man had an uncanny grip and a frustratingly impressive way of knowing just when she was about to wrench and twist it away.

"Let go," she muttered.

"Never," Taernsby shot back without hesitation. "Not if I can help it."

A bubble of laughter rose in her before Lilianna could stop it. *Oh, it is so ridiculous.* The friction between them had to be the cause of all this heat, did it not? The desire rising in her, the laughter, the ridiculousness of it all—he knew he was doing this, didn't he?

Taernsby grinned. "I like this version of you."

Lilianna's hand stilled. "Which version?"

"This one," he whispered. "This carefree version, the one where you don't care what you look like or what anyone thinks of you."

She swallowed. "I…"

What was there to say? That she so rarely experienced it, she hardly knew whether she liked it herself? That there was almost no version of herself she knew except the controlled, buttoned-up, perfect version that she had so carefully constructed for the world to see?

Taernsby was smiling, a softening of his lips like affection, not devastating heat.

Lilianna tried to slip her hand away. "You are too clever by half, you know that?"

She had intended it as almost an insult, but the man grinned. "I know. And you're still trying to get away from me."

"I am."

"Then go."

Lilianna gasped as Taernsby released her hand. The sudden absence of pressure, of his presence, was quite a shock.

The Earl of Taernsby shrugged and placed his hands on his thighs, grasping his legs. "I won't keep you."

She had not expected to feel so… so bereft.

The music continued. It had probably continued, Lilianna realized, the entirety of the hand-being-held-captive debacle.

Strange. She had not heard it. Every one of her senses had been trained on the man seated to her right.

He wasn't looking at her. Lilianna deflated somewhat as he stared at the stage, humming and nodding his head along with the music. It was as though she wasn't there. As though he had completely forgotten about her.

Lilianna looked at her right hand. It was empty.

Did she want it to be empty forever?

"Oh, for heaven's sake," she muttered.

She leaned over, removing Taernsby's left hand from his thigh and placing her own within it. Her instincts made her lace her fingers in between his own and it felt…

Right.

Taernsby was grinning. His wide grin made him even more attractive, and by God, he knew it.

"Shut up," Lilianna said darkly, squeezing his hand.

The Earl of Taernsby squeezed back.

Chapter Ten

March 30, 1840

"**A** LETTER, MY lord."

Arthur looked up, sandwich in one hand and newspaper in the other. "A letter?"

Haslehaw sighed. "A letter, my lord."

It was the most delicate of sighs, but it was audible nonetheless. Perhaps Arthur was a little self-conscious about these things, but he was almost certain that butlers were not supposed to sigh in disappointment about their masters. Not all the time. Not to their faces.

"Right," said Arthur bracingly, taking the envelope from the silver platter proffered by the servant. "Is that all?"

God, he hated the imperiousness in his voice. When had that creeped in? When had it become impossible to speak like a normal man, like he had been only months ago?

When had being an earl changed him?

"I think that is all, my lord, except…"

Arthur leaned back in his seat and raised a brow as he waited for his butler to untangle himself from whatever knot he had managed to create. "'Except'?"

Haslehaw delicately picked off a speck of dirt from his cuff, eyes averted from his master. "Were you not meeting Lady Lilianna Chance for a walk at two o'clock?"

Arthur's stomach lurched as his eyes snapped to the longcase clock. It was ten minutes to two. "Three o'clock, wasn't it?"

"Whatever you say, my lord," the butler said graciously before bowing and leaving the dining room.

Oh, hell. Which was it? Two or three?

Arthur wracked his brains but could not recall. It was a constant challenge when in Lilianna's presence; one's thoughts tended to disappear over the horizon to be replaced, only by giddy admiration and lust.

It was a heady concoction, though it didn't require a great deal of thinking.

Staring longingly at the orange pudding Cook had prepared, which would now go to waste, Arthur stuffed the letter unopened into his pocket and strode into the hall.

Better to be waiting there for an hour if he was correct than be an hour late if Haslehaw was…

As it turned out, the ducks and swans meandered contentedly across the Fish Pond as the minutes slid by and Arthur was left fuming while he sat on a damp bench. He knew it had been three o'clock! What on earth had the old man been playing at?

Ah well. He had that letter, whatever it was. That would pass the time.

Arthur slipped it out of his pocket and broke the seal, a simple wax blob suggesting it was from no one in particular. Only when his focus fell onto the handwriting in the enclosed sheets of paper, five of them, did he realize who had sent it.

Jesus wept. He'd thought she'd understood.

Despite knowing none of the elegant personages promenading up and around the lake, passing him on his bench, could read the tightly scribed lines, Arthur tilted the letter so it could not be viewed by another.

No one needed to know what Celeste had written.

Arthur's eyes scrutinized the paragraphs, hopes sinking with every line.

I knew if I was good enough, you would have chosen to make me your countess, and I had hoped—but my hopes were wild, and I know

now you made me no promises. And yet sometimes, the way you looked at me, I could half-convince myself that you were falling in love with me.

His fingers tightened on the pages. He'd never made her any promises. That did not seem to matter.

His eyes flickered further down the page.

When you came to my bed the last time, I knew it would be goodbye, but I did not know it would be forever. Are you never bored, Arthur? Do you never long for the warmth of my arms? Do you never reach out in the night, hoping your fingertips will graze my—

Arthur put down the letter.

This guilt was far worse than he had expected. This was what it was to truly care for someone, then. He'd never intended it, but unintended consequences were a bad habit of a man who had spent so much time in the arms of women.

One at a time, obviously. He wasn't a *complete* rogue.

Celeste had never been given any assurances—he had always been very careful about that—but clearly, it did not matter. She had fallen in love with him, cared for him, longed for him. And he…

Arthur sighed. He had not thought of her from the moment he had left her bedchamber.

Strange. He had never seen himself in this particular light, and he did not like it. What was he, some sort of heartbreaker? Worse, a brigand? Was he playing with people's hearts just to keep himself amused?

He looked back at the letter, moving from one page to the next, when something caught his eye.

I know that when you find a wife she will be far superior to me. But can she love you like I do?

"What have you got there?"

The letter disappeared.

Arthur snatched at the air where the letter had been but to no avail. It had been completely removed from his grip—and horror of horrors, when he looked up to see who had taken the pages…

"Good afternoon," said Lady Lilianna with a beam. "Have

you been waiting long?"

It was all he could do not to choke on the words. "Letter—g-give back!"

He had risen to his feet—when, he did not know—his pulse was hammering because he had to get that letter back.

He had to.

The very idea of Lilianna reading it…

Arthur snatched at the letter but almost as though she moved purely on instinct, Lilianna jerked the pages away, her laughter delightful in any other circumstance but this. "Taernsby! What is it?"

"It's private," he said hurriedly, his stomach lurching as Lilianna's gaze dropped, just for a moment, to the pages she was holding. "Give it to me, please."

The tension in his voice felt so obvious, taut and strained, yet Lilianna did not seem to understand. She was grinning, almost… almost as if it were a game. As though he were teasing her for her own amusement.

"Love letter, is it?" she said with a hollow laugh, taking a step from him and holding the letters in the air, whirling them about so the paper snapped. Arthur caught sight of the dowdy, young woman he recognized to be Lilianna's lady's maid. She sat on a bench quite some distance away at the other end of the pond, watching her mistress spin about with what seemed like equal wonder to Arthur's own right now.

The panic was fast becoming terror and Arthur did not know what to do. At any moment, she could drop them and they could flutter about the Fish Pond, or she could drop them in the mud and ruin them or—

Or heaven forbid, she could read them.

Arthur knew full well which was the worst outcome. He reached out again, hating that she had them, hating that he did not seem able to grab them.

"Perhaps I had better read it, see who my competition is," Lilianna teased.

Her eyes were bright and her color high, and if this had just been a game, a flirtation, Arthur would have been thrilled. There was clearly a playful side to Lilianna and he had somehow found it—but in the worst possible situation.

She jested about the letter being from a lover. What would she do… if she discovered she could not be more correct?

"Lilianna, please, it's private."

"Not anymore," she said laughingly. "So, what do we have here? 'When you came to my bed'—your… your bed?"

Arthur cursed under his breath. The damage was done. There was no way to recover from this. "Lilianna, just give me the letter."

She took another step back, both hands now on the letter, holding it before her as though she could not look away.

"Don't read any more," he whispered, his voice hoarse.

Lilianna wetted her lips. "'When you came to my bed the last time, I knew it would be goodbye, but I did not know it would be forever. Are you never bored, Arthur? Do you never long for the warmth of my arms? Do you never reach out in the night, hoping your fingertips will graze…'"

Her voice trailed away and Arthur wished he had never met Celeste, or Haslehaw, or ever lived to see this day.

Her face was pale now. The sporting colors in her cheeks had gone, and so had the glint of happiness in her eyes.

Lilianna swallowed, then looked up past the letter. "And *are* you bored, my lord?" she asked quietly.

"That letter." He swallowed. "It's nothing. It means nothing."

"Oh, I don't know. From what I can tell, some poor woman has spent a great deal of time on it," said Lilianna with a forced cheerfulness that tore at him. "Pages and pages of it."

She shuffled them in her hands as though to emphasize just how many there were, her gaze never shifting from his face.

Arthur's hands dropped to his side and he wondered if he should just leave now, before it got any worse. How it could become worse, he could not tell.

Hell, he'd... he'd never made promises to Celeste. And he'd never lied to Lilianna—she had never asked about his past, and he had quite firmly never told her. Why would he? It was before her, before he had ever met her.

"When were you going to tell me about this?"

Arthur's head jerked up. When it had fallen, he couldn't recall. Looking at her was painful, like looking at the sun, but Lilianna deserved to see his pain, deserved to know what it cost him to admit this.

On the one hand, there was the truth. And then there was what he wanted from himself but had never been certain if he could be enough.

"This letter?" Arthur jabbed a finger at it. "Never."

"Not the letter, Taernsby. You know what I mean," Lilianna said quietly.

If only they could be having such a discussion in... in a private room somewhere, just the two of them, where he had the time to explain. Not that he was particularly sure how long it would take. How much time did a man need to explain that he had bedded more women than Lilianna had probably had hot dinners?

But they were here, out in the open, her chaperone within sight if not too close to hear, with the added possibility of strangers walking by them during the conversation and Lilianna looking as though she could bolt at any moment.

Arthur took a deep, painful breath. He'd been forgetting to do that. "My instincts told me never to reveal to you that I had... what I had... who I..."

Damn, but these words were difficult. Since when had speaking been such a challenge? He had always known how to charm the ladies!

Yes, muttered a voice inside his head. *And how well is that going for you right now?*

"Your 'instincts'?" Lilianna raised an eyebrow.

She was all coldness and aloofness and distance again. Arthur could have wept to see the change in her. He'd hardly noticed how she'd taken to him until all the heat had been taken away and he'd been left with the icy expression and distant calm he had first met, when he had caught her in his arms.

It would be difficult to say, but he had to say it. "Yes, my instincts. I thought, when I came to take a wife—"

"I wouldn't start getting any ideas."

He deserved that. "I am afraid you are a little too late for that."

He met her eyes, hoping that through his expression she would understand just what she meant to him. What she had been meaning to him for weeks now.

Lady Lilianna Chance looked calmly and resolutely back at him.

"I thought, when coming to take a wife, I would keep all that hidden. All my past, all that I had been, I would leave it where it belonged, in the past," Arthur said, pushing forward in the desperate hope something he said would reach her. "But you... Since you and I..."

Hell, there's no point in holding back, is there? Look where it's landed me.

Stepping aside for a gentleman and lady who were walking arm in arm, Arthur waited for them to be a few more yards away before saying in a rush, "You make me want to be a better man."

Lilianna's face was impassive. She did not move. Not even a twitch.

Arthur sighed, his shoulders slumping. "You deserve a better man. Not one who had a mistress and cast her off when he..." *Hell, hell, hell.* "When he tired of her."

For a few shimmering seconds after his words had left his mouth, Arthur waited. Waited for the shouts, the screams, the cries, perhaps even the sobs. The gentle patter of soft fists against him. The pleading, the negotiations, and eventually, the tears.

It was all so predictable. He'd caused such reactions in women before and, lord knew, he would do it again.

He braced himself. It shouldn't last too long.

Only after his brain caught up with him did Arthur realize that none of that had happened.

He blinked.

Lilianna was standing there, her focus fixed upon him. Without looking at her hands, she was folding up the letter from Celeste. Then she was stepping forward.

Arthur readied himself.

But there were no shouts. No yells. No fists pummeling his chest. No tears.

Lilianna slipped the folded letter into his coat pocket, her sudden closeness a blessing he had not anticipated. It was gone before he could revel in the intimacy.

"So, she was your mistress?" Her voice was quiet, and her footsteps small, and she was walking away.

Away from everything he had started to hope could be.

Lilianna paused, glancing over her shoulder. "Are you coming?"

Coming?

Arthur almost stumbled over his own feet in his haste to join her. It was too much to hope that Lilianna would ever look past the fact that he'd had a mistress, but perhaps she was not so innocent, so sheltered as he had imagined.

One mistress, fine. Understandable. Forgivable. But the number of women he had bedded…

"She was your mistress."

"Yes." Arthur hated the hoarse scratch of his voice, but swallowing did not appear to make much of a difference.

"And was she the only one?"

He could see her arched eyebrow out of the corner of his vision as they followed the path, curving around to the right.

Hell, but he could lie. She'd never know. There was no possibility of Lady Lilianna discovering just how many women he'd—

But *he* would know.

Damn.

"No," Arthur said quietly. "And I'm not... Christ, this is difficult to describe. But I am not ashamed, Lilianna. What I did with them, it wasn't wrong."

"Society would argue differently," she said, her voice distant. "Would you?"

The widows he had...befriended, for want of a better word, had never had any cause for complaints, but it felt churlish to say such a thing—akin to being a braggadocio, and he was not that sort of gentleman.

He had not intended to grab her arm, to halt Lilianna in the middle of the pathway and demand in that movement that she answer his question. Yet that was what he did.

Lilianna did not pull away. "You... You didn't... You never..."

There was pain in her eyes now, and Arthur waited, pulse hammering in his ears.

Eventually, she murmured, "You didn't ever... I mean, not since we, since you asked me to—"

"No," Arthur said confidently, relief pouring through him that he could answer this one honestly. "No, I've not—not since I met you."

There was a flicker of something in her eyes, but he could not discern what it was. Relief, that he had not been with any other woman during their acquaintance? Surprise, that he had been so forthright?

Lilianna nodded. He'd hoped she would speak, but she remained silent as she gently pried his fingers from her arm and continued to walk. She had not ordered him away, not blamed him, so Arthur returned to her side.

They walked together for some time, her lady's maid keeping an eye on them from a great distance at times from that same bench. At first, the tension in Arthur's shoulders refused to settle, aching in jolts that caused him to flinch, but eventually, the minutes slipping by without hysterics or remonstrances or tears, the tightness melted away.

This was... nice. Walking together. There was something about her company that was infinitely calming.

Finally, Lilianna spoke. "Tell me why."

Why.

Oh, God, how long does she have?

There were a myriad of reasons why, and some of them Arthur wasn't sure he could articulate on a cold, spring afternoon in public. How was a man supposed to tell a genteel woman like Lady Lilianna Chance that sometimes a man needed a... a release?

He prepared a ream of reasons, each one coherent and re-spectable, though all of them disappeared as he looked into her deep, sky-blue eyes.

Eyes that were open. Like her heart.

Arthur's jaw tightened. "I... I was lonely."

Lonely. It was the sort of word that no gentleman ever want-ed to admit to. It was weak. It was pathetic.

"I don't think I realized just how lonely until my father died and my brother—Archibald, you saw his painting—became the earl." *Where is this all coming from?* A deep well had opened within him and Arthur almost watched in astonishment as truths he'd half-buried and half-ignored poured out. "Being the spare, being the boy then man whom people needed but nobody wanted, knowing there was no place for me in the family, in life, no estate or title waiting... My father had little interest in his family, Olive and her parents moved to York when I was small, my mother died when I was very young... I wanted meaning. I wanted purpose. I wanted someone to want me."

I wanted someone to want me.

Christ on a stick, he was pathetic.

The self-loathing Arthur had always worked so hard to push away was rising up like a tide, inexorably and unstable, and he hated it. God, he—

"You wanted to be wanted," Lilianna repeated softly.

It sounded even worse when she said it. But though the instinct rose to deny it, to laugh and say it had all been a jest, to pretend none of it truly mattered, Arthur pushed through it all.

If he couldn't be honest with this woman, the woman he was determined to marry, then with whom *could* be honest?

Did he want to be alone forever?

"I was never meant to be the earl," Arthur said quietly. "But precisely what my father, or my grandfather, ever thought I would do, I do not know. There isn't a separate income from the title, no second castle to be cared for, and though I know it is not the case for every family, the Nelsons have always been firm that a gentleman of my standing would be considered demeaning himself to join a profession. I was—"

"Bored."

"Lonely," he corrected quietly.

Color had returned to Lady Lilianna's cheeks. Some of the ice had melted away, yet there was still a distance between them.

How could he cross it? Would he ever be able to, now he had admitted to such weakness?

Arthur pulled himself together. This was ridiculous. He was out here, in public, admitting to being so lonely that he'd half-leapt, half-fallen into any bed that would have him.

"I always thought my brother would have children and live a long life, that I would have time to—well, to figure it all out," he said bracingly, as though they were discussing nothing more serious than the weather.

"So you believed yourself free to do whatever you wanted until then," Lilianna said quietly.

"Not quite," Arthur said with a wry smile. "I knew I had to be discreet. Knew that... Well."

His gaze returned to her.

Lady Lilianna nodded humorlessly. "Knew a future wife would not want to know of such exploits."

Exploits. Yes, perhaps he had exploited the women he had bedded. Some had exploited him in turn, hoped a little coin would go their way, a few introductions at court. Some, like poor

Celeste, had hoped it would be emotions, not favors, that Arthur would offer her.

"Tell me the truth."

Arthur blinked. Lady Lilianna had halted again, and this time, her cheeks burned with the impropriety of speaking so boldly.

"I *have* told you the truth."

"Not all of it. Not the part of you you're holding back, even from yourself," she said softly. "I can see it, even if you think you're doing an excellent job at hiding it."

And his jaw dropped.

How did she do it? Look past his bluster and his arrogance and his pride, and see—see more than he saw in himself?

"I-I don't know what you mean."

"What do you want, Arthur Nelson, Earl of Taernsby?" Lady Lilianna was standing close, far closer than he had thought possible in public, her eyes trained on him and nothing else. "I don't want to hear the bravado. What is it that you want? What do you want?!"

"Connection."

The word had spilled from his lips before Arthur could stop it, before he could *think* it. Where it had come from, he did not know.

Lady Lilianna's eyes widened.

"I want—I *crave* connection," Arthur said, his words swift now as something within him unlocked as it never had before. "I don't want to crawl out of someone's bed and not remember her name as I leave. I want—I want to know someone. Really know them, all their secrets and the dangerous thoughts they hide, and I want to feel known. I want to look someone in the eye," he said softly, swallowing hard, "and have them tell me that they can see me. All of me. Even the parts I'm holding back. Even the parts I'm holding back from myself. And I want them to love all those parts of me."

He wanted her. He wanted this to be far more than just an impulsive decision to marry the first attractive woman who'd fallen into his arms.

Lady Lilianna was smiling. Her lips quirked and there was joy dancing in her eyes.

She slipped her arm through his. "Thank you for telling me."

"I wanted to—I think I always wanted to," Arthur admitted, his cheeks burning as they started to walk arm in arm. Hell, that part of him had been calling out to her the moment she had refused to marry him, the minx.

"I am sorry for taking the letter."

He could feel the folded pages in his pocket. Somehow, Arthur no longer cared. "I'm glad."

She raised an eyebrow at that. "Glad?"

Arthur nodded. The tension had gone. "It forced me to be honest with you—to tell you the truth. I never want to hide anything from you again."

Chapter Eleven

April 5, 1840

"**I** THINK WE can safely say," said Lilianna with a grin, "that we have never attended a worse ball."

Her cousin giggled as her aunt frowned. *"Really,* Lil! You mustn't say such things."

"No one can hear us, not this far away from the entranceway and with this much noise," Lilianna said dismissively, pulling her pelisse tighter around her as her breath blossomed on the air.

It was a very noisy night. The evening was not that late, which may have explained why the streets were so crowded. There were some, like herself, Evelyn, and her aunt, who were retreating home early from an evening that had not entertained. There were others, it appeared, moving from one location to another in the hope of better entertainment there. And then there were those, and Lilianna tried not to stare, whose natural habitat was the night. Their evenings were only just beginning.

As it was, it was difficult for the three of them to push their way through the crowded pavements.

"I told him to wait as close to the door as possible." Her Aunt Dodo was fretting, twisting her hands together in her elegant, long gloves. "But I can see neither hide nor hair of him!"

"We'll have to keep walking and see where he's ended up," Evelyn said cheerfully. "There's no help for it. Come on."

It was a mite irritating, Lilianna had to admit, that her aunt's coachman hadn't been able to find somewhere nearby to wait in the carriage. Her shoes were not designed for lengthy meanders, but light dancing in a ballroom, and she had to be careful to avoid the little gift a horse had left behind.

Her cousin slipped her arm through hers. "Anyone interesting tonight, then?"

Lilianna tried to smile. "Not a whit!"

Because he had not been there.

She did not say the latter part aloud, but she could almost see her cousin grinning at the words she had not said. The whole family had not yet let her forget about the Earl of Taernsby and his ridiculous flower obsession.

Not that she had ceased to think of him much. Arthur Nelson, the Earl of Taernsby. He was becoming less and less like an earl and more and more like a man with each encounter.

"I never want to hide anything from you again."

Lilianna shivered.

"Cold?"

"Yes," she lied to her cousin.

They halted as Aunt Dodo started speaking to an acquaintance on the pavement, the spring night air just as chilly as it had been in January, to Lilianna's mind.

She had hoped he would be there. At the ball. It certainly would have livened up an evening in sore need of it. But apparently, their hosts either did not know or did not like the latest incumbent of the Earldom of Taernsby, and he had not been there.

A wasted evening.

Lilianna chided herself silently as she and her cousin meandered a few steps from her aunt. How could it be a wasted evening when she had enjoyed it with Evelyn?

And besides, she still did not entirely know where this ridiculous *adventure* with Taernsby, for want of a better word, was going. Yes, he had proposed copious times—but a part of her wondered whether he would actually follow through if she ever said *yes*.

She might give him an apoplexy.

Better that, than lose her heart.

"Mother is taking forever," muttered Evelyn. "I do apologize. It's most irritating."

Lilianna shrugged, though she was in truth a tad frustrated. It was cold, after all, and they still hadn't found the carriage. "It is of no matter. We could keep going, keeping looking for—oh!"

Hands—hands on her behind!

Lurching forward and dragging her cousin along with her, Lilianna felt her cheeks burn as she turned, startled, to look at the person who had just touched her so inappropriately.

It was a man. His greatcoat was a little worn at the edges, but that could just signify a gentleman who had fallen on hard times. It was happening to the best families.

Not hers, obviously. But others.

"*Excuse* me," Lilianna said brusquely, presuming the man would soon apologize for his mistake.

The man grinned. Well, not exactly grinned. Leered. "Hello."

A chill flashed through Lilianna and she clutched on to her cousin's arm with perhaps too much grip.

"Ouch! Lil—"

"Good evening," she said over her cousin, hoping that the man, whoever he was, would take the words as they had been intended: as a departing word.

But he did not walk away. Instead, he walked forward and Evelyn gasped and stumbled backward, dragging Lilianna with her. They both hit the wall at the same time, and it was only then that Lilianna noticed three things.

Firstly, the street had become uncomfortably quiet. No one was walking along the pavement, no carriages were rattling by.

Secondly, her aunt appeared to be nowhere to be seen. Where on earth was she?

And thirdly, she and Evelyn could not outrun this man.

The last thought turned her blood cold. She had been

warned, had she not, about the dangers of men met in pitch-black streets when all alone. It was one of the myriad reasons that her father had always insisted that they did not loiter out of doors in the afternoons in winter, the sun dropping below the horizon at almost three o'clock in the afternoon some days.

"It may seem overly cautious," her father had said. *"But I would rather be overly cautious than overly regretful."*

She had never truly understood what he meant… until now.

The man leered. "What a pretty pair. I hardly know who to start with."

He licked his lips and lunged. One of his hands grabbed Lilianna's shoulder and she twisted away, but his other hand clutched at Evelyn's wrist and she sobbed, trying to pull free but unable to manage it, the man's grip absolute.

"Run!" Her cousin gasped.

"No," Lilianna said determinedly, her mind whirling, hardly knowing what she was doing.

Her feet did. Her right one lifted and kicked the man's knee and he swore, but still, he clung on to Evelyn and Lilianna was hardly going to leave her, but there was no one else on the street and what they would do if he—

"Unhand them, you brigand!"

Storming footfalls, a sense of power, a tall, broad man, a voice Lilianna thought she recognized, but so much fear was pounding through her veins that she could do naught but struggle against the man before them.

But she did not need to. The man was now in a struggle of his own, the incomer wrenching him away from herself and Evelyn, then placing such a punch on the villain's nose that he squealed as blood poured through his fingers.

"You punched me!"

"I would do a lot worse to you if I thought you were worth the time," spat Arthur Nelson, Earl of Taernsby. His gaze shifted from the spluttering man to the two women by the wall. "Lilianna, are you unharmed?"

Lilianna's lips parted, but no words came out. She was staring, unable to take him in.

Yet what a sight he offered. His top hat had been knocked to the ground in the kerfuffle and his greatcoat was unbuttoned, his chest heaving and his hands clenched in fists by his sides.

As though he were restraining himself. As though he were preventing himself from beating the man still moaning and muttering about his nose into a pulp.

It was heady stuff. Lilianna's mind was spinning, but at the whimper by her side, she was brought back to herself.

"Evelyn?" she said urgently. "Did he hurt you?"

"Lady Evelyn?" Taernsby said quietly.

Instinctively, Lilianna put out a hand, keeping him away. The last thing her cousin needed in this moment was another strange man rushing toward her.

But apparently, Taernsby was more instinctive than she'd thought. He had not made any move to even step toward them, seeming to understand that her cousin would need a moment. Perhaps more than a moment.

Evelyn looked up, her eyes blazing. "Let me at him!"

"No! No, that's not how we do things, you know that." Lilianna almost laughed as she was forced to restrain her passionate cousin from beating the man herself.

"How dare he?"

"Evelyn!"

"He deserves to have his lights punched out!" Evelyn rubbed at her wrist. "He hurt me!"

"Yes, yes, but I think his nose is broken, so consider the work done for you," said Lilianna dryly, glancing up at Taernsby.

He gave her a lopsided grin and her pulse leapt.

Oh, this man. Just when she thought she understood him, he suddenly did something to surprise her.

Not that defending a woman in need was surprising. Any man worth his salt would do so—but the restraint. The evident dislike of violence, ceasing the moment that the man had been incapacitated because he'd wished to check on her and her cousin. That had been Taernsby's priority. Not vengeance, but protection.

Lilianna swallowed. "Taernsby, I—"

"I turn my back for one moment and you have two men fighting over you!" Aunt Dodo had run along the pavement and now had a hand on her heart. "I don't know the odds of it happening, surely astronomical—capturing their hearts so quickly!"

It was a complete misread of the situation of course, but as Lilianna glanced at her cousin, she let it be. Evelyn could explain it to her mother in her own time, when they were off the streets.

Which reminded her…

"I found the carriage," said her aunt, inclining her head at Taernsby but evidently giving him no further thought. "Come along, Evelyn. We can drop you home too, Lil, it's no trouble."

"I have already secured that promise, my lady," said Taernsby smoothly, bowing low to the woman. "Taernsby. The Earl of Taernsby. My cousin, Olive, who is in town—"

"Oh, yes, I've heard all about you," said Aunt Dodo eagerly.

Lilianna groaned.

"Is it true that you sent roses and delphiniums?"

"His lordship doesn't have time for this," said Lilianna hastily. "He's very busy."

"And you agreed to escort my niece home, how very obliging of you," said Aunt Dodo, meeting Lilianna's eyes and winking. "Of course, but I can't allow it. She is my charge for the evening."

"I understand. Of course, of course." Taernsby cleared his throat. "My cousin is with me this evening, though. She awaits us in my carriage and will act as chaperone as we escort Lady Lilianna home."

"Lady Barlow?" Lilianna peered around his shoulder, as if the countess might appear from within the shadows. The cousins had played such tricks before.

Aunt Dodo chewed on her lip, then nodded, as if seeming to

make some sort of calculation. She was always making calculations. "That would be acceptable. Of course, the odds of you being on the street at the same time your cousin is within a carriage, just timed so in order to catch sight of my daughter and niece… Then again, far be it for me to step in the way of—"

"Mother, you're babbling," said Evelyn swiftly.

Her aunt's odds, indeed, Lilianna realized with a start. Lady Barlow wasn't waiting nearby in some carriage.

Nonetheless, Lilianna shot her cousin a look of gratitude before Evelyn stepped away, dragging her mother by the arm. "I'll send you a note in the morning," Lilianna promised.

"I intend to sleep all morning," said Evelyn with a yawn. "Good night, Lil. My lord."

In just a few moments, they were gone. In a jingle of reins and a clop of hooves, the carriage disappeared around a corner.

And that left her with…

Lilianna looked up into Taernsby's eyes and knew she was safe. It was a strange sensation. Not that she felt unsafe with other gentlemen. Lord Dalmerlington was a complete petal—a malicious thought had never crossed his mind in his life—and most of her brothers' other friends were harmless.

But she hadn't felt *safe*, as though nothing could touch her now without Taernsby's consent.

She swallowed. And now he was going to take her home. Alone. In his carriage. He *did* actually have a carriage, didn't he, even if he'd lied about his cousin waiting in it?

"My driver is up here," Taernsby said quietly, as though he could read her mind. He was doing that a lot lately. "Are you certain you are not hurt? That—that *brute*, I could have torn him limb from limb!"

"I am glad you didn't. You could have been hurt yourself," Lilianna said softly.

Taernsby snorted. "Not likely. Come on. You must be exhausted."

She was. At least, that was surely why her legs were shaking, her strength gone.

"You were not at the ball tonight."

"No, I was not invited." He chuckled. "Or rather, I *was* invited, but the son of the house owes me a small debt from a bit of gambling."

"'A small debt'?" Lilianna frowned. "Just how small?"

Taernsby grinned. "Not very small. I did not wish to make a scene, but after dining at my club, I thought... Well. I thought you might have attended and so ventured to pass by. Here we are."

Fortunately, the Taernsby carriage was only twenty yards along the road. The coachman nodded to his master as Taernsby opened the door and helped her inside.

"And no falling into my arms this time," he murmured as she took his hand.

Lilianna stifled a smile as she stepped into the welcoming carriage. Was he ever going to be believe her about that moment, that first meeting?

Falling into his arms, indeed...

"Your cousin?" she said, her eyebrows arched.

"I said I would not lie to you. I did not promise to not lie to others—not if it means having even a moment more with you." Taernsby smirked.

The carriage rocked as he entered, sitting beside her and suddenly making it clear that the space wasn't actually that large. Lilianna could feel his knee pressed up against hers, his hip locked next to hers, giving her no room to move.

Not that she wished to move away. Not with this heat spreading through her, sparking her in a way only Taernsby could manage.

Lilianna pushed aside the thought hurriedly. He was going to drive her home, and that was it.

Taernsby must have muttered her address to the driver before he'd entered, for when the door snapped shut, the horses were encouraged to move. The carriage began to pull forward, rattling on the cobbles.

And then he broke the silence. "I apologize on that idiot's behalf. He should have never—the *gall* of him. It is unforgiveable."

"You do not have to apologize. It was nothing to do with you," said Lilianna quietly, folding her hands in her lap. "*You* did not… You did not try to—"

"He didn't, did he?"

His voice was rough, cracked, as though in pain. His features were clear even in the darkness. Her eyes had finally adapted, so long after leaving the ball.

His eyes were raking over her as though carefully looking for any evidence of harm. And this care, this need to keep her safe, settled her nerves in a way nothing else had.

Lilianna reached out and placed a hand on his. "I am fine. I-I promise."

Taernsby grasped her hand before she could remove it, holding it tightly.

He didn't make sense. Rake and rogue, defender and devil, this man was more complex than she had ever given him credit for that first night when he had proposed like a madman.

He was so much more… so much *more*.

"No man should ever touch you," Taernsby said in a low voice, "without you wanting them to."

Lilianna tried not to think of the comforting yet challenging hands now encircling one of her own. "It's why I am… the way I am."

An eyebrow quirked.

"I know people call me a snob. Arrogant, cold, distant," Lilianna said as the carriage rattled on. She let out a laugh that was more a release of tension than anything else. "I am not blind and I am certainly not deaf. But it… it keeps people away, the distance. The coldness. The contempt."

"You are beautiful," said Taernsby slowly.

His remark seemed so completely divorced from her point

that Lilianna could not help but frown.

"I mean, I can understand why so many gentlemen approach you," he added with a shrug. "I couldn't stay away."

"And yet being accosted so continually, the presumption of some men that I would be delighted just to be in the same room as them, breathing the same air..." Lilianna sighed. "It is exhausting. *They* are exhausting."

It sounded foolish when she put it like that, but there was no other way to describe it.

"It's like... they act as though I am indebted to them just for their notice," she added, trying to better explain. "As though I owe them, as though I should be grateful. And they are more often than not dull and insipid and have no thought for me at all, save how they can possess me." Her nose wrinkled. "It's abhorrent."

"I can see that."

Lilianna looked up. "You can?"

Taernsby nodded thoughtfully. "It's interesting. I can—well, not see both sides, but see how it happens. You are beautiful, Lilianna. Beautiful, and charming, and witty—"

"Oh, stop," she said quietly, hardly knowing where to look.

"—yet if they touch you without your consent?" he continued, his voice hardening. "I hate that. I *hate* it."

Lilianna swallowed. There was a vehemence in his voice she had not heard before—at least, other than when he had punched that man in the nose.

"Consent is very attractive," she said, hardly knowing why she was opening up like this. She had never even spoken about such things with her sister, but here, in the darkness, her hand still clutched by Taernsby... "Yet so is determination."

He laughed. "So it's impossible! How is a man supposed to know when he is pursuing a woman who wishes to be caught, and when he is being a nuisance—or worse?"

It was indeed a conundrum. Lilianna had never considered it from that angle, but it was a challenge.

The temptation to do something she almost never did, and flirt, overwhelmed her. Well, she was safe here, wasn't she? Taernsby was hardly going to do anything to her; she trusted him, perhaps better than any gentleman outside her family. And they were in a carriage. What could he possibly do to her here?

Besides, they must surely almost be to her home.

So, a little light flirtation. *Why not?*

"Consent and determination must come together, I suppose," she said through her lashes, a gasp catching in her throat at her own boldness. "Being able to read the person you're with... Yes, that's the difference. That's when you should know whether when they say 'not a chance in hell' what they really mean is—is *kiss me*. Now."

For a moment, nothing moved.

And then he was kissing her. Lilianna gasped in his mouth, half-shocked that what she had said had gained such a reaction, reveling in the way he pressed her against the carriage seat with complete abandon.

One of his hands in her hair, the other at her waist, Taernsby groaned as Lilianna parted her lips for him and welcomed him in.

Oh, she *welcomed* him in.

Taernsby trailed a line with his tongue along her lips before plunging into her warm mouth, eking out a tingling pleasure that made Lilianna gasp.

"Taernsby—"

"Arthur," he moaned, pushing her farther down the seat until she was almost horizontal. "Call me 'Arthur.'"

Who was she to deny him? How could she, when he was worshipping her so thoroughly?

"Arthur."

And it was like she had sparked a tinderbox to a flame. His torso was covering hers and the weight of him was welcome, her hands around his neck, grasping his shoulders, pulling him closer.

She wanted him closer, deeper. Lilianna did not have the words, but all this space between them, the layers of clothing—it had to go.

His kiss deepened. Arthur seemed to know precisely what she wanted, his tongue ravaging her mouth, tasting her, and the strength of his ardor inflamed her. Lilianna was so hot, burning under his touch.

Her leg nearest the center of the carriage slipped off the seat, but she hooked it up over his own and Arthur broke the kiss, lowering his head to her neck.

"God, Lilianna, you don't know what you—you do to me."

"I have a good guess," she murmured, quivering as he trailed kisses down her neck toward her décolletage.

There were stars spinning in her eyes as Arthur lifted his head and grinned, the swaying of the carriage continuing under her as her head spun.

"Do you like this?"

Lilianna swallowed, her throat suddenly dry.

"Consent and determination must come together, I suppose."

"Y-Yes."

"Good," he said, his eyes flashing with desire. "Because I want to keep going. You can stop me if you want."

Lilianna reached for him. "Don't stop—"

His lips crushed against hers, the strength of his passion twisting an aching heat between her legs. She squirmed, trying to fix the ache, though she knew not how, her body instinctively rubbing against him.

Arthur moaned in her mouth and suddenly, his hand was no longer at her waist, but near her thigh—no, her knee. Somehow, he had found the hem of her skirts and he was doing something. Lilianna could not see what and she could barely think. His lips pressed against a delicate spot beneath her ear as he—

"Arthur..."

She had moaned his name and he did not stop. His fingers fluttered past her knee, rising along her thigh, stroking and caressing, and Lilianna was quivering with the anticipation she knew she should not feel, because he was about to touch her...

Touch her… *there.*

"I've wanted to do this," Arthur breathed in a jagged voice, lifting his head to look into her eyes. "For so long."

Lilianna gasped as his fingers halted, twisting under him. "Please—please Arthur, please…"

"Please what?" There was delight in his eyes, a hunger she had never seen before. "Ask for what you want, Lilianna."

She whimpered, the words alien to her tongue. She had never thought of this, never dreamt of it, but now to miss out merely because she was not brave enough to say, to beg for what she wanted…

"I want—"

"We're here, m'lord."

Lilianna's eyes widened. The carriage was not moving. They had arrived?

Arthur lowered his head to her neck, brushed a solitary kiss against her skin, then swore quietly.

Then he was moving, pulling her up on the seat, shifting her so that she was upright, and Lilianna could have wept, the need in her was so urgent, but it had to be abandoned.

Of all the timing in the world, it had to be like this?

"I thought I had more time," Arthur said ruefully.

Lilianna tried to smile, and tried not to say, *Take me. Take me right now.* "H-How do I look?"

He chuckled in the gloom. "As though a very bad gentleman has attempted to have his way with you."

Her stomach lurched. "Well, then. At least my story will match Evelyn's."

Arthur swore again. "I should have punched his lights right out."

"I know."

"I would have stopped, if you had asked me to."

"I know," said Lilianna quietly as the carriage door opened beside her. She allowed herself to be handed out of the carriage by the footman, who was studiously avoiding her eye.

There was her home, and yet for the first time in her life, she did not want to enter it.

"Lilianna?"

She turned. There was an expression of genuine concern on Arthur's face. "I never would have... If you had wanted me to stop, I—"

"I know," she said for a third time, and a little wickedness sparked within her as she spoke before walking into her home. "But I wanted to let you."

Chapter Twelve

April 9, 1840

"IT'S ALL GOING to plan," said Arthur proudly as he pulled on his coat. The spring air was sultry this morning and he was going to relish it.

"I am overcome with delight, my lord."

Arthur grinned as he glanced over his shoulder at his butler. "There's no need for your sarcasm, Haslehaw."

"I suppose not, my lord," said the older man stiffly. "I trust you will enjoy your walk?"

"As do I," muttered Arthur as he opened the door. "As do I."

It was the information that the little urchin Kay had given him, what felt like years ago, that had done it. Though it was slightly mortifying to discover that in fact Lilianna had been cognizant of his methods, the details discovered were at least still useful.

Arthur strode along the street with a tingling expectancy. Knowing Lilianna's habits had at first been just a clever way to make sure he could accidentally run into her. Then it had been a pleasant way to irritate her, to see the red sparking in those cheeks when she grew frustrated with him.

And now…

Now it was a way to keep her safe.

Today is a Thursday, Arthur thought as he side-stepped around a pair of gentlemen arguing about what sounded like cards. That meant she would be delivering a parcel to Mr. Creighton again, as she did every Thursday. That meant at about this time, a church bell chiming helpfully, she would be on Milsom Street.

So that was where he would be.

Arthur wasn't sure what had made him decide to do it. Lady Lilianna Chance was, after all, the daughter of a marquess. Based on the rules of society, of the etiquette she knew far better than he did, she should not be meandering about the place alone, unchaperoned. Last time he had observed her during this task, she had parted from a woman he knew now to be her cousin. He could only hope she was with her cousin or maid today.

Of course, her cousin had not been enough to save her before. After seeing her almost attacked on that dreadful night, Arthur had promised himself that any time he had to spare, if he knew where she would be, he would be there too.

Not *with* her, not necessarily. But there. Keeping an eye on her.

Keeping her safe.

Within five minutes, Arthur was leaning in a shadowy doorway and watching as Lilianna conversed with the same old man with whom he'd seen her before, her lady's maid at the end of the alleyway, looking about nervously.

"—temperate evenings now, so my rheumatism is much better," Mr. Creighton was saying.

Lilianna placed a hand on his arm. Arthur straightened, just for a moment, so he could rush forward if the old man took advantage of her kindness, but he sank back against the door-frame as the man chuckled and continued to speak to her kindly and politely.

"Don't worry about us old folks. We'll do fine."

"But you must tell me if you need anything in particular. There will still be cold evenings coming."

Arthur watched her, his eyes hungry. She was so beautiful— and when she was like this, calm and relaxed, knowing she was safe, the joy he now knew she often forced down blossomed.

It made her... not a different person. Just... more the person she was always meant to be.

Mr. Creighton was bowing now. "And my wife's best regards, m'lady."

"And I return them," said Lilianna, her voice carrying in the quiet lane. They were a long way from Milsom Street. "Until next week, Mr. Creighton."

Arthur watched as the man meandered off, clasping the basket that the noblewoman had given him. How many people did she help like this? Quietly, without pomp and ceremony, without the dramatics that ladies of the *ton* like Lady Romeril required before they could be kind to anyone.

She was a most interesting woman.

He followed at a respectable distance, making sure he was not too close, as Lilianna walked slowly along, her lady's maid a few steps behind her. Her basket now gone, there was a lightness about her shoulders that Arthur delighted in.

She deserved to be happy. If he could give her happiness...

"Lady Lilianna!"

Arthur stiffened. He stopped, standing behind a large bush that gave him cover when peering out at the pair. Lilianna, *his* Lilianna, and another man.

Not *his* Lilianna. Not technically. Not yet.

"—and if I had any interest in accepting those dinner invitations, you would have seen me sooner," came the ringing, cold voice of a Lady Lilianna who was having none of it. "As I said, Mr. Lister, the sooner you learn that I have no interest in your invitations, the sooner you will save money with your calligrapher. Good day."

The man looked utterly crestfallen as Arthur passed him, following in Lilianna's and her maid's footsteps, and he could not help but be delighted.

There was something so arch, so refreshingly direct in Lilianna's approach. No gentleman could ever claim that he did not know where he stood with her.

His stomach lurched. Except him.

"You have not a chance in hell."

A great deal had changed in the last few weeks, to be sure, and in a way Arthur could hardly tell what would come next. He admired her, yes, he cared for her, wanted to keep her safe. Calling her *beautiful* was almost an insult to the word, for she was so much more than that. More than the word *beauty* could contain.

Lilianna appeared utterly unconcerned that she had dashed the hopes of what appeared to be a polite enough young man. She continued walking at a slow pace, palpably not eager to arrive wherever she was headed. Then, to his horror, she pointed ahead of her, causing her lady's maid to step forward and gaze about, and with the maid's back turned, Lilianna slipped down a lane.

When Arthur reached its mouth, he saw it was more an alley than a lane. It was dark, the gap small, only a few feet wide.

And she was walking here, alone?

Arthur shook his head as he followed her. Did the woman never learn? If she was going to avoid being accosted by some troublesome lout, she couldn't be walking along places like this.

He was but a few inches away when he said, "Lil—"

She acted immediately.

The basket had been given to Mr. Creighton, but there was still a reticule on her arm. The instant he had uttered the first syllable of her name, Lilianna had whirled around, reticule flying, and whacked him across the face with it.

"Christ!" he shouted.

"Let go of—Arthur?" she said, blinking.

Arthur was blinking too. It was the only way to prevent his eyes from watering.

"God in heaven, what is in that thing?" he said thickly. "Is my nose bleeding?"

It certainly hurt enough. Stars popping in the edges of his vision, Arthur shook his head as though that would rid him of the pain.

When he stilled his gaze it was to see Lilianna staring, hands to her face, clearly mortified.

"Arthur! I thought—I mean, I was alone and someone said my name. I thought—"

"Yes, yes, I can see I was an idiot," Arthur said thickly, grimacing through the pain.

God, she has a good swing to her.

"But why are you alone? Your maid was with you but a moment ago. I left her standing back on the sidewalk, searching for you."

She swallowed. "Yes, well, I feel bad about that. But Father and Mother have been annoyingly concerned about by safety since that night. I might not have told them, but my aunt did, once she realized what had happened. I just thought... Well, surely, I'd be all right for a short while on my own." She tugged on the brim of her bonnet, as if that were enough to keep people from recognizing her. "Clarke will know where to meet me if I *happen* to get parted from her in the crowd."

He arched a brow. "You've given her the slip before?"

She pursed those kissable lips. "A time or two."

He wanted to laugh, but it hurt to smile. It was his own fault, he could see that as he leaned against the wall, blinking the pain away. There didn't seem to be any blood, thank God, but there would be an interesting bruise on one side of his face where the catch of her reticule had swept past his cheek.

"What is in there?"

Lilianna flushed. She was standing beside him now, clearly battling between laughter and mortification. "It's Frank. She asked me to pick up something for her."

"What, a brick?" said Arthur with a weak smile.

Her cheeks pinked. "A hammer, a specialist one, she said she needed it for a project."

Arthur groaned, pinching the bridge of his nose. "Trust me to try to talk to you while you're carrying a—did you say *hammer*?"

She nodded. "Frank ordered it especially, and as I was coming into town, I said I would collect it."

That hit must have been heavier than he thought, for Arthur could have sworn Lilianna had said "Frank" and "she." Well, that would keep. He had more important things to think about.

Like the woman in front of him.

"Well, at least I don't have to worry about you walking the streets on your own anymore," he said sheepishly.

Lilianna's eyes widened. "Is—Is that what all this is about?"

"Perhaps," Arthur said cagily.

Now he'd said the words aloud, he wasn't certain if she would take offense at such a thing. Lord knew, he wouldn't appreciate being followed about the place.

"You've been following me. You noticed as soon as I left Clarke behind." The slight puckering frown between her brows suggested she was thinking on similar lines. "Because you don't think I can look after myself."

"Because I know what men are like, and you gained a taste of that yourself four nights ago," Arthur said urgently, stepping toward her, pain in his face forgotten.

She did not step away and this brought him far closer to the woman he cared for than he had expected.

"And another thing," Arthur said, relishing his subject now that he had broached it with her. "I think it's very admirable, what you're doing for Mr. Crighley."

"Mr. *Creighton*," she corrected him with a wry smile. "Arthur, you—"

"But it was not a clever idea to walk down this alleyway on your own," he said sternly.

Lilianna's lip quirked. "Oh, I don't know, you seem to have come out worse. You're bleeding, Arthur."

Bleeding?

Arthur blinked. "You called me 'Arthur.'"

"You asked me to." Her eyes were liquid, suggestive, reminding him of that moment in his carriage when he had almost been carried away. "I did not think the request was limited to times when you were kissing me senseless."

He groaned, forcing himself not to think about that delectable moment. Then he frowned. "I'm bleeding?"

"Here." Before he could ask what she was doing, Lilianna had opened up her reticule.

"Not going to hammer me, are you?"

"Not this time, Taernsby," she said softly, pulling out a spotlessly clean handkerchief. "Now hold still. If you will barrel into things like this, I'm afraid you will have to take the consequences."

It was hardly a bad consequence, really. Arthur stood, trying to fight against the instinct to pull the woman into his arms and kiss her senseless as she had so recently described. Lilianna in turn resisted the temptation perhaps to bop him on the nose as she delicately wiped away a small amount of blood from his cheek.

"I think it was the catch of my reticule," she admitted quietly. "I am sorry."

"I should not have startled you." Arthur breathed, drinking her in as she stood on tiptoe, so close, he could almost hear her pulse.

Lilianna gave a laugh. "I should get accustomed to it, I suppose. Some of the people I help they… Well, they don't live in Royal Crescent."

Clenching his fists by his side to prevent himself from grasping her and shaking a promise out of her that she would never go there again, Arthur said instead, "Oh?"

"And don't you start. Clarke can barely bring herself to accompany me, always itching to leave. And Frank is already mortified that I go there at all."

Ah, well. At least she had a brother like Frank to look out for her. "And you don't listen?"

"I've not listened to a word Frank has said in years," Lilianna said dryly, returning her handkerchief to her reticule. "There. You're presentable enough."

She did not step away.

Not that it would have been particularly easy to do, in an alley this size. It reminded him of Squeezegut Alley, in Whitstable, the seaside town to which his father had taken him as a child. As his father had grown older, and rounder, it had become impossible for him to enter.

"You should be more careful," Lilianna whispered.

Arthur snorted sardonically. "What, like you were? Lilianna, anyone could have approached you."

"But they didn't," she pointed out. "It was *you*."

Yes, it was. This time.

Arthur's stomach clenched with fear at the thought of a time when he wouldn't be here to protect her, to accept the hammer to the face from a startled woman. What would she do then?

He pushed aside the dread. He could not, would not, give into it. "You must—"

"You can't 'must' me. I will live my life as I choose." Her voice was soft, but there was iron at its core. "I am not the only woman in Bath, Arthur. I know what I'm doing."

"Like you knew what you were doing today?" The words slipped out before he could stop them.

Lilianna grinned. "I'm sorry, who has just had blood wiped off their face?"

"You know what I mean."

"You know what *I* mean," she quipped quickly. "And before you start riding about on that high horse of yours, Arthur Nelson—"

His pulse spiked. "I am not riding on any—"

"—you should recall that you yourself have spoken rather directly and at times, crudely, to a woman in public," Lilianna said softly. "To myself, for example."

It was a most uncomfortable moment. There was silence in the alley, nothing but the chatter of far-off people living their far-off lives. In this moment, in this place, there was no one but themselves.

And it was uncomfortable. Arthur shied away from the truth

of her words, but it was a discomforting thing to be faced with the truth of yourself.

He swallowed. "I speak plainly."

Lilianna raised an eyebrow.

"Fine, *very* plainly."

"Is that what you call it?" she said lightly.

Arthur tried to shrug. "I only speak that way because I wanted to catch your attention. And it worked. Here we are."

Her smile was stifled but not successfully. "We're here because you followed me down an alley, you dolt."

And it was the delicate insult that made him swell and his spirits soar. Arthur had been cut down, cut off, and now literally cut *by* this woman, both in public and in private. He had kissed her and tried desperately to do more, yet it was in this moment that he felt closest to her.

Not just because she was standing before him, her breasts grazing his chest when they both inhaled at the same time.

But because they were happy. Together. Here, in this moment, she had called him a "dolt" and now he never wanted to be called anything else.

"Lord, if my mother could see this." She sighed. "It doesn't exactly fit the picture of a perfect daughter."

Perfect. It was the right word to describe her, yet a shadow had passed over Lilianna's face as she had spoken.

"'Perfect'?"

Her cheeks pinked. "It's… Well, I *am* the eldest daughter of a marquess. I am a Chance. There are certain expectations—"

"Lofty expectations, by the sound of it," Arthur interjected gently.

He couldn't take his eyes from her face. It was the most vulnerable he had ever seen her; the admission that she was seeking some sort of validation, that her parents had requirements of her.

Lilianna's brief smile was heartbreaking. "I've always tried—I mean, I want to be the perfect daughter. The perfect Chance, the perfect… I know my worth, I know my value. I know the sort of person they all want me to be. Being perfect, it's hardly easy, and—"

"You are so precious," he said quietly.

Lilianna stilled, her laughter evaporating like the tide along a shore.

"Lilianna, you… you are so precious," Arthur said, his voice cracking. "Damn, what I mean is—"

"I know what you mean," she said softly, lifting a hand to his cheek and brushing past a part that hurt, but not as badly as his stomach. "I know, Arthur."

And then she was kissing him.

Arthur could hardly believe it was happening, his mind still unable to accept that she had done something so forward and so bold, but she was. Lady Lilianna Chance, the ice-cold daughter of a marquess who had cut him down to size the first time they'd met, was kissing him, pushing him up against the wall, the reticule dropped to the ground, her hands now in his hair and her moans on his lips.

He had promised himself restraint the next time he drank from her, but he had forgotten just how sweet she tasted.

Clutching her to him and exulting in the delicacy of her waist, Arthur poured as much of his technique into the kiss, pushing back the brim of her bonnet with his forehead, parting her lips gently, then ravishing the inside of her mouth.

Oh, she tasted so sweet. So succulent. So innocent, waiting for him to progress the kiss, despite her eagerness at the beginning.

Well, he could teach her.

Shifting his feet and delighting in the way she squeaked in surprise, Arthur took a step forward, pushing her against the opposite wall. Before she could say anything, he had captured her lips with a passionate kiss, but he didn't stop there.

"Oh, Arthur…"

Her bonnet falling askew off her scalp and to the ground with the roughness of his pressure, her head lolled back as his hand found her breast, squeezing gently at first and caressing just where her nipple would be under all this damned fabric. His mouth moved to her neck, nipping and teasing kisses down until her reached her collarbone. Here he sucked, desperate to taste her afresh.

Lilianna quivered in his arms. "Oh, yes, yes…"

Her moans thrust him forward, tempted him to take liberties he had not considered. He nudged her feet apart, thrusting himself forward between her legs and almost crying out himself at the sensation of coming home.

This was where he belonged. With Lilianna's arms around him and the taste of her skin on his tongue and the warmth of her core tangible through the fabric of his trousers—trousers that would not be keeping them apart for long—

And that was when he forced himself to stop.

"S-Stop." Arthur groaned, staggering to the side, away from this woman, who was quite clearly going to be the death of him.

Lilianna was blinking as though surfacing from a deep pool, and he thanked the stars that this wasn't night or he would truly have been in trouble.

As it was, he wasn't sure precisely how he was going to walk.

"Why?" she asked, lips bruised pink with the strength of their ardor.

Arthur forced himself to swallow twice before responding. It wouldn't do to say exactly what thoughts had been cascading through his mind but moments ago.

"Because—Because otherwise, I won't," he said simply. "Stop."

Lilianna's shock, her wide eyes and parted lips, was momentary. It was swiftly replaced by a grin. "And if I didn't want you to?"

"Dear God, woman, you're going to destroy me." Arthur groaned with a dry laugh, trying to force himself not to look at her heaving breasts, the way he had marked her on the neck. Christ, he'd *marked* her. Made her his own.

Think, man!

"Good," she said with a grin. "I want to destroy you. I... I want you to know what it is to be looked at by you."

She was more than he could ever have expected, more than he deserved—certainly more than he'd bargained for.

Arthur hesitated, then said the words he'd wanted to say for days. Words that meant something different now. "So does this mean you will marry me?"

Lilianna stepped back, leaning against the wall opposite him as she appraised him with a blatant glance up and down his form. Arthur was not accustomed to such an approach and discovered to his horror that heat was cascading up him.

His eagerness to hear her speak was only just restrained by his determination to let her think. If she could agree... If she was about to say that she would be his...

"Perhaps," Lilianna said, her voice almost a whisper. "But we've got to do something first."

Oh, this is more like it.

"You took the words right out of my mouth," Arthur said, his fingers scrabbling to undo the buttons of his trousers. "God, I never thought that we... That you'd want to—"

"Not *that!*" Lilianna was laughing, and his shoulders slumped as he realized just what an idiot had been. "You think I want my first time to be in an alley?"

"No." *No, of course not.* He was a complete fool. "But then... what?"

Lilianna grinned.

Chapter Thirteen

April 12, 1840

"Y OU PROMISED ME you would behave!"

"And you believed us?" Samuel scoffed. "More fool you, say I."

Lilianna tried not to smile. "Yes, I'm starting to see that now."

It was easy to forget sometimes that her brothers were five and twenty and seven and twenty respectively. They were gentlemen—Samuel would be the Marquess of Aylesbury one day—God forbid that it happen anytime soon, like if their father decided to follow in their Uncle William's footsteps and abdicated his title before death—and they were members of Society. Respected members of Society. At least, they were supposed to be.

And that was why she had presumed that a promise from their lips that they would behave this evening, of all evenings, would be kept.

Why she had been so foolish, she did not know. She never expected much from Frank.

"But I am busy!" Frank scowled, dropping onto the sofa with a glowering expression. "Can't a girl stay in her workshop at all hours so that she can fix the—"

"No," came the answer from Lilianna's lips. She grinned to hear their father chorus with her.

Frank's scowl deepened.

"I am not saying you cannot spend any time in your... your *workshop*, for want of a better term," said their father.

Lilianna watched as her sister glared. "You don't have to call it a 'workshop' if you don't want to. Call it 'the room that no one wanted and so when Frank begged for—'"

"But when there is an important family event, yes, I expect you to attend," continued their father hastily, pouring himself a large glass of brandy. "Myself and your mother—oh."

Lilianna, standing near the door to the hall, stifled a grin as her mother entered the room, took the glass of brandy out of her father's anticipating hand, and took a large sip.

"Steady on there, Florence!"

"It's a b-big night," said Lilianna's mother, staring perceptively. "Isn't it, Lil?"

Benjamin was reading a book in an armchair but looked up at their mother's pronouncement. "Is it?"

"I w-wish you'd had Clarke do m-more with your hair, d-dear," fussed their mother, approaching Lilianna with eager fingers.

Lilianna dodged her attempts to re-pin her hair as Benjamin piped up, asking, "But *why* is it a big evening?"

"You've not been paying attention, have you?" Samuel grinned from the fireplace, warming his hands.

Frank was giggling and Lilianna flushed. Well, surely, it wasn't up to her to explain things to her brother—he was a man, after all, not a child any longer.

"But why is tonight—"

"Mother, my hair is perfectly—"

"I suppose I should pour myself another brandy," mused their father.

"But why is it—"

"Oh, Benjamin, *for heaven's sake!*" snapped Lilianna, pushed beyond all endurance, her nerves frayed enough as it was. "Because the Earl of Taernsby is coming to dinner and he wants to marry me!"

There was silence in the drawing room. Silence, that was, other than Benjamin's astonished spluttering, Frank's giggles, the crackle of the fire, and the sound of brandy sloshing in a glass.

"Right," said Lilianna awkwardly, hoping to goodness they would presume the red in her cheeks was from the flickering of the fire. "Glad we've got that sorted. Brandy."

She wasn't usually one for strong drink, that being far more the purvey of her brothers, but tonight of all nights it was probably acceptable.

When she approached her father and reached out to take the second glass of brandy he had poured, however, it was made clear to her that it was *not* acceptable.

"Not on your life," her father said forcefully, tugging it away. "You're going to want a clear head for this evening, Lil. Trust me."

Throwing back his head, he downed the entire glass in one.

Lilianna stared. "And you don't?"

"Oh, I came to this dinner with a mussed head to begin with," said the Marquess of Aylesbury with a smile.

Her stare became one of slight panic. "Oh, Papa! Of all of them, I had depended on you to be... Well. Normal. You mean you've already had a glass of something?"

"What? Oh, no, no, that isn't what I meant," her father said swiftly, placing a reassuring hand on her arm.

Lilianna examined him closely. He did not appear to be intoxicated. It would have been rare for her father in the first place, but he *had* said...

"Why can't I ask him his intentions?" Frank was saying behind her to a stuttering Mama. "I just think, the first gentleman she's ever bothered to ask to dinner—"

"It was just... Well. I am nervous," said the marquess.

Lilianna's attention snapped back to her father. "Nervous? *You*, nervous?"

She could not recall the man ever being nervous before. He was her father. He was Papa. He was always tall, and proud, and strong.

The Marquess of Aylesbury nodded ruefully. "Well, I… Ahem. No one has ever come to actually take my daughter away from me. You've always been very good at batting them back, but now…"

He looked a little lost.

Lilianna's affection swelled as she threw her arms around her father's neck and kissed him on the cheek. "No one is taking me away from you. Not truly."

And that was when the jangling sound of the doorbell echoed through the house.

Lilianna stiffened.

"Hell, he's here!"

"*Samuel!*"

Her mother's remonstrance to her brother continued, but Lilianna could not concentrate as she released her father and gave him a nervous smile. "You are not the only one who is tense," she confessed.

Her father grinned and brushed a lock of her hair from her eyes. "That's a good sign, if you ask me. I was terrified of impressing your mother when I knew I loved her."

"*When I knew I loved her.*"

It was the sort of sentence Lilianna wished she had time to consider, to ruminate on, to ask her father precisely what he meant—but there was no time. The door to the hall was opening and in stepped Humphreys accompanied by—

Her breath caught in her throat.

Well, he did look particularly handsome, dressed like that. The finest of suits with the most expert of tailoring, his hair finely coiffed in a way that felt far more formal than she'd ever seen, and—was that a gold pocket watch chain?

"The Earl of Taernsby, my lord," said Humphreys stiffly.

Lilianna gave the servant a nod before stepping forward. She'd had a talk with the butler, with all the servants, that very afternoon. If the family was going to disgrace themselves, and she had a horrid feeling that they would, the servants at least would treat tonight with the solemnity it deserved.

Humphreys bowed, took a step back, then winked behind Arthur's back before leaving the room.

Forcing herself not to sigh—*could no one in this place be trusted?*—Lilianna instead curtseyed to Arthur, who bowed in turn.

"My lord," she said softly.

"Lady Lillianna," he returned.

Just those three syllables were enough to make her legs quiver, but as she straightened, Lilianna concentrated on not quite meeting his eye.

That would be the end of her, she knew. And as she appeared to be the only sane one of the lot.

"C'mon, then, let's have it out!"

Lilianna gasped as her eldest brother strode forward and nudged her out of the way. "*Samuel!*"

"And who are you, then?" asked Samuel sternly, glaring at the newcomer. "Come to bewitch my sister and take her away?"

"I rather think that's *my* job, son," said their father with a smile as he stepped forward. "Aren't I supposed to be the one who speaks to the man?"

Frank raised her hand. "If anyone should interrogate the blighter, it should be me!"

Lilianna groaned, lifting a hand to her temples in exhausted disappointment. After all her preparations, and their promises to behave…

"F-Frank, it really should be your f-father," their mother was saying.

It did not appear to matter. Frank had risen from the sofa and elbowed their brother away from the bemused earl. "I'm her sister, and I'm the one who knows her best! How do you intend to keep her happy, eh?"

"*Frank,*" hissed Lilianna under her breath, trying to tug her sister away. "This really isn't the time for—"

"'Frank'?" Arthur said with a slight frown. "But I thought—

aren't *you* Frank?"

Lilianna glanced around at the brother to whom Arthur was referring.

Benjamin blinked up from his book. "Sorry, got lost in my novel—who are you?"

If they were purposefully attempting to disgrace her, they could not have done a better job. Lilianna wondered if it were possible to disown the lot of them and just—well. Marry Arthur.

She swallowed the rising panic and confusion. Not because she was in love with him. No. Most definitely not.

When she turned back to their guest, her sister was explaining the confusion.

"—but I never liked *Francesca*—"

"Such a p-pretty name," said their mother, who was clutching her brandy glass on the sofa. "My b-babies are all grown up."

"—so I'm Frank," said Frank inflexibly. She glared up at the interloper. "Is that a problem?"

Lilianna swallowed. So many gentlemen attempted to coddle Frank, to treat her like a delicate flower. She was more a wrench than a wisteria.

"No, I don't think so," said Arthur airily with a shrug. "What do I care what you call yourself?"

Frank's eyes widened. "You... You don't think it is unlady-like, uncouth, and without charm?"

"*Frank!*"

"Well, that's what you said last week, Papa," she said with wide-eyed innocence.

A slow smile started to creep across Lilianna's face as Arthur snorted.

"It may be unladylike, uncouth, and without charm," he said easily. "But if you like it, I don't see what anyone else's opinion has to do with it."

Lilianna watched as her sister beamed.

"*See*, Papa!" Frank said triumphantly. "And he's an earl, so I would say that's one for and one against. You're acceptable,

Taernsby."

"Thank you, Frank," Arthur said with a grin, as though daughters of marquesses who demanded boys' names and then immediately addressed him as if they were his equal were an everyday experience for him.

"Can I get you a drink, young man?" asked the Marquess of Aylesbury. "Something strong to fortify yourself to deal with this rabble in which you've found yourself?"

It was like watching a play. Lilianna did not wish to interfere, not all the time, at least, and it was important to her that he could survive this on his own. If... Well, if she were to accept his advances and finally agree to be Arthur's wife, then this would be the family he would step into. A loud, rambunctious, often nonsensical family.

And this was only *their* branch of the Chance family. Her father's three brothers had their own varieties of foolhardiness to contend with.

Arthur inclined his head, evidently grateful at her father's suggestion. "That would be most pleasant, thank you."

"What tipple do you favor?" asked her Papa, striding over to the drinks' cabinet and waving aside a footman who had appeared, almost like magic, to be helpful. "I have brandy, port, whiskey, wine..."

Lilianna caught her mother's eye and beamed as they watched. It wasn't a test, not really, but at the same time, it very much was. There was only one right answer to this, and Lilianna prayed Arthur was smart enough to see it.

Arthur had followed the Marquess of Aylesbury over to the drinks cabinet and was perusing the numerous bottles within it. *No, that isn't right. He needs to say—*

"What would you recommend, my lord?" Arthur asked quietly, looking up at his host. "I am happy to be guided by you."

Both Lilianna and her mother breathed sighs of relief.

The marquess beamed. "Oh, the brandy, most definitely. Its rich smoothness is perfect for a spring afternoon like this! The honey notes of this '47—"

"I *adore* the '47. It's one of my requirements for a good dinner," said Arthur jovially. "But have you tried the '56, my lord?"

The knot in Lilianna's stomach unwound itself as she watched two of the men who meant the most to her converse happily.

"I'd be more than happy to send a set of six bottles along to your butler, with my compliments," Arthur was saying.

"That is most generous of you, my lord."

"Oh, please, call me 'Taernsby,'" he said with a charming smile.

With the way his shoulders relaxed, the dimple in his cheeks, Lilianna saw her father's approbation gained in that moment.

"And you must call me 'Aylesbury.' Everyone does," Papa said with a laugh. "Brandy, Samuel?"

"Please, Papa."

"Here, let me," said Arthur swiftly.

Picking up his own glass and accepting the fresh one that his host had just poured, their guest for the evening strode across the room to the fireplace, where Lilianna's oldest brother had returned to warming himself.

"Thank you," Samuel said stiffly.

Arthur inclined his head then held his glass out for a small toast. Just as her older brother lifted his own in return, his mouth moving, Arthur also muttered something she did not catch.

Lilianna glanced at her mother, who mouthed, *"What did they say?"*

She only had time to shrug before both Arthur and Samuel were crowing with delight, clapping each other on the backs, and generally treating each other like long lost-brothers.

What on earth?

"I had no idea you were also a member," Samuel was saying eagerly. "There aren't that many of us in Bath."

"I suspected you were from the moment I saw your cufflinks," Arthur returned with a dry laugh. "It seemed too good to be true, but I thought I would try the code word."

"Terrible shame we haven't made your acquaintance before," said Lilianna's brother cheerfully. "Lil, he's a—"

"Member of that silly secret club of yours," supplied Frank from the sofa, a glare of concentration on her face as she frowned at her notebook. Where she'd pulled it from, Lilianna could not guess. "The one that doesn't allow ladies."

Oh, of course. Understanding dawned in Lilianna's mind as her eldest brother and Arthur chattered away happily, swapping stories of how they had joined.

Well, she could never have predicted that. So, that was her sister, her father, and one of her brothers swiftly charmed. He had already, of course, charmed her mother at the concert. Arthur was working even quicker than she could have predicted.

Lilianna swallowed, sipping the glass of wine that her father had brought over to her. It was all going so… so well. Better than well. Better than she had hoped.

But that still left…

Her mother asked Samuel a question about this secret club of theirs, one her brother at great pains tried to explain that he wasn't permitted to explain, and Arthur meandered across the room to the armchair where her younger brother was seated.

Lilianna's shoulders tightened. Benjamin's reputation was not as it should have been, to the constant chagrin of their parents. He did not appear to be able to stop himself from getting into scrapes. He was, in a way, the perfect companion for the Earl of Taernsby, who appeared to have bedded half the country.

But she knew Benjamin. He was soft, and sensitive; he wouldn't respond to the roguish secret club guff that their elder brother loved so much.

Benjamin stiffened with awkwardness at the stranger's approach, placing a bookmark in his novel and looking up warily.

"Are you enjoying the book?" Arthur asked politely. His voice was quieter, now, softer, modulated differently. "It's *The Mysteries of Udolpho* by Ann Radcliffe, isn't it? I adored her *A Sicilian*

Romance."

And in that moment, her final sibling was won over.

"Have you read it? I have found it most difficult to find a copy—the lending library here in Bath is subpar," said Benjamin eagerly, brightening up.

"I have a copy signed by the author, as it happens," Arthur said, dropping into the companion armchair and nodding. "Yes, I was fortunate enough to encounter someone who had met her before she passed on one of my trips to Italy, and when I asked them what she had said about the setting…"

"He's d-doing v-very well."

Lilianna turned at the soft words to her mother, seated beside Frank.

"A little *too* well," grumbled Frank.

"Th-There's no such thing as too w-well when it comes to m-meeting a family," their mother said, chiding her daughter. "And he is imp-portant t-to you, isn't he, Lil?"

Lilianna swallowed. She turned back to her youngest brother, who was gesturing wildly now as his discussion on novels continued with Arthur Nelson, Earl of Taernsby.

Yes, he was important to her. Far more important than she liked to admit. Here was a man who had been warm yet not condescending with her sister, respectful and generous with her father, laddish and bold with Samuel, sensitive and cultured with Benjamin. All he had to do now was marry her, and her mother would adore him for all eternity.

There was so much to this man—but a part of her could not help but wonder whether any of the facets of Arthur she had seen this evening were true. Were real. Were him.

"You'll have to borrow the volumes," Arthur was saying.

Benjamin's eyes widened. "No, I couldn't possibly. Signed by the author? I wouldn't dare!"

"I've gained a great deal of enjoyment from them and I see no reason why you shouldn't, either," said Arthur firmly. "I insist. Enjoy them!"

"Gosh, that's very kind of you."

The dinner gong echoed from the hall, halting their conversation.

"Oh, good, food," said Lilianna's father, who looked to her mind as though he'd had quite enough brandy for one day. "My dear?"

The Marchioness of Aylesbury rose in a rush of silks and smiles, and Lilianna could not help but smile to look at her. Her parents had truly been made for each other. The story of how they had found each other had been told so many times she could almost recite it.

Her pulse lurched. And was this part of the story she would tell one day… to her own children?

As though he could read her thoughts, Arthur was grinning when she looked up to meet his eye. "Shall we?"

She had never been taken through to dinner by a gentleman who was courting her before. Lilianna hated how her hand shook as she placed it upon his arm, and she tried not to notice Frank's smirk as her sister rose and took Samuel's arm.

The dining table was resplendent. Lilianna had been most careful in her instructions to Cook and Humphreys, and both had surpassed themselves. The silver service gleamed in the brilliant light of copious candles and candelabras, the floral decorations astounding and the pineapple atop the central display truly impressive.

"You've gone all out for me," muttered Arthur with a grin as he helped her to a seat.

"Don't be silly," Lilianna said archly as she sat. "We dine like this every day."

But her cheeks flushed as he lowered himself into the seat beside her.

Surely, he could see that it was for him, that she wanted to welcome him into the family, to show him what living as part of the Chance family was like.

"Ah, thank you, Humphreys," her father was saying as the

butler poured Lilianna's mother a glass of wine. "I must say, the place looks—"

"Completely normal," Lilianna said, the heat in her cheeks blossoming as she felt Arthur's eyes on her. "Thank you, Humphreys."

The butler grinned. "Anything you wish, Lady Lilianna."

The footmen stepped forward as one and began to serve the family. Frank was chattering away with Benjamin about the need for reform within the world of engineering—"I mean to say, if we prevent ladies from entering the field, are we not halving the ingenuity of the pack in a stroke?"—while Samuel was talking about politics to their father, their mother listening in sagely and interjecting at all the right places.

Lilianna looked at her plate and nodded to herself approvingly. Roast pheasant with a plum sauce and roasted vegetables to start. Excellent.

It was all going to plan.

"So, are we on schedule?"

She started at the soft whisper from her left, and smiled at Arthur, who returned it. "I am sure I don't know what you mean."

"You know exactly what I mean," he retorted. "I know you, Lilianna. You like order, you like a plan. This evening—it's all been planned out, hasn't it?"

Of course it had been. Did the man think a spectacular dinner like this just happened by accident?

"I couldn't say, I'm sure," she said, sipping her wine. The heat and flare of the spices in the red wine could not beat the heat in the man's stare.

Arthur took a bite of his pheasant and moaned slightly with delight, which was not particularly helpful in calming Lilianna's racing pulse. "This dinner is absolutely delicious. I'll have to send my cook round to beg for the recipe."

"Or I could just send Kay around with it," Lilianna shot back in a low voice, laughter dancing in her tones. "She knows the way, after all."

Arthur rolled his eyes. "You're never going to let me forget that, are you?"

"Most definitely not," she said quietly.

No, she did not wish to forget a single moment of this. Of any of it. This was to be her love story, Lilianna was starting to realize, and it was perfect.

"You've charmed my family."

Arthur grinned. "Good. That was my intention."

"Such different things to different people. I was dazzled by the variety," Lilianna said lightly as Frank slammed her cutlery down and started sniping at their brother. "I suppose the question is, who are you, really? The charmer, the lout, the great reader?"

Sipping his wine before answering, Arthur winked. "Whoever you want me to be, Lady Lilianna."

Grinning as though he had spoken the most amusing joke of all time, he returned to his pheasant.

Lilianna could not eat another bite. Her mouth was dry, her appetite gone.

"Whoever you want me to be, Lady Lilianna."

"I was afraid of that," she said quietly, turning away to mutter something to a footman.

It had been a convenient excuse—that candlewick really did need trimming; it was almost criminal that Humphreys had let it go on like that—and out of the corner of her eye, Lilianna could see that Arthur, rather than looking self-congratulatory at his winning remark, instead looked crestfallen.

Chapter Fourteen

April 14, 1840

H E WAS GOING to wear out a hole in the carpet if he wasn't careful.

Arthur snorted and kept walking. Up and down, up and down, along the long portrait gallery. He'd been here so long that the shadows had crept around the room and finally disappeared. When a footman had appeared to light the candles, the servant had been forced to step around the pacing earl.

It was all so—so goddamn frustrating.

"I suppose the question is, who are you, really? The charmer, the lout, the great reader?"

"Whoever you want me to be, Lady Lilianna."

What had possessed him to say such a thing?!

He knew full well. He had been attempting to be charming. Teasing. As though that was what Lady Lilianna Chance wanted—he knew better than that!

Castigating himself all evening when he had returned home had not helped. Blaming himself all of yesterday for ruining a perfectly good dinner with the woman he… he *loved*, dammit, there was no point in lying to himself… with the woman he loved had not resolved the issue.

And today, he'd spent almost the last six hours pacing.

Pacing! Like a lovesick swain!

Arthur muttered something to no one in particular. "Stupid,

idiotic, foolish brute!"

That was all he was. Two days ago, he'd had the chance to impress the entirety of the Chance family and most importantly, the woman he'd been asking to marry him for weeks.

And what had he done?

Well. At first, he'd been brilliant. But then that line, dismissing her, immediately reducing himself in her eyes… he'd been an absolute imbecile.

"You can't just stay here worrying about it," said a voice.

Arthur did not look up from his pacing. "You don't know a thing about it."

He wouldn't have been so rude, except that it was rather a liberty for the man to speak like that at all.

His butler came into view and shrugged. "Servants talk, my lord, and not just within their own households."

Arthur glared at the man then resumed his pacing, his gaze dropping to the floor.

Yes, he was sure half of Bath knew what a complete fool he'd made of himself at the Aylesbury townhouse. The gossip had probably floated away on the lips of footmen and maidservants, initially, but it would be all over town now.

"I sent a note," he said curtly.

Haslehaw cleared his throat. "I know, my lord."

"I mean, I sent a very politely worded letter thanking them," Arthur burst out, tugging his cravat, which was far too tight. "I sent it to the marchioness as hostess. That was right, wasn't it?"

This damned earling business—it is far too complicated.

"Yes, I would have said so."

"But nothing back from the marchioness?"

His tone was almost pleading, as though he could somehow coerce his butler into receiving a reply.

The servant shook his head.

Arthur swore. Of course there wasn't. The woman had probably heard all about his inane remark from her daughter. Lilianna had been disappointed—disappointed in him. He'd given her a reason to doubt. That doubt had undoubtedly spread through the family.

"And there has been no reply to your other note, either."

Turning on his heels, Arthur froze. "'Other note'?"

No one was supposed to know about the other note.

Haslehaw was smiling. "Yes, the other note. The one you wrote specifically to Lady Lilianna. I presume you sent one, my lord. That would be the done thing."

The done thing. How far had doing the done thing gotten him? *Not bloody far.*

Yes, damnit, he'd sent a note. "And no reply?"

"None, I am sorry to say, my lord."

He'd spent a great deal of time on that note. Arthur had never had to send an apology letter to anyone; his mistresses or conquests had always been left very well satisfied, at least by their own accounts, and Arthur had been careful to stay clear of any sort of politics. With his brother as earl, he hadn't had much else to do.

So yesterday, he'd been faced with his writing desk, sheaves of paper, pen and ink, and absolutely no idea what to say.

~~Lilianna, I am sorry. I didn't mean~~

~~I don't know what came over me. I just wanted to im-press~~

~~I will be anything you want me to be, anything. Just tell me what~~

It was no good. No matter what he tried to write, the words were inadequate. Nothing could encapsulate the panicked feeling that overwhelmed him whenever he thought of that moment.

"Whoever you want me to be, Lady Lilianna."

"What is happening to me?" Arthur asked curtly, glaring at his servant. "No woman has ever done this to me!"

"I think you will find this is what happens when one falls in love, my lord," the butler said delicately. "Not that I am an expert."

In love. Yes. He'd told himself as much.

In lust, he'd known that from the start. Arthur had known he had wanted Lady Lilianna Chance from the moment she had fallen into his arms. Hot, and squirming, and looking as though she were the devil incarnate.

Her determination not to be impressed by him had only inflamed his desire.

And now... now he was pacing up and down his portrait gallery trying to work out how to win her back, and he wasn't even sure why he'd been such a damned fool as to lose her.

"What can I do, my lord?"

"Nothing," Arthur snapped, fury at himself redirecting to his servant. "Nothing at all!"

His butler's nostrils flared. "In that case, is there anything *you* can do?"

For a heartbeat, Arthur just glared at the man. Then he swore under his breath and made for the stairs.

In less than five minutes, he had donned a greatcoat and top hat, ignoring his gloves, and marched out onto the street. There was no time to ask Haslehaw to have the carriage sent round or to call a hackney cab; Arthur half-ran, half-walked through the sodden Bath streets after what must have been a downpour he had not noticed. His shoulders were heaving by the time he reached the Aylesbury townhouse, but that did not matter.

A note—what had he been thinking? This sort of apology required an in-person effort.

Precisely what he was going to say had been rehearsed carefully in his mind during the ten minutes of frantic rushing through Bath streets. It went something like this.

Lilianna. You know how I feel about you, and I do not think I have hidden my desire to marry you. I wished to make the best impression possible on your family, whom I know you greatly adore and respect, and so I was careful to bring forward different aspects of my personality to impress them. I wanted to impress them. I wanted to impress you.

Please, I am literally begging you. I will get on my knees and beg if need be.

Fine, the ending needed a little work. But the beginning was sound.

When Arthur pulled at the doorbell, he had expected the well-oiled machinery of the Chance household to spring into action. He had already calmed himself sufficiently to present a tranquil expression for whichever footman opened the door.

But it did not open. A full minute passed, and Arthur was just considering pulling at the bell again, when the door finally creaked open slowly.

"My good man," Arthur began. "I would like to see—"

"I am not your 'good man,'" said Lilianna with a raised eyebrow. "And I never intend to be."

His mouth fell open.

This—this was not part of the plan. Where was the footman? Why on earth was Lilianna, a daughter of the house—a house of a marquess—answering her own front door?

"I… I… Wh-What…?"

This was the moment, Arthur told himself furiously, to pull himself together. Hadn't he spent all day hoping she would reply to his letter? Hadn't he marched over here because he couldn't wait any longer?

Speak, man!

Lilianna's eyebrow remained raised. "Well?"

Well, indeed. Arthur swallowed, mouth dry, but all the clever phrases and the well-reasoned argument that he'd put together faded away into the oozing mess his mind was apparently now made of.

Lilianna. You know how I feel about you, and I do not think I have hidden my desire to marry you.

"Desire," Arthur croaked. "Marry you."

Christ, that isn't it!

Lilianna's other eyebrow had raised to join the first. "I beg your pardon?"

Arthur rubbed his temple and wondered what on earth this woman had done to him. There had been a time when he had been charming. There had been a time when he had been coherent.

And now here he was, standing on her doorstep—*why had Lilianna answered the door?*—blabbing about desire and marriage.

"What do you want?" Lilianna asked quietly.

Arthur looked up into her sky-blue eyes and said the only thing that was true. "You."

Her face softened. "Well. You had better come in, then."

He half-fell, half-stepped into the Chance house. The place was just as he had remembered it from two days ago, although the sense of bustle and noise was gone. It was quiet. Very quiet.

Too quiet.

"Erm…" Arthur said hesitantly, looking around for a footman to take his greatcoat and hat.

No one appeared. Lilianna did not appear to care; she was stepping across the echoing hallway into a room he had not been in before.

What was he supposed to do now?

Arthur did the only thing that made sense: he followed her.

By God, I would follow that woman anywhere.

When he stepped into the room, he saw it was a breakfast room. The small table was still covered in breakfast things, although it was nearly four o'clock in the afternoon. A single candle was lit in a holder on the sideboard and the curtains were drawn, which was early. There was the same sense of emptiness here, the same… absence. Arthur could not put his finger on it.

Lilianna closed the door behind him and he swallowed. He knew what he *did* want to put his finger on.

"How may I help you, my lord?" she asked quietly, stepping past him without a second look and seating herself on a chair at the table.

Arthur swallowed. It was an excellent question. "I… I am not sure I know how to answer."

Lilianna's imperious look—puckered lips, chin in the air—had returned and it broke his heart. This was the woman he had first met, the cold, aloof version of Lilianna whom he had adored yet wanted more from. He had broken her barriers, crept under the ice-cold sheet around her, knew her better than this.

So why had she retreated?

Other than his abominable rudeness the other day, obviously.

"Aren't… Aren't you going to ring for tea?" he said helplessly.

Tea, yes, that was it. The bastion of good society. With a hot cup of tea and perhaps a slice of cake, perhaps he would be prepared to face the onslaught that was surely coming.

A strange flicker moved across Lilianna's face. "There is no point. No one would come."

Arthur frowned. Something was wrong here. "Look, what is going on—where is everyone?"

"Gone," Lilianna said curtly. "Most of them. What are you doing here?"

"What do you *mean*, gone? You're not on your own?"

Arthur had spoken without thought, but his eagerness had slipped out in his tone before he could stop it.

Lilianna, alone. The two of them alone together. Able to say what he wanted to say, able to do what he wanted to do. Touch her, kiss her, worship her, show her just what she meant to him in ways he was almost certain she would appreciate.

"I am sorry, you know," he said aloud, partly to break the silence and partly to break the stream of sensual images streaming past his eyes. He blinked. The real Lilianna, the one still glaring, swam back into view. "I shouldn't have—I wanted to impress you. I wanted to impress you all."

"I wanted the *real* Arthur Nelson, Earl of Taernsby, to meet my family," Lilianna said stiffly. "What I got was a caricature."

"No, no, that's not—"

"Just the same old Taernsby who has charmed so many women and undoubtedly their families," she said, her voice thick with emotion.

Arthur stepped over and knelt before her, desperate to be close to her, to look her in the eye as he revealed what he had to admit. "Look, I *was* honest. I *was* real."

"But you were so—so different!" Lilianna sounded pained and he had done that to her. He had hurt her. "How can I trust anything you say, any way that you act?"

He bowed his head for a moment, trying desperately to recall the brilliant speech he had put together on the way over. *What was it, something about aspects of personality and care and that sort of thing?*

"I… There's more to me than just being a rake."

Out of the corner of his eye, Lilianna had gone very still. "What did you say?"

Arthur swallowed as he looked up, still kneeling before her. "I said, there's more to me than just being a rake. I love Ann Radcliffe. I have all her books, and as I said to your brother, most of them are signed. It's just… It's never come up before."

Lilianna's face was blank, as though attempting to understand what he was saying. "And… And the brandy?"

"I've been—well, let us call it *importing* it for some time," Arthur said with a wry smile. "At least, my family has. I think the Taernsby cellar has one of the greatest assortments of brandies in the country. It would be no trouble at all to send a few to your father."

"It's not about the bottles, it's about—you gave him the choice of your drink," Lilianna said, as though she were accusing him of kicking a puppy. "I thought…"

"Is it not polite to do that?" Arthur said, confused now. "I just wanted to be a good guest. I wanted them to like me. I want you to see me as… as part of your family."

It was horrendous, spilling out these thoughts before her like gifts for a queen. But Arthur would do it all again, kneel at her feet like this and try to explain, if he could achieve the impossible.

A slow smile quirked Lilianna's lips. "It was really you."

"It's not the me who most people see, I will grant you that," he admitted quietly. "It's easier to trot out the rake, and don't get me wrong, that is a part of me too."

"But not the only part of you."

Arthur shook his head slowly. "Not at all."

She examined him closely, as though hunting for some additional truth in his face. Then she sighed, shoulders slumping. Only then did he see the tiredness, the worry in her eyes.

"Humphreys has come down with scarlet fever," Lilianna said softly.

Arthur leaned back on his haunches and sat, ignoring the impropriety of sitting without being invited, on a chair beside her. "Your butler?"

She nodded. "How on earth the man has managed to get through life without catching it by now, I do not know. But then, neither has Frank."

Frank. The sister—the one he had presumed would be a brother.

Fear gripped Arthur. "She has it?"

"The doctor advised that she leave Bath immediately," Lilianna said hastily. "As far as we know, she is unaffected, but staying here…"

"Not worth the risk."

Her nod was sage, quiet, concerned. "Mama and Papa took her to Stanphrey Lacey—it's the family seat. Really, it's the property of my Uncle William, but they returned to London last week and so it was empty. Samuel went too."

Well, that would explain the quiet in the place. But the second brother, and the servants, where were they?

"It all got somewhat complicated," Lilianna said with a laugh, in that unerring way she had of reading his thoughts. "Benjamin has taken Humphreys to a convalescent home, as he'll get the best treatment there, and most of our maids went with my parents and Frank to Stanphrey Lacey. They'll need the additional help. Two footmen haven't had scarlet fever, either, so they've gone to their families on full pay…"

She trotted out the list of where everyone in the household had gone, but Arthur wasn't listening. He was far too busy making sure that he did not lean forward and kiss this woman firmly on the mouth in his relief that she was unaffected.

Scarlet fever… a terrible sickness, one that could rush through a family and steal many lives.

That explained why the marchioness had not replied to his note. Selfish though it was, Arthur could not help but be a tad relieved. He had not offended the Chance family. He did not have to redeem himself.

"—which leaves myself," Lilianna said with a wry look. "There was insufficient room in the carriage for me to accompany Frank, and… and I wanted to stay here."

Arthur frowned. "Why?"

"Because of you," she said simply.

Excitement sparked. "So… So you're here all alone?"

Now this was a turn up for the books, and no mistake.

Lilianna's glare was potent. "*Arthur Nelson!* Absolutely not. I am here with my maid, Clarke. She agreed to stay behind. Her mother is a cook and so she will see to my meals."

"But not to cleaning up?" Arthur said, gesturing at the table covered with dirty plates. He should have guessed something was wrong—only two sets of plates. "And she's eating with you?"

"Why not? It seemed silly for me to eat alone up here and for her to eat alone downstairs," Lilianna pointed out.

So the maid was still here. That ruled out some of the more delectable things Arthur had immediately started to hope for.

"What are you thinking?"

"Nothing," Arthur said hastily.

Not hastily enough. Lilianna grinned—and there she was, his Lilianna, the one he had coaxed out of her ice palace and held and kissed.

"You're a terrible liar, Arthur. Which I suppose is all to the good—because it means I can trust you—but *honestly*. You think I don't know what you were thinking?"

It's a trap, isn't it?

"Ahh," Arthur said helplessly, shifting on his chair with no idea what to say next. "I… Uh…"

"You've had enough mistresses for me to know precisely what you want," Lilianna said, leaning back and perusing him as if he were a book. "Don't think I don't know what you want."

He swallowed, mouth dry, pulse throbbing in his ears, loins tight. *And am I going to get it?*

Not a question he could ask aloud.

"Why are you here, Arthur?" Lilianna asked softly. "I need to know."

"I wanted to explain, to apologize—"

"I don't mean *here, now,*" she said, interrupting him and reaching out to take his hand. "I mean… Why are you pursuing me? Why me?"

Arthur tried to think as her soft fingers placed a gentle pressure on his own. How precisely he was supposed to think, he was not sure.

"And I want the truth."

Of course she did. The trouble was, Arthur wasn't entirely sure of the truth himself. He'd told himself he loved her. But how did he explain that to her? Explain why she, of all women, had been the first—the only—to inspire such declarations from his soul?

He looked up, catching her sparkling eyes and seeing the need in her. Not just the need to be touched, to be satisfied by him, although that was certainly there. No, there was another need. The need to hear the truth. To be trusted.

Arthur took a deep breath. "I told you before, weeks ago, that I needed a wife. Heirs."

Lilianna nodded. "The portrait gallery."

The first deep breath had not been enough, but Arthur did not seem able to coerce his lungs to take another. "Well, that is true—but it's not the only truth. These things, they are not never that simple."

"Like you."

He let out a laugh. "Something like that."

Strange. In this breakfast room in the silent house, inhabited by only them and a maid somewhere about the place, it was easy to fool himself into thinking that this was their home. That their life together had already begun.

"It was easy to fool myself into thinking it was the only reason," Arthur said haltingly. "Easier to think that than to admit that I was lonely. And when I saw you... Christ, I'd never believed in love at first sight."

"You do now?" Her voice was taut, uncertain, curious.

Forcing himself to meet her gaze, Arthur told the truth. "I don't know. What I felt for you in that moment, it defies logic. It defies everything that I thought I was."

"A rake."

He had to laugh at that. "I suppose so. I knew I was more, but I'd kept it hidden away. I hadn't seen the point in bringing it forward. No one wanted to know the younger brother of an earl. And you—Lilianna, you're so impressive and—"

Lilianna's scoff halted him. "Don't give me the routine, Arthur, I'm not one of your conquests."

"I know you're not! You're a woman who knows what she's worth!"

Something in his words stopped her laughter. Lilianna's eyes fixed on him, flickering only momentarily to his mouth before she said, "You truly think so?"

Arthur leaned forward and captured her free hand with his own. Here they sat, hand in hand. *If not now, when?* "Lilianna, I had not even known what I was looking for, until I found it. Until I found you. You're... You're everything I want. Everything I will ever want."

It felt strange, exposing himself like this. Arthur had always looked down on men who had been so devoted to their wives. And yet that was all he wanted to do for this woman, *his* woman. Betray his own strength, tear down his walls, and show her, *bleed* out his affection.

Dear God, I am long gone.

"I want you," he revealed. "I meant it, at your front door. You are what I want, Lilianna. And I know there's only a small chance in hell that you'll have me, but—"

"Then have me," Lilianna said, interrupting him with a smile that was paired with flushing cheeks. "Have me, Arthur."

Arthur blinked. "You—You'll marry me?"

"Yes," said Lilianna simply as a mischievous grin crept across her lips. "After you have me."

Chapter Fifteen

THE WORDS—HER ACCEPTANCE, her *demand*—echoed painfully in her ears, but Lilianna could not find any regret in her for having said them.

She wanted him. She'd wanted him for too long to hold back now, not when he was opening himself to her, revealing the Earl of Taernsby she had never quite believed had been there.

And yes, she was being bold. Yes, the perfect wife would be an innocent on her wedding night, that was what her mother had always told her. That was what Society said. That was what Society expected.

But what was the point in waiting? Within weeks, she would be marrying this man, becoming his wife. A shiver rushed through Lilianna's spine. What difference would it make?

Arthur's lips were parted and his eyes were wide, but there appeared to be something wrong with him. The man wasn't speaking.

Lilianna grinned. "I have flummoxed you."

"I—not—flummoned."

"Flummoxed," she supplied, trying not to laugh. Oh, it was wonderful to put this arrogant and clever man on the back foot.

He'd been direct and sharp and unrestrained the moment she had met him, never failing to speak what he wanted. And now she had done the same, and he had fallen apart.

It was rather endearing.

"I-I… You… not," Arthur managed. He cleared his throat and

Lilianna tried not to follow the bob of his Adam's apple or the sharp line of his jaw. "I don't think you quite understand what you're asking of me."

"I understand perfectly. I may an innocent, but I am not ignorant," Lilianna said, heat flooding her cheeks at the merest hint of impropriety. Oh, this was going to be difficult. "I mean, I… I know roughly what… what is involved."

It seemed that her uncertainty gave Arthur back his own. His roguish smile returned. "You do?"

"Basically," she said primly, pulling her hands away in the flush of embarrassment that rocked her. "I do have brothers, you know. I listened at doors to their nonsense over billiards. Very illuminating game, billiards."

Well, she could hardly hold his hands while talking about such things, could she? Except that very soon, if she had her own way, she would be doing those things…

Lilianna's attention raked over the man seated before her. Only now did she permit herself to linger on those broad shoulders, the hint of muscle flexing through his jacket, the way he always sat with his knees parted…

Giving his manhood room to breathe.

The mere thought made her splutter, just for a moment.

"Lilianna? Are you well?"

"I am quite well," she said quickly, halting any further concern. "Now, are you going to ravish to me or not?"

Once again, she was the one advancing, and though Arthur did not retreat, he was clearly not entirely comfortable. "I… I mean, *Lilianna!*"

"What?" Lilianna ensured to blink innocently. "Ladies cannot proposition their betrotheds?"

"It's just that—"

"Because we are betrothed, aren't we?" she added. It would never do to progress without being absolutely certain of the agreement here. She'd heard enough gossip about certain young ladies to know that it did happen.

Arthur's smile was earnest. "We are betrothed. God, I never thought you'd ever say *yes*."

"Neither did I," Lilianna said ruefully. "So there is no reason why you can't bed me, is there?"

Because she desperately wanted to be bedded. To feel him against her, feel his arms around her, his tongue…

Arthur was spluttering again. "I mean to say, Lilianna! Your-Your maid is here. I can't think what we would… I mean, if we were caught…"

"Oh, did I say that my maid is here?" Lilianna watched in triumph for understanding to dawn on his face. "I should have said that my maid *was* here."

He blinked. He was very still, just staring. "'Was here.'"

She nodded. "She's started to feel unwell and so I sent her straight to the convalescent home—well, you can't be too careful. I have sent a note to my parents and they'll be returning a maid to me. She'll arrive… oh. Tomorrow? The day after?"

It had not been a plan, exactly. Lilianna loved a good plan, naturally, but this one had fallen into her lap without any great effort on her part. Clarke was genuinely unwell, and with scarlet fever so recently in the household, there had been no possibility of her staying. It wasn't as though she, Lilianna, could care for her.

And so here they were. Alone.

Arthur appeared to be having an apoplectic fit. "I… What a pretty painting!" He jabbed a finger at the wall. "Did—erm, did you paint it?"

"As a matter of fact, I did," said Lilianna, impressed that of all the paintings in the entire house, he had managed to select the one she had indeed painted herself. "It's not very good."

"It's beautiful."

His eyes were on her now, not the painting, and Lilianna smiled. "Forget-me-nots. My favorite flower—but you're changing the subject. Are you going to ravish me or not?"

His voice was croaking now, but Arthur gave her a wry look.

"Never change, Lilianna."

"I don't intend to," she said primly, delighted. Oh, after all those irritating men with bad breath and even worse conversation, she would be Arthur's wife. The Countess of Taernsby. Then her eyes narrowed. "You *are* going to marry me, aren't you?"

"I thought *I* was the one who was supposed to ask *you*," he said with a laugh.

"I suppose you are, but then you have asked so many times, I thought it was only fair that we start to even up the numbers," Lilianna said with a grin.

Arthur was shaking his head. "You are ridiculous."

Perhaps she was. This whole situation felt like a dream, like she could wake up at any moment and Frank and Mama and Papa and all of them had only just left.

But this was real. She was seated at the breakfast table in the late afternoon, shadows creeping across the room and the solitary candle lit hardly enough light, with a rake who wanted to marry her.

Her rake.

"You didn't fall in love with me because of my shy and retiring nature, though, did you?" she whispered.

It was perhaps too far. He had never said—he'd spoken a great deal on his attraction to her, but love?

Arthur stood up and for a moment, Lilianna thought he was about to leave. Then he grabbed her hand, pulled her upright, and kissed her hard on the mouth.

Time stopped. So did her pulse. Lilianna could do nothing but accept the onslaught of hedonism that he poured onto her lips.

When Arthur pulled away, there was something shifting in his eyes, and Lilianna luxuriated in it. "I didn't fall in love with you until I knew I had to have you."

"Then have me," Lilianna whispered. "Have me now."

It was not the most eloquent thing she had ever said in the world, but it did not need to be. Here they were in their own little world, a world without others, without interruptions, without Society and its rules—just themselves.

Just Arthur, dotting kisses across her neck as his fingers clutched at her buttocks, drawing her hips against his.

Lilianna gasped, hardly able to draw enough breath. The whole thing was so intoxicating. She had never known anything like this, never experienced such longing that kept her awake at night—and now she was going to know what it was to be ravished, completely.

By the Earl of Taernsby.

It was too much, and not enough, and her senses were being crowded in a way that made Lilianna's head spin. Surely, this was far too much for any woman to bear, and yet parts of her were awakening and crying out that it wasn't enough.

More. She needed more.

"More," Lilianna whimpered against his lips.

Arthur grinned. "Good."

Her gasp was almost lost in his kiss as his tongue swirled in her mouth, tasting her, rocking her on her feet, but Arthur's strong arms were around her.

No—only one arm was around her. Where was the other?

Only when her hair started to flow down her shoulders did Lilianna realize what he was doing. Pins started to fall to the floor and her pulse raced.

"You're so beautiful," Arthur murmured.

"I… I've never been like this before a man," Lilianna said bashfully, lifting a hand to tuck her hair behind her ears.

His face twitched. "There'll be a lot of firsts like this tonight."

Tonight…

She had awoken that morning trying to think of the right words that she could write to Arthur, to tempt him to come to her house now that the unimaginable had happened and her family had departed. Now she was standing by the breakfast table, hair mussed, being kissed thoroughly by that same man.

Her future husband.

Lilianna's fingers moved hurriedly as Arthur sucked on her lower lip in his kiss, her hands unable to move coherently when he did such a decadent thing.

"What are you doing?" he murmured.

"My gown," Lilianna said feverishly. "I need to take it off."

He pulled back at that. "'Take it off'?"

"I… I want to be close to you." It was hard, admitting to such a thing, but Lilianna knew he would understand. "And your waistcoat, your shirt—I need them off."

"Oh, you do, do you?"

Lilianna smiled as the ties to the side of her bodice finally gave up, the ribbon cascading to the floor. "I most certainly do."

She watched, delighting in the way Arthur's eyes widened as she lifted the bodice of her gown over her head. Her chemise under her corset was a pleasant, light-cream color, but it did not remain on for long. Her fingers pulled at the mother of pearl buttons of her overskirt and then that was gone and—

"Slow down, Lilianna."

Her name was a benediction on his lips, but she did not understand why he halted her, why he had captured her hands with his, a knowing look on his face.

"But—But we're—"

"I know. We will," Arthur said softly, reaching up and brushing her hair out of her eyes with hands that had no business being that soft. "But there's no need to rush, Lilianna. I want—I want this to be good for you."

Good for her. Yes, she had heard some mutterings about the pain of lying together as one. And the pleasure. Pain first, pleasure after. The sooner she got through the pain…

"Why don't you wait a moment?"

Lilianna started. "Wait?"

Arthur did not reply. At least, he did not reply with words. Instead, he took a step back, Lilianna almost whimpering at the distance, and, without dropping his gaze, started to remove his coat.

Oh. Lilianna had never experienced anything like it. The sudden intimacy, the silence save for the brush of fabric against fabric, the way that each second brought her closer to seeing more of him…

It was intoxicating. Her mind giddy, her pulse racing, her core throbbing in a way that was most unladylike, Lilianna watched with hungry eyes as Arthur slowly removed his shirt, then his waistcoat, then—

"Oh, my."

He was far superior to anything she could have imagined. The broad planes of his chest undulated with muscles she could not have conceived. Wiry hair dusted down from his neck, his throat finally uncovered by the cravat, which followed his clothing onto the floor, then wound its way down to his hips, a slight V curving over the top of his trousers.

Lilianna swallowed. Trousers that most definitely had a tenting effect that had not been there before.

"Do you like what you see?" Arthur asked in a teasing voice.

It was all she could do to nod. She didn't want to see. She wanted to *feel*.

As though he understand the need within her, Arthur stepped forward, his arms remaining passive by his sides. "Then touch."

Lilianna managed to keep the moan of longing deep within her as her fingertips brushed over his collarbone. Warm, and soft, and yet with the unexpected coarseness of his hair. Her fingers explored, pushing against the resisting flesh.

Oh, he was so handsome.

"I… You are…" Heat scalded her cheeks. "You probably think I'm a fool."

Here she stood, acting as though she had been the first in the world to see such a splendid sight, when there had been women galore who had experienced all this before.

That knowledge, the crushing realization that this was all new and special for her yet commonplace for him, weighed on Lilianna's shoulders like an anvil.

She stepped back, eyes darting about the room, wondering how swiftly she could get dressed again. Oh, she looked ridiculous, standing here in naught but her stockings and underskirt and corset! What had she been think—

"Whoa, there."

And she was in his arms and the intensity of the feeling of his scalding skin against hers was almost too much, and Lilianna fought him.

"Lilianna, what the hell's gotten into you?"

"It's all new for me and you—you've done it all before," she cried out, not bothering to censure herself. "I can't… It's all too much and you… you…"

She raised her eyes to his, almost fearfully. He would think her the most preposterous ninny.

Arthur was looking at her with devotion, his lips soft, his eyes focused. His fondness was so startling, Lilianna gasped and her words faded.

"This is not my first time, not in the same way," he said quietly. "But it's *our* first time. That's the most special thing—you are the most special thing… Lilianna. You're… You're Lilianna Chance. And you're mine."

The calm and possessive way he'd said it, it made her unsteady. Lilianna swallowed all the objections that had risen in her mind. "You… You don't care?"

"I want you to feel loved and exceptional. That is all that I care about," Arthur said simply. "If you want to stop, we'll stop—God knows I would never force you—but stop because you don't want to do it, Lilianna. Not because it scares you."

Lilianna attempted to take deep, calming breaths. Then something of what he had said registered in her mind, and she tapped him on the chest. "I am *not* scared!"

"The Lilianna I know would never be scared," he teased, his lips quirking.

Oh, he was the most aggravating, most intolerable—

She kissed him full on the mouth and he responded in kind,

opening for her, welcoming him in. Shyly, with increased boldness with each passing heartbeat, Lilianna tasted him, teased her tongue into his mouth and knew what it was to possess a person.

How did anyone stop once they had started?

As the pair's kisses continued, Arthur's fingers were not idle. Lilianna gasped as he pulled at the ties of her corset, loosening it more moment after moment, until he pulled away and dragged the thing from her body.

Corsetry and lacing fell to the floor and she was without any defenses.

But she was Lilianna Chance. She met his eyes, proud and resolute, refusing to be cowed into shame merely because she was naked.

Well. Almost naked.

"You missed a bit," she whispered.

Arthur's eyes widened. "'Missed a bit'? What do you—oh, Christ, Lilianna."

She had removed her underskirt. Beneath it was naught but her stockings and… herself.

His focus raked over the curls in the wedge between her thighs, the way her stockings rose up her legs topped with blue ribbon, and she saw the unrestrained need pulse at his jaw.

Perhaps there was something to be said for being brave.

Reaching down, Lilianna's fingertips grazed the tops of her stockings—

"Leave them on," Arthur rasped, his fingers fumbling at the buttons of his trousers.

"*Arthur!*"

She'd had no choice but to exclaim. Leaving his trousers on, which to her mind was most counterintuitive—*would he not need them off?*—Arthur had stepped to the breakfast table and in one swift movement, swept everything upon it to the floor.

"Arthur, that's—"

"I'll clean it up later and pay for any damage," he said, turning to her with hungry eyes. "Now come here."

She was not in the habit of obeying men's orders, or *any* orders, for that matter. But he could have demanded that she march to China in this mood and she would obey him.

Lilianna squealed as Arthur's strong hands clasped her waist and lifted her, placing her on the edge of the table.

What on earth was she here for?

Arthur knelt before her. *Now this is getting silly,* thought Lilianna through a lust-hazed mind. *He could never reach my mouth from there, so how is he going to kiss—*

And then he kissed her. But not on the mouth.

"Arthur!"

"If you want me to stop," came his muffled voice, "all you have to do is ask."

Lilianna clutched the edges of the table and thanked the heavens there was no one in the house to hear her moan. Dear God, she had never expected, never thought... that a man would...

Arthur's tongue curled into her secret place and she quivered. "Arthur..."

Evidently, he understood her silent request that he continue, for he slowly began to lap at her warm folds, shoots of elation sparking across her body, her shoulder shaking as the dull ache between her legs became more sharp.

Lilianna's eyes closed. *Oh, this is—this is—*

His rhythm changed. His tongue ventured deeper, curling against her, exploring her, tasting her, and Lilianna's breathing became labored, her knuckles digging into the table.

It was too much, and yet not enough, and he seemed to know that, curling his tongue delightfully around a bud within her that throbbed with aching pleasure and—

"Arthur!" Lilianna cried out.

She was exploding. She was falling apart, cascades of *need* flowing in ripples. Her whole body was shaking and she would fall, but Arthur's hands held her hips down as he mercilessly lapped at her sweet nectar.

When he finally released her, Lilianna stared with burning cheeks and a shaken frame. "That… That was…"

"I know," Arthur said swiftly, rising to his feet and throwing off his boots and trousers. "I could taste it."

If anyone else had said those words, Lilianna would have expired on the spot, but as it was, it was just what she needed. She wanted him to know, to taste, to *feel* what he had done to her.

What it appeared he was going to do to her again.

"I know it's not exactly couth to take your innocence on a table," Arthur said with a hungry expression, pushing her to the center of the breakfast table and clambering onto it himself, nestling between her legs. "But I have a feeling that our marriage is not exactly going to be like everyone else's."

Lilianna grabbed his shoulders, pulling him closer, tasting herself on his lips. "Our courtship was hardly standard—why change now?"

Arthur grinned, twisting his hips slightly to push his warm and rod-thick manhood against her. "God, I love you."

And that was when he entered her: when she could still hear his words of affection roaring in her ears and all she wanted to do was live in this moment. This moment: with Arthur's manhood slowly sheathing itself into her and her wetness welcoming him in, pulling him closer, tighter.

Lilianna gasped. "You—You're—"

"I'm not hurting you?" Arthur asked urgently, his voice tight.

The tablecloth was gathered awkwardly under her, but above her was the most precious man she had ever known.

And he was worried. Worried he was hurting her.

And now she came to think of it, he wasn't. Hurting her, that was. In fact, she felt—

"It's wonderful. *You're* wonderful," she murmured. She lifted up her lips for a kiss.

Arthur pulled himself almost completely out of her then

plunged himself back into her just as he kissed her and Lilianna shuddered, the promise of bliss that she now recognized sparking within her.

"Oh, yes…"

He knew the rhythm she liked, had practiced with his mouth, and Lilianna could do nothing but hold on to his shoulders as Arthur feasted on her body. Harder, and faster, and deeper, he slid into her with kisses intermingling their shared cries. The minutes slid by in a haze of pleasure and Lilianna knew she could never be the same again after this. After *him*.

His mouth was on her nipple and before Lilianna could stop herself, could relax into this moment and revel in it for all its glory, she was crying out his name and digging her fingers into his shoulders.

"Arthur, oh, Arthur—yes!"

The pleasure was exquisite. It was different this time: not better, just altered, and as her body clenched around him, tugging at his manhood, tightening around it, Arthur swore and poured himself into her.

When the heavens slowed their race across her eyelids and the room started to settle, Lilianna managed to open her eyes. It was to discover that the breakfast room ceiling was still there, much to her astonishment. There was also a man lying beside her—lying on the breakfast table beside her.

Oh goodness. That was… That was…

"I'll never be able to sit down at this breakfast table again," she said with a laugh, "without thinking of you."

There was a chuckle beside her. "I hope you're never able to sit down *anywhere* without thinking of me."

There was a throbbing need between her legs and Lilianna squirmed. She had given everything to him, and he had taken it— yet given back far more in return. He was hers.

"Perhaps," she said quietly. "But I think for that to be certain, you may have to impress me again."

Arthur snorted as he leaned on his side, peering at her with a sated smile. "Again?"

Lilianna nodded, rubbing her thighs together as the need he had awoken in her started to ache again. "Please, Arthur. I need you."

It was wanton, and it was wicked, and she did not care.

The desire in his eyes told her that Arthur had few complaints. "I don't suppose there's a chance in hell that you'll let me leave tonight?"

Lilianna grinned, reaching out for his hand and nestling it in her curls as she tried to say, "No."

Chapter Sixteen

April 15, 1840

I T WAS NOT difficult to carefully step through the back door of his Bath townhouse.

The place was awake. Arthur knew that his servants rose early, but he had not realized there would be quite so many in here.

Cook raised an eyebrow. "Interesting night, m'lord?"

Arthur grinned, his limbs weary. He was desperate to see Lilianna again as soon as he could. *"Very* interesting."

And it had been. Ravishing Lady Lilianna Chance had been unlike anything he could have imagined. The temptation to remain there all morning and show her another few routes to pleasure had been intense, indeed, but the impending arrival of another lady's maid had sadly made that impossible.

For now.

"But I have a feeling that our marriage is not exactly going to be like everyone else's."

Arthur gave a happy sigh as he stepped along the servants' corridor and emerged into the wide hallway.

Well, he was engaged, which was a bizarre thought. The Arthur of a year ago—hell, two months ago—would not have credited it. Yet here he was, promised to a woman who made him feel...

Feel as though he could conquer the world if asked. As

though nothing would be too difficult if it put a smile on her face. As though the rest of his life was going to be a great deal more interesting than he had expected.

So. That meant preparations needed to be made.

Though his bed cried out for him, tiredness tugging at the corners of his eyes, Arthur made instead for his study. There he could rattle off a few letters to the relevant people and start getting this wedding underway.

The sooner, the better.

The study was just as he'd left it. Strange. To think that when he had departed this house only yesterday, he had not known, could not have known, in what state he would return.

A state of bliss.

Arthur sat heavily on the chair behind his desk and leaned back, a grin on his face.

"I'll never be able to sit down at this breakfast table again without thinking of you."

He'd made love before. No, that wasn't quite right—he had *bedded* women before. The mechanics were not unknown to him, and he'd certainly found completion with other women. But he hadn't found what he'd discovered with Lilianna. That had been new.

A connection—a meeting of minds and bodies and souls. A surrender, a need to give her everything, to delay his own gratification totally if it meant she was given everything that she wanted.

"I don't suppose there's a chance in hell that you'll let me leave tonight?"

"No."

Arthur swallowed, trying to prevent himself going hard. That would hardly be useful.

Letters, that was what he was here for. Letters, then he could go upstairs and collapse into bed, drifting into dreams of his Lilianna…

He had almost completed the first letter, to his banker—

jewels, he needed jewels—when the door opened.

"My lord," said Haslehaw serenely. "You have returned."

Arthur grinned as he glanced up. "I have, indeed."

"And?" the servant asked delicately.

Well, he deserved to know that he would be welcoming a new mistress, didn't he? But that didn't mean that he couldn't have a bit of fun.

"I don't know what you mean, Haslehaw," Arthur said with wide, innocent eyes.

Perhaps not innocent enough. "Really? I was under the impression that you departed yesterday to offer your undying affection to Lady Lilianna Chance, with the hope she would reciprocate." His butler cleared his throat delicately. "I hope that you carried out your plan and did not lose your nerve, my lord."

Arthur was able to resist rising to his own defense, but only just. "In fact, Haslehaw, I did not. I did barely sleep last night, however. I was… otherwise occupied."

He grinned. *Well, what did he care if his servants knew?* Lilianna was going to be his wife, and they were going to engage in a great deal more amorous congress between now and then. After she was his countess, he would be able to sleep in the bed beside her, wake up every morning to find her there, the woman he loved…

Someone cleared their throat. Arthur jumped.

Haslehaw's eyebrow was raised. "A successful evening, then, my lord?"

"*Very* successful," Arthur replied, privately thinking it was a very good thing he had returned home this morning. There could be an element of openness in his own household, true, but perhaps he was being rash, considering it being broadcasted further. Ah, and now he came to think about it… "Have a hamper of Cook's finest treats sent over to the Aylesbury townhouse, will you?"

That surprised him, as the man blinked perceptibly. "I beg your pardon, my lord?"

"Cook's best pies, dishes, puddings, that sort of thing." Arthur waved a hand in the air by way of explanation. "You know. The very best."

"I rather thought you would wish to have Cook focus on tonight's dinner."

"No, make the treats and send them to Lilianna—to Lady Lilianna Chance as soon as possible," he said firmly. "Each and every day for the next, oh, say week?"

How long was it that people have scarlet fever for, anyway?

"And I believe we will need to sit down and plan a wedding," Arthur said with relish.

At last his butler looked pleased. "Ah, you have gained the approbation of her father then, my lord."

Damnation, he had completely forgotten about that. "All in good time," Arthur said aloud, making a mental note to write to the marquess post-haste. "I will need your assistance in ensuring the plans are enacted promptly."

"You wish to marry before the autumn, my lord?"

Arthur snorted. "Before the month is out, man!"

Haslehaw's second eyebrow now rose to join its pair. "I do not believe you will have sufficient time to plan such an affair."

"Well, as soon as possible," Arthur said, waving away his servant's probably very reasonable objections. "I want Lilianna in this house, established as its mistress, as quick as we can."

"And breeding."

Arthur blinked. Surely, he had misheard that. His butler could not have said…

"That is, after all, the reason why you are marrying in the first place, is it not, my lord?" Haslehaw said delicately. "To breed? To have heirs, for your title?"

Arthur's lips parted in astonishment.

Because the man was right. At least, he *had* been right. That was where this had all begun, had it not? Him needing an heir, not minding too much who was willing to give him one.

And now here he was, absolutely besotted with one woman. Hell, if they never had children, what would it matter? He had her.

"Preparations for a wedding, Haslehaw," Arthur said firmly. "Go on. Be off with you. And mind your tongue around your future mistress, yes?"

Haslehaw's jaw tightened, but he nodded. The door closed behind the servant, leaving his master to sit in silence and think. Think of the delight he felt whenever he was with her. Think of her beauty, her kindness, the way she snorted when she believed he was being ridiculous.

A foolish grin creased his lips. Oh, to be her husband—it was more than he could have dreamed. Part of him wished he had remained with her. Part of him wished she had come here, unable to stay away.

She could slip in through a side door, Arthur thought dreamily. *Wander along a corridor, hoping no footman saw her, then arrive at my study with that knowing smile—*

The door was thrown open—but it was not the woman he wanted to see who walked through it.

Instead, it was a beauty with sharp edges to her face, red ringlets falling out of place from the messy pile of hair atop her head, her scarlet dress somehow both ostentatious and a little worn-down—and a little too big.

Arthur groaned. "Look, Celeste, you can't just come in here."

"I have never been forbidden entrance to your study before," said Celeste with a slow grin, stepping seductively into the room and closing the door. "As I recall, you and I have shared many a moment in this room. On that chaise. On that desk. Your brother never suspected."

He couldn't deny it. *I'll have to get rid of most of this furniture,* Arthur thought ruefully, *before Lilianna becomes my wife.* He could hardly take her on the same desk that he had taken his mistress, after all.

Even if it was an antique desk with brass fittings.

"What are you doing here?" Arthur sighed, leaning back in his chair.

It was going to be an awkward conversation, and there was no point in avoiding it any longer. Plainly, the letter he had sent to her had been misplaced. Or misunderstood. Or misconstrued.

Celeste smiled and Arthur felt... nothing.

Nothing at all. It was a bit of a relief, Arthur's shoulders sagging as the tension sparked yet could not find a hold.

He was free of her, free of all the other women he had bedded and moved on from. It was Lilianna he wanted, and the affection he felt for her was far greater than anything he had ever felt for—

"You are not listening, Taernsby."

Arthur blinked. *Was she talking?* "Look, what we had—it's over."

She meandered over to his desk now, her fingers placed on its edge as she beheld him. "I don't understand."

Her willful misunderstanding aside, Arthur thought he had been very clear—and very patient. "You do, Celeste, you just don't *want* to."

"We were so good together, Taernsby," she purred, leaning forward and giving him an eyeful of her—

Arthur looked away hurriedly, though he was reassured by the complete lack of stirring in his loins. Damn, Lilianna really was the only woman for him now. It was astonishing, really, that he was so untouched by Celeste's charms.

A year ago, even three months ago, he would have already stripped off his shirt and would have her bent over the desk.

And now... now all he wanted to do was get back to his letter. To keep making plans for his marriage to Lady Lilianna Chance.

And ask Haslehaw to order him a new desk.

"Look, Celeste—"

"I love it when you say my name like that," she murmured, her gaze flickering over his form.

His body stiffened. "Like what? All I said was your name." He shook his head, his eyes closing. "Look, you have to understand that this is over. Has been for months. When I told you last October that we would not see each other again—"

"You miss me, though, don't you?"

Arthur hesitated, but only to search within himself, and he found… nothing. No desire for her, no interest, not even a passing fancy that he could take this opportunity, private as they were here in his study, to take a final taste of a woman he had bedded a not inconsiderable number of times.

No, everything within him cried out for one woman, and she was not here.

"I am in love with another," Arthur said simply, his eyes locking on to hers.

Her nostrils flared. "You can't be! You're a Nelson. You don't fall in love!"

"And yet I have, and quite without the expectation of doing so," he said, smiling at the memory of that incorrigible woman. *"You're Lilianna Chance. And you're mine."*

"I don't believe it. I *won't* believe it," Celeste said softly. "I know you, Taernsby, and you aren't the sort to fall in love."

She was leaning even closer now in a most possessive way, and Arthur was certain that sort of thing would encourage many a man to lean forward in turn and taste those lips. But not him. Not anymore.

"I love another," he repeated softly.

There was a glitter of malevolence in Celeste' eyes. "We'll see how long that lasts."

And suddenly, she had lunged forward, closing the gap between them and her lips were on his and Arthur recoiled, but she followed him, climbing onto the desk and it was wrong, it wasn't Lilianna and he tried to wrench his head away—

As the study door opened.

"Arthur, my new maid won't be coming until tomorrow and I—" Lilianna stood, hand on the doorframe, eyes wide, pain visible in her expression.

Arthur was not breathing. He *could* not breathe.

Celeste giggled, propping herself up on the desk and wiggling her hips. "I didn't know you wanted someone to join us, Taernsby."

"It's not—I wasn't—" *Speak, man, speak!*

But the damage had already been done.

"I can't… I can't believe you would—"

"Lilianna, it's not—"

"I trusted you!"

The pain in her voice was visceral, scraping over Arthur's skin like a blade. It cut, sharp and true, and he could almost feel the agony in his own body.

"Who's this, Taernsby?" Celeste grinned. "This is the next one, is it?"

For a brief moment, a mere heartbeat, Arthur closed his eyes in horror. This was going from bad to worse and worst of all, there did not appear to be anything he could do to stop it. To stop her.

"Get out, woman."

Celeste arched an eyebrow. "I only said—"

"And I said, *get out!*" Arthur barked, rage subsiding in his lungs as his hoarse words flew about the study.

Lilianna was still there, thank God, looking at him through crestfallen eyes. He could explain, couldn't he? It would be easy enough to get Lilianna to understand, once he had explained—once he had promised her that nothing, save a kiss he had not wanted, had occurred.

"It sounds to me like you two have a great deal to discuss," said Celeste delicately with a grin Arthur hated. "Why don't I give you two a little time alone to talk this through?"

Her smug attitude was displayed in her walk. Arthur had never seen a woman walk like that, as though she'd achieved something truly great. As though no one had ever done something so clever, so impressive.

As Celeste approached the doorway, Lilianna stood her ground, forcing the other woman to step clumsily around her. It gave Arthur hope, hope he dared not even consider in case it fled, that this was all going to be resolved.

Celeste disappeared from sight. Lilianna stepped forward into the study. She closed the door behind her.

Arthur finally coerced his lungs to work. "Dear God, Lilianna, I thought there for a minute—"

"I should have known."

He blinked. "'Known'?"

Lilianna was leaning against the door as though she could not get far enough from him and remain in the same room. "Yes, known. I should have known all of this, this joy, this—this happiness I felt…"

Felt. Past tense.

Arthur's stomach lurched. "She means nothing to me. You must believe me!"

"Will you speak that way of me?" Lilianna whispered.

He didn't understand. She wasn't making any sense.

"When you grow tired of me, and you can happily throw me out of your study, will you speak of me that way?" she said quietly. "Like I was nothing. Like what we shared, what we had was nothing."

"It isn't like that. Lilianna, she's just—"

"Just a woman you bedded, and now can't seem to give up," she finished for him.

Incorrectly, thought Arthur through a haze of panic and anger. What, she would just assume the very worst of him the moment that she saw him? Did she not wish to hear his side, to know what the truth of the matter was?

"Celeste is—*was* my mistress, yes, but that has been over for months now," Arthur said, trying to bring some rationality back to the conversation.

Lilianna flinched. "'Celeste'?"

Why did that matter? Arthur nodded, hoping to move on. "You have to believe me. She—"

"She was the one who wrote to you."

Arthur stared, uncomprehending, trying to understand her words. Wrote to him? Plenty of people wrote to him. How was he supposed to remember—

And then the memory returned. A letter stuffed in his pocket. A moment to read it before Lilianna—but she had arrived early, hadn't she? Grabbed the letter from his hand. Seen some of its words.

Evidently, she had seen the signature at the end of the letter.

He rose hurriedly, chair pushed out behind him, as though that would give greater credence to his words. "Lilianna, *she* wrote *me* a letter. I cannot stop—"

"Kissing her, it seems," said Lilianna in a brittle voice he had never heard from her lips before. "Oh, Arthur, what were you thinking? When you and I had an appointment to meet here?"

"It wasn't like that. I wasn't hiding—"

It was the wrong thing to say. As panicked words attempted to rise up inside him and better explain, Lilianna just shook her head with a dull look in her eyes.

"You weren't hiding it, I see. It was just myself who did not know. Your whole household knows."

"Lil!"

"Do not call me that," she said sharply. "I am Lil to those I trust."

This could not have been happening—it was a nightmare, a bad dream. Perhaps he had fallen asleep at his desk, the evening's activities—for want of a better word—entirely exhausting him. Because he could not be standing here by his desk seeing Lilianna examine him like... like she did not know him. Like she had never known him. Like it would take a miracle for her to trust him again.

Arthur took a deep breath. *There had to be a way out of this. There always was.* "Celeste wanted to resume our old—our old connection, and I said *no*."

"By kissing her," Lilianna said coldly.

"Damnit, *she* kissed *me*!"

"And you let her, Arthur. You let her! I walked in here and saw the two of you together!"

"What you saw wasn't—"

"I swear to God, Arthur, if you try to tell me that I did not see what I saw, then I am going to get very angry indeed."

And she sounded it. She also sounded like the cold, icy, distant Lilianna he had first met. Before his eyes, Arthur watched the wholehearted woman he had grown to know disappear, frozen in the sight of him kissing another woman.

It was all going horribly wrong and yet he did not know what to do.

"How can I prove it to you?" Arthur said desperately, stepping around the desk and advancing toward her.

And halting. There was something so intensely unwelcoming in her expression that no man could have progressed farther.

"You can't," she said simply.

His breath stuttered. "But I must be able to…"

"No," Lilianna said sharply, red now tinging her cheeks. "No, you can't just have it all your own way, Arthur! You can't just shout down or out-argue me merely because you wish it!"

Arthur hadn't realized just how desperately he was panting, but he did now. His hands were heaving, a tingling sensation aching in his fingertips, and it was all going wrong. It was falling apart before his eyes: his perfect life, his future with Lilianna.

And there was nothing he could do to stop it.

She was speaking in a low, quiet voice, as though almost to herself. "I should have known I could not trust you, you were and are a rake."

"People change," Arthur said, taking a step forward.

The look she gave him would have quelled an army. "Not you," Lilianna said quietly. "There was not chance in hell you could truly change."

"But I love you!" he said desperately.

It was not enough. He could see it in her eyes, the way she held herself, the scrabble of her fingers on the door handle.

"Really?" Lilianna said softly. "I would hate to see how you treat those you say you despise, my lord."

"Lilianna!"

And she was gone. The door had opened and she had slipped through it before Arthur could reach her. Wrenching it open, he caught just the merest glimpse of her before she turned the corner of the corridor. She must have been running to reach it so quickly.

Running away from him.

Arthur slumped against the doorframe, his mind whirling. He needed to go after her, but what was there to say that he had not already said? He had told her Celeste had kissed him, that he'd wanted nothing to do with her, that he loved *her*, Lilianna… and still, she did not trust him. Still she would rather walk away, run away, than listen.

A giggle reached his ears and his pulse leapt, just for a moment, before he saw…

"I suppose it's just you and me, then," Celeste said archly, stepping out from behind a curtain in the hallway. "Poor Taernsby, you look sad. Perhaps I can help cheer you up?"

"Haslehaw!" Arthur roared.

With the unerring skill of a servant who had butlered for a good many years, the butler appeared immediately. "You yelled, my lord?"

"Take this woman and throw her out onto the street," Arthur said bitterly. "And make it clear to her, and all the footmen, that she is never to be permitted entrance again."

Celeste's eyes widened. "But—"

"Did you think this was a jest, Celeste?" Arthur hissed, pouring all his frustration out onto the woman before him. "Get out of my sight."

She disappeared from his house with a great deal of shouting and complaining, but Arthur heeded her not. He was too busy stepping into his study, closing the door, and slumping onto the chaise.

"I would hate to see how you treat those you say you despise, my lord."

Arthur dropped his head into his hands. Now what was he supposed to do?

Chapter Seventeen

April 17, 1840

“ **A**ND THAT WAS when I realized, it was the blue that wasn’t working. Time and time again, I had mixed it, and it was only when I looked at the…”

More words were said. Lilianna was almost sure they were. They washed over her like a slow tide over pebbles, hardly disturbing her thoughts.

Not that she knew what her own thoughts were.

Her Aunt Dodo had apparently decided that, after news that the maid her parents had hoped to send had also been feeling unwell, if her niece did not wish to move in with the third branch of the Chance family, then Lilianna could not be left alone for yet another whole day. Clarke had returned, though, feeling much better and never having succumbed to the fever, so Lilianna wasn’t actually alone anymore. But that hadn’t deterred her aunt. She had sent Cousin Evelyn, who was nattering on as Lilianna held a cooling cup of tea without moving.

Just thinking. Thinking and trying not to think, trying to block out the pain that had been her entire existence since—

“People change.”

“Not you. There was not a chance in hell you could truly change.”

Lilianna’s jaw tightened and she tried to heed the words pouring from her cousin’s lips.

“The trouble is that finding good models, or *any* models for that matter, is becoming almost impossible. One would almost think that being an artist was something to be ashamed of! I never had this much difficulty in London, but I heard from a friend that even she is finding it a challenge to find someone to sit for her."

Lilianna nodded automatically as Evelyn paused to draw breath. This was apparently the right thing to do, for her cousin immediately continued.

"I have even considered advertising, though of course my mother would be horrified and I almost think my father would consider taking my easel away. As though I could function without it!"

"Indeed," Lilianna said quietly. It had been almost ten minutes since she had last said something and it felt appropriate to comment.

Evelyn sighed, cheeks flushing somewhat as she said, "Advertising… It would be a most radical thing to do, and as a lady… Well, I do not believe many ladies have considered such a thing. And yet the men, they can advertise any way they please!"

Yes, men have a far greater freedom, Lilianna wanted to say. *Freedom to kiss anyone they like without any repercussions. Freedom to lie, and to steal one's heart away, then stomp on it so hard—*

"Don't you think?"

"What?" Lilianna said, blinking.

Evelyn was seated on the opposite sofa and stared at her cousin's rudeness. "I said, don't you think?"

Precisely what she was supposed to be agreeing with, Lilianna was not sure—but as Evelyn did not appear willing to explain for a second or arguably a third time, she merely nodded her head.

Evelyn sighed. "If I could leave behind my art, then I would, you know. It has brought me naught but trouble, and heartache, and frustration. Yet without it, I don't know who I am."

Lilianna's stomach lurched.

You are not supposed to be thinking about him, she told herself firmly. Thinking of him only brought pain, and she had hoped that taking afternoon tea with her cousin and hearing about her art and the like would distract her entirely from the man she was most definitely not thinking about.

Not at all. Not even a little.

"It has brought me naught but trouble, and heartache, and frustration. Yet without it, I don't know who I am."

Unbeknownst to her cousin, she could not have said anything more likely to make Lilianna think of Arthur Nelson, Earl of Taernsby.

But she could give him up. She was determined to. Lilianna was not about to betray herself and everything she stood for and accept back into her life and arms a man who could—

Nausea rose as the image of Arthur, seated at his desk, kissing that woman rose in Lilianna's mind.

Her grip tightened on her teacup, which shook in its saucer.

She was not going to think about it.

"Last time I had a really good model, his wife got all upset about it, as though I would ever—as though I could…"

Lilianna blinked. Whatever her cousin was talking about now, it was something most peculiar. She had never seen Evelyn's cheeks that shade before.

Her guest cleared her throat. "I mean… as if I would!"

"As if," Lilianna said, agreeing to whatever it was her cousin was talking about.

Evelyn appeared to take encouragement from Lilianna's words. "That is what I said! But she did not listen, and so I am once again on the hunt for a model. I return to London next week and hope to goodness, I will be able to find someone."

Nodding occasionally, humming agreement and gasping at all the right places, Lilianna found it was relatively easy to navigate a conversation with Evelyn about her love of art without having to give anything she said much thought. It was rude, yes, but it was also manageable.

It also unfortunately left Lilianna's mind perfectly able to go about thinking of Arthur.

It was almost impossible to believe. If she had not seen it, seen him, seen them with her own eyes, she would not have credited a rumor.

But there he had been—mere hours after she had given herself to him, gifting him her innocence without a hesitation, Arthur had been locking lips with another woman.

"There was not a chance in hell you could truly change."

"But I love you!"

"Really? I would hate to see how you treat those you say you despise, my lord."

The words rolled in her mind, unceasing, no matter what Lilianna attempted.

After all her decisiveness not to credit him with any decency, after resisting him for so long, after ignoring those foolish proposals of marriage like a sensible woman... she had fallen for it.

Oh, how could I have been so foolish?

"The curvature of the cheek, you see, is so different to what I had anticipated. I am finding the piece very difficult, but I am sure with the right red—you cannot get good paint here, for love nor money! When I return to London, then I shall perfect..."

Lilianna swallowed a sob as she took a sip of her tepid tea.

She was ruined. Ruined, forever. Not only had she given Arthur her innocence, something she could never take back, but she had risked—after all, they had not prevented... Thanks to her brothers, she knew how children came to be. Right now, this moment, she could be...

A twist in her stomach made her place the teacup and saucer onto a small table beside her. There was no need to panic, not yet. Her monthly flux was not due for another week. Only then would she know—

"You are being very rude, you know."

Lilianna blinked.

Evelyn was staring with a curious expression, half-censure, half-appraisal. Lilianna felt somewhat like one of her cousin's models must have felt: closely examined with the expectation that the artist in the family was about to portray her angles and expression onto canvas.

Rude? Rude, me? The outrage!

"I think you'll find," Lilianna said in her most icy tone, "that it is *you* who—"

—is boring me to tears. Won't stop going on about this art project of yours. Can't appear to cease complaining about Bath and how difficult it is to find paint, and models, as though those things matter!

Lilianna bit down the words.

Perhaps, months ago, she would have said them. There would have been no need to censure, no interest in keeping someone else happy.

All that had changed. Damn him, he'd changed her. Made her weak.

Swallowing hard, she said softly, "I apologize for my tone."

Lilianna was not totally sure what she had expected from her short and admittedly curt apology. In a certain light, it was impressive: both that she had apologized, and that she had managed not to say the words that would have so offended.

It was therefore greatly surprising that instead of graciously accepting the apology, perhaps delicately murmuring that it was she, Evelyn, who should apologize, her cousin's jaw dropped.

"Goodness," she said, in a most unflattering manner. "I do not think I have ever heard you apologize."

Lilianna frowned. "'Ever' is a bit of an exaggeration, don't you think?"

"No, I don't think that it is," said Evelyn slowly, clearly giving the matter some thought. "I cannot recall the last time you apologized, to me or anyone else. What has got into you, Lil?"

It was a very good question, and it had a myriad of possible answers—none of which Lilianna particularly wanted to share.

Her shoulders slumped. "Was I really so rude that receiving an apology from me is a surprise?"

It was the perfect opening for Evelyn to immediately reassure her that no, Lilianna had never been that bad, and in fact it was an overreaction on her part.

Evelyn grinned. "Yes."

Lilianna groaned as her cousin laughed. "That isn't particularly helpful, Evelyn!"

"Well, I was sent here to be helpful by my mother, and so I suppose I should make a greater effort," her cousin said breezily, setting aside her own cup of tea. "Besides, I wanted to come and see you. There has been a great deal of chatter in the family about you recently."

She should have known. If there was one thing the Chance family liked, it was gossip. Well meaning, and often wildly inaccurate, and usually limited to what was happening in the family itself—but still. Gossip.

"What's the worst of it?" Lilianna said with a sigh.

At least she did not have to worry about a sudden interruption from her mother. Both her parents and Frank were still at Stanphrey Lacey, and her brothers… Well, Lilianna was not sure when they would be returning. "Soon" was the latest from Samuel. Benjamin had not bothered to reply to her letter.

"Mostly, that you have been scorning a very respectable earl and he keeps proposing to you regardless."

Lilianna started. "That—That is what the family is saying?"

"But I think there's more to the story," Evelyn said, her voice softening as her eyes raked over her cousin. "Come on, Lil. We've known each other forever. What's truly going on with this earl of yours?"

Her voice was hoarse. "He is no earl of mine."

"It certainly sounds like he was, for a time. And you've changed, Lil. Not for the worse, necessarily, or the better, just… changed." Evelyn sighed. "Do you want to tell me what happened?"

Not particularly. It was still raw, still painful. Lilianna still saw them, the two of them together, every time she closed her eyes. Arthur, pressed up against that chair, his fingers clutching the desk. That woman, leaning over it, claiming him as she had thought she herself had claimed him.

Lilianna's mouth was dry as she swallowed, but it gave her throat no release.

What happened?

Everything. Nothing. Her heart growing with joy then broken, its shards so delicate, it could never be mended.

"Lil."

Lilianna blinked through tears she would not shed, and her cousin reached out. Her hand grasped her own, just for a moment.

"You can tell me," Evelyn said gently. "You… You fell in love with him, didn't you?"

Grasping the soft cotton of her gown as though that would ground her, Lilianna nodded. "I… It all happened… I don't really know how it started."

"I suppose we will just have to get married, then."

A grin graced her cheeks, despite herself. "I fell into his arms."

Evelyn's eyes widened. "I thought Cousin Benjamin was jesting!"

"I mean, it sounds far more dramatic than it actually was," Lilianna said hastily. "It was a mistake, just an accident—"

"He is devastatingly handsome, though," mused her cousin. "There was the night he rescued us, but I saw him at one of the Duchess of Axwick's picnics, last year, in better light. Before he inherited the earldom. Tall and far too good-looking for his own good."

That about summed him up, yes. "The Earl of Taernsby and I, we… He… He kept proposing to me and for a long time, I believed he was jesting, and—then it felt real. I truly thought he— but then I discovered…"

Lilianna's voice gave out and she reached out for the now cold cup of tea. Anything, any liquid that could help her speak.

What precisely she would say, she did not know.

Evelyn waited for a moment, then said delicately, "So… So

you are not engaged to be married."

"Not anymore," Lilianna said, forcing her voice to be harsh.

Because she couldn't allow herself to feel anything. It would be ridiculous, mourning a relationship that had brought her nothing but pain at its conclusion.

"The Earl of Taernsby," mused Evelyn. "A great womanizer, I heard."

Lilianna's stomach jolted. "I… Well, I suppose so, but he appeared to… I thought he had left that way of life behind him."

She had believed him when he'd said he wanted a wife, had wanted her. Believed him when he'd told her she was beautiful.

Her fingers twisted together in her lap.

Evelyn was nodding. "A terrible man, from what I've heard— and only a Nelson, not from a great family at all."

"He is an earl," Lilianna pointed out, almost despite herself. "A Nelson, true, not in the league of the Lindows—"

"Or the Chances," her cousin said quietly.

"It's not that—I do not believe that he is particularly below me, or anything like that. I mean, perhaps I did at first, but the more I got to know him…" Lilianna said in a rush. "He was… He is…"

Precisely how to describe the man who infuriated her and dazzled her in equal measure was difficult. Lilianna's attention meandered around the room, as though searching for insight, yet she could find nothing but warm memories.

Warm memories seared with pain because they were over. She would never experience anything like them again.

"I hear he has a different mistress every day of the week."

Heat flared throughout her body. "And where did you hear such an egregious rumor?" Lilianna snapped.

Evelyn's expression remained calm and placid, as though she faced a furious cousin often. "It isn't a rumor, though, is it? If it's true."

"That was Arthur's—I mean, the Earl of Taernsby was like that, I think, before he and I… He wasn't like that when…"

Lilianna swallowed. "You're laughing."

"I'm grinning," corrected her cousin.

And she was. The smile was almost a smirk, a knowing look that made Lilianna feel silly and uncomfortable all at once.

The grin did not disappear, and Lilianna frowned. "But why are you grinning?"

"Oh, Lil, don't be so dense!" Her cousin's cheeks colored, the directness unusual. "You still like him!"

Lilianna almost recoiled from the sentiment. "I don't."

"Here I am, giving you half a dozen reasons why the man is someone you should not even pass the time of day with," Evelyn said quietly. "And everything I say, you defend him."

Heat was suffusing up her. "I'm not… I haven't…"

"You like him," said Evelyn, her voice hardening. "And don't try to tell me that I'm wrong, because I'm not."

It was on the tip of Lilianna's tongue to say just that, but she swallowed, the words bitter in her throat.

Because she did not like him. She did not! There was nothing about him that she liked, and any connection they'd shared… Well, it had just been hopes and dreams, hadn't it? She'd hoped, and she'd dreamt, and he'd still… he'd kissed…

Lilianna closed her eyes for a moment and the image of Arthur and that woman appeared again.

Her eyes snapped open. "I don't like him."

Evelyn frowned. "I think you—"

"I love him," Lilianna whispered helplessly.

Perhaps in a different situation, the words would have felt triumphant. She would have been celebrating something beautiful, sharing with one of her favorite cousins the beginning of the rest of a happy life.

The words sounded hollow now. Cheap. They could do nothing, mean nothing.

"Who falls in love with a man who would do that to you?" Lilianna murmured, half to herself.

Evelyn's frown only deepened. "Do what to you?"

There was no possibility of revealing the depths of the betrayal to her cousin. Speaking aloud the words would make it real in a way she could not yet fathom. Accepting it had happened at all had been difficult enough. Lilianna had hastened from that house without any desire to ever return—but telling someone else…

Not for the first time, she wished her sister had not been whisked away to avoid sickness.

"He kissed another woman," Lilianna said in a rush.

"No!"

"I don't want to talk about it," she added, bile rising in her throat. "I don't… He…"

And the pain from that moment reared its head as though she had just caught sight of him mere moments ago. Despite the days between then and now, the pain had not dimmed or darkened. If anything, it had grown, the sense of betrayal fermenting, curdling in her stomach.

"Fine. You don't want to talk about it. What are you going to do, practice the pianoforte and conversation and attract a new earl?"

Lilianna scowled. "I hate the pianoforte."

"I know," said Evelyn with a sigh. "Come on. Tell me about it."

Lilianna shook her head, no words needed as tears scratched at the corners of her eyes.

"Paint me a picture," Evelyn urged. "I want to understand. I want to help."

"Nothing can help," Lilianna said quietly.

The worst of it all, as though it could *get* any worse, was that Arthur had done nothing. He had not run after her, or sent messages to her home. He had not arrived on her doorstep, pulling on the bell and banging on the door, demanding to be given entrance so he could explain.

Because there is nothing to explain, Lilianna told herself fiercely. *And the sooner I accept that…*

"Go on, Lil, paint me a picture," her cousin said. "I want to understand."

Lilianna snorted, pain and disdain mingling in the reflex. "'Understand'?! I do not think it is possible to understand how a man can sit at his desk while a woman, his mistress, leans over it and kisses him!"

Just saying the words was like suffering through it all over again. Lilianna dashed away the unshed tears fiercely, loathing her own weakness. She would not, could not cry about this.

She would not cry over a man who could so easily betray her.

Looking up, she expected to see a look of outrage on her cousin's face. She expected Evelyn to be mortified on her behalf and start talking about duels and forcing Arthur to marry her...

She would not force a man to marry her, just for the sake of her reputation. How could she look him in the face if she tied him to her?

"It... Well, it sounds to me... Well. Like this mistress, whoever she was, was the one kissing the earl."

She scoffed. "Yes, he insisted as much. He's not a gentleman who spurns kisses, I must say."

Evelyn cocked her head at that, as if about to ask more—like how Lilianna might know that fact about the earl's kissing habits. But instead, she said, "You misunderstand."

Lilianna frowned. "What do you mean?"

"Well, by the way you describe it," Evelyn said slowly, "and I am not an expert in these matters, you understand... but it sounds to me like the mistress was kissing him, rather than him kissing the mistress."

"And what difference does that make?" Lilianna said sharply. "They were still kissing! If he did not wish to kiss her, all he would have to do was... was..."

She stopped. She wasn't sure what she had expected him to do. Shove the woman to the ground? He wasn't a beast.

"But you don't know what came before it, do you? I mean, what precipitated the kiss," her cousin said quietly. "For all you know, he was telling her that there was no possibility they could be together again."

"Then why would she kiss him after hearing that?"

"I don't know," Evelyn said with a sad shrug. "I just… Well, it does not sound like you have the full story. It sounds like the sort of thing you would want to talk to your earl—"

"He is not *my* earl!"

"—about before you rushed to any particular conclusions."

Lilianna sighed and twisted her fingers in her lap. She had hardly rushed to a conclusion, had she? She'd seen the two of them kissing, with her own eyes.

It was tempting to hope there was something more to the story. Tempting to think if she'd permitted him to speak, a different story could have been told. Tempting to hope their story could end differently.

"And you love him."

Swallowing, Lilianna looked up. Across her cousin's face was an expression of pity, the woman's small mouth puckered in an elegant frown.

"You love him," she repeated, "and you are not going to be able to stop loving him, are you?"

"No," Lilianna said, her voice breaking. "But—oh, Evelyn. How can I ever entrust my heart to someone that I can't trust at all?"

Chapter Eighteen

THERE WAS A very slight damp spot just in the top left corner of the ceiling. Strange. Arthur had never noticed it before.

But then, he had never spent two hours slumped in an armchair in the library staring up at the ceiling before.

The shadows moved slowly. He had half-expected them to disappear, for clouds to come and cover the sun and make it impossible to see. Why should the sun shine when he felt like the world was ending?

Slowly, the shadows crept over the ceiling, moving from east to west. Eventually, the light faded, a footman stepping quietly into the room to light the lamps. He stepped right past Arthur, who remained slumped there.

Arthur said nothing.

The footman completed his duties and left, shutting the door behind him. Arthur remained looking up at the ceiling, his fingers cold from the lack of movement.

"There was not a chance in hell you could truly change."

"But I love you!"

"Really? I would hate to see how you treat those you say you despise, my lord."

He closed his eyes, squeezing them tightly. Perhaps if he just fell asleep here, he would wake up and that dreadful conversation would never have happened. Perhaps he could will it away, hope he could have another attempt at explaining.

"Celeste wanted to resume our old—our old connection, and I said

no."

He relaxed his eyes though kept them shut. He did not want to move. What was the point in moving? Where would he go? What would he do?

There was a possibility that Lilianna would speak to him. He could go to her home, bang on the door and demand entrance, and all she would have to do is stay on the other side, not letting him in.

Her lady's maid would be there by now. For all he knew, a footman or three had arrived. It would not be difficult for them to remove him, and then what would he do?

Bring disrepute and shame onto Lilianna.

Arthur gave a heavy sigh. Oh, it was such a mess—and it was all of his making, though of course not directly.

He'd been slapdash when he'd written back to Celeste.

He'd never properly explained that he was seeking a wife, not a lover.

Christ, there was so many opportunities now he looked back that he could have altered this outcome. He hadn't known at the time, worse luck, but then no man ever did.

It was only after the wave had come crashing down on your head that you realized the tides had changed.

What a damn fool he was.

As he stretched out his toes, a crick from his back echoed around the room. He was going to sit here forever. What was the point in moving? Where would he go? What would he do?

A throat cleared itself. "And when, precisely, do you intend to join the land of the living?"

Arthur's eyes snapped open. There was a face above him. The face looked, as it often did, indignant. Its curls framed its face beautifully, yet the expression was like thunder.

"Oh, hello," he said weakly.

The face sniffed. "I don't suppose you want to explain why you've been sitting in this armchair for several hours, worrying your servants half to death?"

His cousin could be so comforting sometimes.

"I haven't been worrying my servants half to death," Arthur pointed out, from the admittedly weak position of both staring up at Olive and not knowing where his servants had been for the last few hours. Except the footman. Hadn't there been a footman?

She frowned. "And so I return to my original question. When will you be joining the land of the living?"

Something harsh caught in Arthur's throat. "I don't deserve to."

A dark eyebrow raised. "Ah. That bad, is it?"

Arthur closed his eyes, just for a moment, and tried not to think about the last conversation he had shared with Lilianna. It was cruel, for Celeste to come into his perfect life and ruin it just as he had found the woman he wanted to spend the rest of his life with—and, most importantly, after he had finally convinced her to do just that.

She'd never forgive him.

"You have no idea," Arthur croaked.

How long had it been since he'd had something to drink? Hours. But what did that matter? He had nothing important to say anymore. Anything meaningful had been stated to Lilianna and she had not listened.

She had walked away from him, and out of his life.

Dear God, when had he become so pathetic?

"I see," said Olive sardonically. "So you *have* fallen in love, then?"

Fallen in love. Why did anyone do it? Only pain and disappointment and heartache. It left you alone, and miserable, and sitting on your library floor for hours at a time.

Arthur groaned. "In love? Yes. For the first time, and it's the worst I have felt in my entire life."

His cousin's face disappeared, but she did not depart from the library. Instead, there was the sound of a chair scraping along a rug. The noise grew louder until it ceased, and instead, the rustle of fabrics shifting as a person sat echoed about the place.

"Your entire life has been excessively spoilt and gilded, if you ask me," said Olive calmly. "With that in mind, I am not astonished to hear that falling in love has been more adventurous."

"More adventurous"? Why, if she knew what I got up to with a marquess's daughter.

Arthur managed to swallow back the words before they escaped his tongue. No, that was probably not the best idea. Olive was a most understanding cousin and he was fortunate to have her… but even their relationship would be stretched if some of those revelations were to come to light.

"In love," mused Olive. "I never thought I'd see the day."

"Can we concentrate less on the 'in love' and more on the 'worst I have ever felt,' please?" Arthur knew he sounded petulant, his overall tone not helped by the fact that he was still slumped in the armchair.

The trouble was, he felt so lethargic, so utterly devoid of energy. What was the point of getting up, anyway? Where would he go? What would he do?

Nothing. He would always be wishing to be with Lilianna, and as she wouldn't see him…

"I do apologize, how remiss of me," came the cutting sarcasm of his only living relative. "The worst you have ever felt. Pray, tell me more."

Arthur decided to ignore the blatant rudeness and instead concentrate on the fact that someone was listening to him. "Well… I was so lonely after Archibald died. You can't imagine—"

"And I am going to stop you right there, you selfish, self-centered idiot," rang out his cousin's calm words. "Did it ever occur to you in that breath that I very well could imagine? That in fact I too lost a cousin, and worse, I then lost my remaining cousin to the earldom and you completely vanished overnight? I have been your only family this entire time, you fool. You could have come to me. You *should* have come to me."

Silence settled onto her words like softly falling snow.

Arthur sat up so hurriedly, stars popped into the corners of his eyes. He blinked them away. "I... I should have done. You're right."

His cousin was snorting and muttering something about how she was always right, but Arthur could not heed her words because so many thoughts were whirling about his mind.

Olive would have understood. She had lost Archibald, just as he had. He could have gone to her—more than for amusing interludes of hiding behind screens and in general making a complete ass out of himself.

Why on earth hadn't he done so?

Because, a nasty little voice at the back of his mind pointed out, *because you discounted women. You still do! You don't expect much and so you don't get much.*

"I... I have been a terrible cousin, haven't I?" Arthur said in a small voice.

He'd expected Olive to smile, preen for a moment, then console him.

He hadn't expected her to say, "Yes," in such a definite tone.

"*Olive!*"

"Well, you have," she said sternly. "Fairly awful, all told. You haven't asked me how I'm feeling for about six months, by the way, and if you had bothered to do so, you would have discovered something rather to your benefit."

Arthur blinked. "I would?"

He couldn't think what on earth Olive could say to make him feel better, but evidently that was the wrong answer, because his cousin sighed and leaned back against the chair.

"If your mother had lived longer, she would have had a great influence on you. As it was, Uncle and Grandfather took more of a hand in your education and... Well. It shows."

Heat scalded Arthur's cheeks. "You know, I am not *completely* useless."

"Really?" Olive was laughing now, and he couldn't for the life of him understand why. "Lord, you are dense sometimes. Ask me how I am, Arthur."

Arthur frowned. "How—How are you, Olive?"

"Very much with child, thank you for asking," his cousin said with glowing cheeks.

"'Very…'?" His eyes widened. "You're not."

"I am, in fact, extremely with child," Olive said with a laugh. "You really haven't noticed? It's been all over town the last week. I presumed the rumor had reached you by now and you had not sent your congratulations because you were all wrapped up with your lady love."

Olive… with child?

Well, it was a fairly common consequence of marriage, Arthur had to give her that, but—

"You're going to have a baby!" he said in a croaking voice.

Olive's eyes were full of pity. "That makes you an uncle, I hope you realize, for I find myself without siblings entirely and as Barlow has no siblings, that leaves you the only one. Potentially an heir to your sorry earldom, if he's a boy and I have other sons. I hope you are determined to make a good go of being an uncle, by the way, or I may have to skin you. Alive."

A baby—a new child, a new life, who to him would be a niece or a nephew.

Arthur could hardly take it in. A baby. Another part of the family, not a replacement of who came before, but an extension of who could be in his life today.

Though now he came to look at her, Olive was looking a tad rounded in the stomach area. Nothing to shout about, nothing that a casual observer—*damn, like himself*—would have noticed. She may as well have eaten too many cakes.

Olive was smiling. There was that glow, the glow he should have noticed if he hadn't been so self-centered for the past…

Arthur hesitated. *Month? Year?*

When was the last time he had worried, truly worried about his cousin?

"You are well, aren't you?" he said urgently, fear rushing

through his bones. "You and the baby, you're both in good health?"

"Dr. Walsingham seems to think so, and he's been in practice long enough to know what he's doing," said Olive airily. "Barlow has been a complete nuisance—"

"Yes, well," Arthur interrupted.

His cousin shot him a glare. "You should be nicer to him, you know."

"I suppose I should," said Arthur, another layer of guilt coming on thick and fast. Truth be told, he had never made much of an effort. Olive had married the man a week before Archibald had died, and the burden of the estate had rather distracted him. "But you're healthy? The baby, it'll come soon?"

"Oh, yes, soon."

"What, like now?" Arthur rose swiftly, as though a baby could shoot out of her at any moment.

Olive laughed. "Oh, Arthur, before you get married, I am going to have a little talk with you."

His stomach lurched. "Hell, I don't need the birds and the bees talk with *you*."

"You need a good talking to, that's all I'll say," she said darkly. "You've hardly noticed me these last few months, and I tell you now, Arthur, you have missed out. You'll never get that time back again and I want you to know that you've been quite irritating."

His reflexes told him to shout back, to deny it, to refute every word she said.

His instincts knew better.

"Oh damn," he said quietly. "I have been a terrible cousin."

His cousin's giggle was not exactly comforting, but it did suggest a more lighthearted approach to the whole disaster than he would have attempted.

"Come here, you clot," Olive said, patting the seat beside her.

It was a chaise and not a chair that she had dragged across the room. Now Arthur that knew of her condition, guilt resurfaced.

She shouldn't have been lugging furniture around—that was his job!

Well. Not necessarily his, exactly. One of his servants'.

"Look," said Olive firmly as Arthur dropped onto the seat beside her with a grump. "You weren't raised to have emotions. Neither you nor Archibald were. You were raised to be—"

"Idiots," Arthur said dully.

"Men," said his cousin sharply. "Though the way you're behaving, I can see why you were confused."

She didn't need to push the knife in any deeper, and the thought must have shown on his face because she sighed.

"You weren't brought up to have emotions, and most definitely not to express them," Olive said quietly. "It's not your fault. Not entirely."

Arthur snorted. "First time for everything."

"Are you just going to wallow, or are we going to have a proper conversation?"

There was the Olive he knew of old. Arthur grinned. "You're going to be a wonderful mother, you know that?"

"Of course I will," his cousin said primly. "So. You have managed to get yourself into a pickle."

Heat seared his cheeks. Lord, this was not the sort of conversation one wanted to have with one's cousin. Especially not when she was examining him with her head tilted, her mouth soft—a knowing, almost pitying expression.

"Whatever you have heard," Arthur began, not quite sure how to approach this conversation, "about a—a mistress, or—"

"It's probably true, I am sure," said Olive with a grin.

The heat in his cheeks was almost certainly visible, but there wasn't anything Arthur could do about it. He flopped back on the chaise and groaned instead. "How could this have happened?"

"I see," his cousin said quietly. "True enough for you to have given up on her, then."

Arthur cringed. "It's *she* who has given up on *me*."

"Oh, I see. You were tempting her back by… lounging

around your library and moping."

He shot her a look. "You know, you're not being very comforting here. I had expected sympathy."

"Well, this is what you're getting," Olive said sharply. "No one said anything about having to mother your cousin after he was of age, and to be quite frank, Arthur, I have bigger problems than you and Lady Lilianna Chance not being able to communicate for more than five minutes together."

His back stiffened. "Don't you speak about her like that! I won't have it, you hear? If Lilianna—if Lady Lilianna Chance is to be spoken of at all, it's to be done with respect."

Arthur did not recognize the expression in his cousin's eyes for a few seconds, and when he did, he groaned. Again.

"You look pleased."

"Well, it's pleasant to see you defending her. You've never spoken about any woman like that," Olive pointed out calmly. "You truly care about her, you dolt, which begs the question: what are you doing here, and not going after this woman you claim to love?"

Arthur swallowed.

How could he make her understand? There were such complexities, such layers to his interactions with Lilianna. It had all started out as something completely different to what it had become, and he had hoped, longed for it to become even more.

But he wouldn't force her. He was not the sort of man to batter down doors and put a woman in an awkward position.

Lilianna would not thank him for that.

"She…" Arthur hesitated, but barreled forward. "She deserves better than me."

"Probably," came his cousin's unsympathetic reply.

He couldn't help but laugh, even if it was a laugh of impatience. "You are most unhelpful, you know!"

"I don't see anyone else lining up to help you," came the cool response.

Arthur's swift reply caught in his throat and died away.

There was no bitterness in her eyes, no cruelty, yet the words cut deep. Mostly because they were true.

He had never been one for friends. Friends were just people who would want something from you, and besides, he had Archibald. Why have friends when you could have a brother?

When he had died…

At first, he hadn't noticed. Why would Arthur notice when he had being an earl and sorting out land estates and title deeds and trying to memorize all the servants' names to keep himself busy?

Only now, with Olive beside him and no one else bothering to check on him, did Arthur realize just how alone he had become.

That will change, Arthur vowed to himself. It would have to, now he had lost Lilianna.

"You say that you don't deserve her," came his cousin's quiet voice. "And perhaps you don't. But you want her, and more importantly, you want to deserve her. Sometimes that can be enough."

Arthur laughed bitterly as he recalled the look on Lilianna's face—the last look of hers he would ever see. "There is not a chance in hell that she would ever accept me."

"Arthur—"

"I don't think she would even consider speaking to me," he added, pain radiating through him at the thought. "She's… She's gone, Olive. And I didn't explain, not fully—not properly. It all happened so fast."

They fell into silence as Arthur's mind whirled. There was more he could have said, *should* have said—but the shock of Celeste, then Lilianna, it had been too much for his brain to contend with.

"I suppose you know that she would not accept you," Olive said delicately. "Having gone over to the Aylesbury townhouse, and apologized, and explained, and apologized again, and then received the 'no' you're so sure about."

She met his eye with a quizzical expression.

How did they do it? Was this something all women were taught upon reaching the age of majority? The way she could look at him, stern and yet polite, all sweetness and light and rock-solid steel underneath?

Arthur bit his lip and shifted his hands awkwardly in his lap. "Well... Well, no. Not exactl—ouch!"

A heavy cushion with a velvet covering smashed into his face.

When it departed and he had blinked sufficiently for his sight to return, it was to see an irate Olive, her lips trembling and a vein surfacing at her temple. "You complete dolt!"

"Olive—ouch!"

The second whack with the cushion should have hurt less, not more, Arthur thought, his head spinning.

"What do you mean, you haven't gone over there?"

"Well, I—*really!*"

The third whack with the cushion came so fast that although Arthur intended to catch hold and prevent his very—no, *extremely* with child cousin from whacking him again—it slipped through his fingers.

Olive was panting heavily and glaring. "I can't believe you. I thought this, all this moping, was because you had gone after her and failed! You mean to tell me that you haven't even tried?"

"She doesn't want to hear my excuses—I mean, my very valid explanation," Arthur added hastily, his head slightly spinning from the repeated whacks.

"Oh, well, if you want to walk away from happiness, be my guest," said Olive with a sigh as she placed the cushion down— out of Arthur's reach, worse luck. "I suppose you know best."

Arthur's jaw tightened.

He had thought he had. He had been so sure Lilianna would never open the door for him, never wish to hear his explanation—and his appearance would surely cause comment, cause a storm of scandal to descend upon her.

He wouldn't wish that on any young lady of the *ton.*

No one knew the beautiful Lilianna had given him her virtue—there hadn't even been a servant there to wonder. And his own servants, well… Haslehaw knew not to spread such rumors. She'd avoid scandal that way, even if she never allowed him to do the honorable thing and marry her.

For he could not force the issue. It was *her* honor to protect. And so it was her decision.

But was there a slight opportunity—and Olive appeared to think that there was, and after all, she was a woman—that Lilianna wanted to hear from him?

Wanted to relive that awful moment, if only to see if they could reconcile? Be together?

Be happy?

"And where do you think you're going?"

Arthur cursed as he ran toward the door. "Damn you, Olive, for always being right!"

His cousin's laughter followed him as he threw himself through the door. "I suppose we know now why you never ask for my advice—good luck!"

Good luck. Well, he was going to need it. Arthur had given no hint of exaggeration to his cousin when he had given his honest appraisal of the situation: there was not chance in hell this was going to work.

But he could never live with himself if he didn't try.

Chapter Nineteen

I T WAS VERY difficult to practice Mozart when one's doorbell was jangling so unpleasantly.

It was a convenient excuse. With a great sense of relief, Lilianna closed the lid of the pianoforte and checked her gown for any marks or scuffs. There was clearly someone coming to visit and it would not do to be untidily dressed.

Even if her entire family was away, there was no need to let the side down.

"Y-You must be perfect. You m-must always be p-perfect!"

The marchioness's words resounded in Lilianna's head as she settled herself gracefully upon the sofa, ensuring to tuck one ankle behind the other and keep her head upright.

There. She was ready.

Unfortunately, that did not appear to matter a great deal. The doorbell kept jangling, the clanging echoing resounding louder and louder in Lilianna's mind as she waited for…

Her shoulders slumped. "Of course."

After living with servants her entire life, it was still getting difficult to remember that she was here alone with only Clarke for company. And as hard-working as she was—and Lilianna had never realized how difficult it was to press a gown until her maid had roped her into helping in the laundry room yesterday—it was perhaps too much to expect the only servant in the house to do everything.

Which left… her.

"Clarke?" Lilianna called out hopefully.

After all, she'd already made the mistake once of opening her own door. Look where that had led.

Pushing aside the memory of her and the earl upon the table sternly and chastising herself for even allowing the thought to meander into her mind, Lilianna turned and leaned over the sofa, as though that would help her voice travel farther.

"Clarke?"

No one answered. Not her, and not the door.

Lilianna sighed. "How long does it take to recover from scarlet fever, anyway?"

Surely, it could not be long until Humphreys was well again and Frank out of danger—then her family could return, and all the other servants, and her life could go…

Well. Not back to how it was.

She could never do that, not now she knew what it was to love and be loved. Not now her innocence had been taken from her. Not now she could never look another man in the face without flushing and knowing, or at the very least guessing, what was lying underneath his trousers.

Lilianna cleared her throat as the doorbell continued to jangle. *Well, no one else is going to answer it.*

Sighing as she swept out of the drawing room into the hall, she wished not for the first time that her Papa had listened to her desperate please to update their front door. The fashion was quite different now, with an elegant triptych of colored glass being quite the thing. Not only would it look better, she had argued vehemently last spring, but it would make it easier to see who was approaching the door before it was opened.

As it was, John Chance had said it was a frivolous waste of money and that front-door fashions, if there were such a thing, would soon swing back around to solid doors.

And so Lilianna unlocked the door and grasped the handle firmly, ensuring to place her coldest, most aloof expression on her face before she opened the door to the mysterious stranger.

Just half an inch of gap was enough for Lilianna to slam it back into place.

"Lilianna!"

"Absolutely not," she muttered fiercely as the door slid back into its frame.

But it hadn't. Somehow, despite the rapidity with which she had moved, Arthur Nelson, Earl of Taernsby and general tyrant, had managed to get a toehold into the crack of the door.

It was quite literally a toehold. Lilianna resisted the urge to tread on the very tip of his boot that had managed to wedge itself into the gap and instead glared profusely at the man who was attempting to force his way into her home.

Her home!

"Go away!" she snapped.

Arthur groaned. It surely hurt, Lilianna realized, to have one's toes the only thing preventing solid wood and solid wood from colliding, especially as she was putting her entire weight against the door.

Good.

"Lilianna, I just want to speak with you."

"I said, *go away!*"

"You're really hurting my—"

"Good!" Lilianna cried, heaving her body against the door and wishing to goodness she had a brother or two at home to assist her.

When she halted, she caught the momentary gaze of the man who was attempting to shove his way inside. His mouth was open, his eyes dull, his posture stooped. And he arrested her with his searching gaze.

He was… devastated. It couldn't just have been the pain in his foot that was making him look that wretched, could it? She had never seen a man look so injured yet so besotted. It gave him a look of agonizing desire and she did not know what to do about it.

Pulse quickening, stomach twisting, core aching, Lilianna

tried to think, but her full attention was caught by the twin focuses of pushing the door closed—or attempting to—and the look on Arthur's face.

The man she—

She did not, could not, would not love him. How could she betray herself so utterly by loving a man who was so treacherous?

"You really are hurting my foot," Arthur said, his voice strained in the effort to keep the door open. "But if it will help you forgive me…"

His voice trailed away, cheeks a burning red as he caught her eye again.

Lilianna blanched. How did he—it was most unfair that he could do that. Treacherous men should not be able to look so… so innocent! Betrayers should not be allowed to look betrayed.

Swallowing hard and hating that he had managed to wrong-foot her with just a few words, Lilianna looked away from his face. Perhaps that would help. Perhaps ignoring his pleading eyes was the only way she could keep herself resolute.

Unfortunately, that meant she had to look at something else.

Lilianna's eyes widened. "That's… That…"

Her mind could not fathom and therefore her words could not explain what she was seeing. Because it couldn't be.

"You're holding something," she whispered, her shoulder still leaning against the door. "You… It's…"

It wasn't a roomful of roses, like the first time the Earl of Taernsby had attempted to gain her attention. It wasn't a thousand delphiniums—Frank had been most meticulous and counted—which had made her mother sneeze for three days.

It was a forget-me-not. In a pot.

Lilianna swallowed. All the fight drained out of her, her shoulder lifted from the door, and Arthur gasped as his foot was released.

He did not attempt to push forward, for which she was grateful. In this moment, in this state, she was not sure she was cogent enough to stop him.

"A forget-me-not."

Arthur appeared confused. "Of course."

"Of course"? There was no "of course" about it.

"You remembered," Lilianna said, forcing herself to meet his eyes. They were still sky blue, still passionate and brimming with emotion.

She swallowed. He was still, in many ways, the Arthur with whom she had fallen in love. But no, he was also the man who had betrayed her, who had kissed another woman just after they had—

"Lilianna," Arthur said firmly, slamming a hand against the door just as she attempted to close it. "I remember everything you say."

"I don't want to listen to you." She spoke through tears, tears that threatened to fall at any moment.

"You must hear it. You must hear me." Arthur spoke with an urgency Lilianna had never heard from him before. "You must because I am falling apart without you, and—and I love you."

I love you.

Three small words. They shouldn't mean anything, not when spoken by a rake who had clearly no real understanding of just how painful it had been to see him, watch him take up with a mistress mere hours after they had shared... shared everything.

Yet they were the words she craved to hear from him again, and again, and again. Words that promised so much and yet so little. Words that were meant to be shared between two people who were committed to each other. Who could not imagine life without each other.

Who trusted each other.

Lilianna swallowed. Oh, it would be all too easy to be taken in. That handsome face, those features arranged in a most contrite manner. A man she wanted to believe.

The charming, bragging, confident man she had met—he had been enchanting, yes. But it was the other Arthur, the one only she had seen, who was so endearing.

She saw him now. The bluster, the fight, was all gone, and there instead was a man who truly felt his loss. The loss of her.

Try as she might, Lilianna could not prevent warmth from suffusing through her. He missed her—truly missed her. It wasn't that other woman's door he was crashing through, trying to beg for forgiveness.

It was hers.

"You hurt me," she whispered.

She'd let go of the door. She couldn't fight it and him, and the determination to resist the charms of Arthur Nelson, the Earl of Taernsby, was taking a toll.

Slowly, Arthur opened the door. He did not step in.

"I know," he said quietly, pain etched across his tense face. His fingers gripped the potted plant tightly.

"I don't know how to forgive you," Lilianna said softly.

"I know," came the solemn response.

"I don't know if I can trust you again." It hurt, saying these words, but it was almost like the poison of the betrayal was being drawn out with every syllable.

Perhaps it was being with Arthur. To be with him was to adore him, worse luck, and Lilianna had tried to fight off his charms before and knew it was a losing battle.

She needed him. Part of her always would.

"I know."

"You don't deserve to be forgiven," she heard herself saying stiffly.

She noticed the slight slump of his shoulders, the bob of his Adam's apple as he appeared to collect himself, the overall demeanor of defeat.

And it was intoxicating.

"I know," Arthur said in a cracked voice, his eyes dropping to his hands and the plant within it.

She was about to make a decision, one she could not easily take back. She might regret it, yes.

She might live the most incredible life.

Sniffing back a chuckle and hardly knowing if she was going to laugh or cry, Lilianna managed to say, "It is most irritating that it is getting easier to forgive you with each passing second!"

Arthur grinned, and it was the perfect medley of shy and uncertain and bold and brash. "I know."

Her Arthur. Hers.

It was almost too much, but Lilianna managed to hold herself together.

She was a Chance. She was the eldest daughter of the Marquess of Aylesbury. She was not going to burst into tears on her front step.

Probably.

"I… I thought love would be easier than this," she confessed before she had time to draw the words back.

A shadow flittered across Arthur's face. "I know—so did I. Though if I am entirely honest—"

"And you had better be, my man, because I have had it up to here with your surprises!"

"I just… I was going to say…" Arthur swallowed and a shiver of fear flickered up Lilianna's spine.

What on earth was he trying to say? Was this, in fact, not a reconciliation—merely an apology?

Her pulse skipped a painful beat. Surely, life would not be that cruel. Surely, Arthur would not be that thoughtless, raising her hopes to a peak before forcing them to tumble off a cliff?

"I never thought any woman would want me," Arthur said in a rush.

Lilianna could not help it. She laughed. A snort would have been unladylike, and therefore, it most definitely could not have been a snort that had left her nose, but it had been something very akin to one.

"You don't expect me to believe that, do you?" she said incredulously. "What, because you were too handsome, or too charming, or too skilled in the bedchamber?"

She had spoken the words to be derisive and anyone else

would have flinched at such coldness.

But Lilianna saw to her great surprise that Arthur did not. He held her gaze, strong and yet not forceful, preventing her from looking away as her stomach flipped over.

"No," Arthur said softly. "Because… Because I am not good at being honest. Not all the time—but I am getting better. I want to get better, be better, for you."

Lilianna hesitated. It was charming, in a way, but it was also painful. No one liked to admit that they had any faults and Arthur had therefore been brave to admit to such.

But no one liked to think that the person they loved had any faults, either. None of the princes or heroes in her novels ever had any faults, other than a predisposition to accidentally tear the clothes off their lovers' bodies, which, in Lilianna's opinion, could happen to anyone.

Standing here, looking deep into Arthur's eyes and knowing that they had almost lost whatever this was because of their pride and disinclination to speak, Lilianna had to accept that Arthur had faults. He was not perfect.

And neither was she.

Forcing down the panic that rose, Lilianna took a deep breath. "I am not perfect."

"You said that as though you were admitting to murder," Arthur said with a lopsided grin.

She shoved him hard on the shoulder, but he took the momentum and did not step back. "I am being serious!"

"So am I," he teased. "'Perfect'? You think I want perfection, Lilianna?"

Years of upbringing rose up in her defense. "What man doesn't want a perfect wife?"

"And I would quite agree with you there, except it appears that our definitions of 'perfect' are not the same," Arthur pointed out. He was still holding the forget-me-not plant in a terracotta pot. "For example, I think you most perfect when you are irritable and angry at someone, shooting them down with deft language and a sneer that a queen would envy."

Lilianna tried not to smile. "You're being ridiculous."

"Perhaps we both are," he said gently. "Perhaps we both love each other, and foolishly wanted perfection, and instead have an even better perfect. The perfect we make together."

The perfect we make together.

It was a heady thought, and not one Lilianna could fully understand. Perfect… together? Perfect was always something she had to do alone, achieve alone, maintain alone.

Perfect was being alone, after all: set apart, different, better than everyone else.

The idea of being perfect together, of their imperfections washing away the sharp edges of their characters…

Lilianna laughed helplessly. "I desperately wish to stay angry at you."

"And?"

"And you know full well I can't," she admitted. "I love you, that's the trouble."

She loved him. It felt strange to say it like this, in these circumstances, on the front step of her Bath home, where any passerby could see them.

She wouldn't have it any differently.

"You—You do?"

Lilianna scowled. "Don't give me that, Arthur Nelson. You know full well how I feel."

"Yes, but you haven't said it before," said Arthur, his grin growing. "God, it's wonderful. Say it again."

"No." Heat seared her cheeks.

"Please?"

"Absolutely not," Lilianna said, drawing herself up sternly. "You've heard it once. Let that satisfy you."

"If I get on my knees and beg, will you say it again?"

The heat was descending now, past her décolletage, past her breasts, settling in her core and burning an ache in her that Lilianna knew could only be quenched by Arthur's touch.

She was most definitely not going to smile. "Fine. I love you."

The bland tone with which she spoke did not appear to matter. Arthur was almost vibrating with happiness and Lilianna could not help but laugh at the transformation.

"You are daft."

"Probably," said Arthur ruefully. "And you're not the only one to think so, so who am I to argue with the majority?"

Lilianna stiffened.

He wouldn't... Surely, he wasn't referring to other women now. After all of this.

Evidently, the concern was revealed in her eyes, for Arthur's own widened in panic. "No, not—I meant my cousin! My cousin, the Countess of Barlow, she came to see me. She thinks I'm a complete dolt."

Lilianna considered for a moment. "Good."

"She's also very much with child."

"You mean she'll have the child soon? And you did not know?"

He winced. "I think 'extremely' was the word she used," Arthur said, shaking his head. "It's most trying, discovering that you were so wrong. I hope that the next time I need to apologize to you, she won't be there to make me feel like a complete clod."

The next time...

Lilianna reached forward and took the forget-me-not pot out of Arthur's unresisting hands. She placed it on the floor in the hall and turned to the man whom she knew now she could not live without.

"Arthur," she said seriously.

His lips twitched. "Lilianna."

"I'm being serious."

"So am I," he said with a grin.

She shook her head and sent him what she hoped was a wry look, completely unable to dislike this man who had at first forced, then schemed his way into her affections. "I need to know. About her."

His smile disappeared and his brows puckered, but he did not shout, or scream, or step away. Instead, he said, "She was my mistress, last year. I last saw her—October? November? It's been over for months, certainly for me. I suppose I was not clear enough with her. You… Well. You saw the letter."

She had. She had also seen a kiss.

As though the blackguard could read her mind, Arthur nodded. "I didn't expect her there and I never initiated a thing. I mean, I didn't want what she did. It's over. It never really began, not really. I didn't feel anything for her comparable to what I feel for you."

Lilianna tried to listen, really listen to his words. Not just his words, but his tone. His honesty. The depth of pain in his words.

He was telling the truth.

"We're going to argue all the time," she said quietly.

Arthur grinned and somehow pulled her into his arms. The safety and security and need of his gesture poured through Lilianna's gown, unable to be ignored.

"I know," he said, his grin broadening. "Isn't it wonderful?"

Lilianna sighed as she wound her fingers in his hair and knew, as she felt his pulse throb through her arm, that she was home. "I suppose so."

The kiss was slow, and reverential, yet still packed so much heat, Lilianna whimpered in his mouth. Needing him, craving him, was nothing like finally being sated by the crush of his lips or the teasing aches of his touch.

Arthur tipped her head back, deepening the kiss, and Lilianna welcomed him in as the only man who would ever possess her in this way. Every part of her leaned against him, desperate to be closer, to abandon herself to the pleasure this man could give her.

His tongue swept across her own, sparking tingles of need through her body, her nipples aching to be touched as she ground her breasts against his chest.

More, more, she needed more—and he would give it to her. Soon.

Even in the giddiness of the kiss, however, Lilianna was vaguely aware of the sound of a carriage slowing to a stop just behind the man who was kissing her so thoroughly. When Arthur pulled away, both of them panting heavily, a voice erupted behind him.

"I trust my daughter on her own for a *few* days! Always insisting she'll be fine alone, that nothing will happen to her!"

"J-John, d-don't—"

"Get off me, Florence, I need to rip this man apart!"

"*Papa!*"

"Frank, I don't want to hurt you or your mother. Let go!"

"Ah," said Lilianna helplessly as Arthur turned around with wide eyes. "I think we may have some explaining to do."

Chapter Twenty

April 25, 1840

THERE WERE HUNDREDS of them.

"You put that back right now, I haven't finished with it."

"You're never going to hit the post. I don't want to wait for—"

"Ouch! You did that on purpose!"

"You got in the way! What was I supposed to do?"

Arthur had never been on a battlefield. He knew that was a fairly fortunate thing—he had a great deal of things to feel fortunate about, and not ever having to brandish a weapon in true anger was one of them.

Still. Even without having to fight for queen and country, he had a relatively good idea of what the viciousness of battle looked like.

And this? This did not compare.

A woman younger than Lilianna wrenched the croquet mallet from the man's grip and brandished it like a sword. "I told you what would happen if you touched my balls, Michael!"

"Erm," said Arthur helplessly, gesturing in their direction.

"You were taking too long, you arrogant monster!"

"Erm, Lilianna?" he said again.

The sunshine was pouring down on the vibrant lawn, though if he were any judge, there would soon be some sort of massacre upon the green. The numerous Chances whose names all intermingled with one another's were crowding now, some taking the young woman's side and some taking the young man's.

And it was getting heated.

"—boil your own head in—"

"Lilianna?" Arthur attempted again.

"I beg your pardon?" said Lilianna breezily, turning away from an older couple who must have been an aunt and uncle, and smiling. "Ah, I see Gwen and Michael are at it again."

"—come any closer and I'll—"

"They look like they could really hurt each other," said Arthur, a little unsure.

True, he did not come from a large family, but he was quite certain that sisters were not supposed to gesticulate like that.

"They might do, I suppose," said Lilianna without a hint of concern. "Those are two of my cousins. They've been fighting like that for—oh, what would you reckon, Uncle Frederick?"

"Since birth?" the older man said in a quiet voice, a wry smile across his high forehead. "It alarmed us at first, but to be honest, we've just got used to it. They never actually hurt each other."

"Well…" said the woman beside him who had to be his wife. She was long-limbed and possessed an elegant beauty—even with the fine lines on her face and the silver in her hair—as if she had been carved from marble into an ancient Greek statue.

"Only the once," Lilianna said hastily. "What's a broken wrist between family?"

Arthur tried to smile. "Ah. Right. Yes."

There were very few situations in which he found himself that he felt completely overwhelmed, but as it turned out, meeting one's future wife's entire family in a rambunctious house that sprawled over many floors and appeared to hold more family members than he knew what to do with was one of them.

Dear God, there was so much to take in. Over there, a pair of aunts, he was almost certain, nattering away on a picnic rug that had been spread under a wide oak tree. There were two gentlemen on horseback riding about the place, one of which was a brother of Lilianna's but Arthur could not see from here which one. There were a trio of cousins laughing about in a secretive circle, evidently discussing something hilarious, and one who was sketching alone in a notepad, brushing off any attempt one made at conversation. Two more cousins—*dear God, how many cousins did she have?*—appeared younger, him reading a book, her embroidering something that looked strangely like a mallet cover.

And there was the noise of the croquet lawn.

"Look, let's just start over again," said the broad-shouldered gentleman whose mallet appeared to be the offending one in the circle of Chances. "Then we can—"

The derisive laughter from his elegantly attired sister made Arthur wince. "You would suggest that, just as you were losing!"

"You aren't going to… I don't know," said Arthur helplessly to Lilianna. "Intervene?"

She raised an imperious elbow. "What, and lose an eye?"

"Careful, there!"

It was fascinating, Arthur had to admit. He'd met the Aylesbury branch of the Chance family before and considered them all rather sedate and calm, other than Frank. Nothing wrong with that, of course. But still. Calm. Quiet.

It was only now that he had been introduced to the whole plethora of Chances that he realized why. Clearly, it took a great deal of calm to remain in a family like this.

Chaos. It was chaos!

"How—how many cousins do you have again?" Arthur asked quietly as her aunt and uncle disappeared back into the house, the heat of the sun apparently too great for them.

Lilianna's eyes twinkled. "Twelve, at the last count. Why?"

"Twelve," he repeated faintly.

How she managed to keep track of them all, he did not know. It would take keeping an intricate list of parents, dates of birth, and personality traits for anyone to keep sane and maintain an understanding of them all.

At the very least.

"I don't know what you're worried about," Lilianna was saying. "They all like you."

"Ah," said Arthur, his shoulders relaxing.

"Most of them," she said lightly before stepping away, her light-green gown flowing behind her.

He blinked. "'Most of them'?"

She was laughing by the time he'd caught up with her, and Arthur nudged her gently with his shoulder. "Now, was that nice?"

"No, but it was hilarious—the look on your face!" Lilianna grinned.

Their mingled laughter joined with the shouting of the croquet lawn and the remonstrances from the two aunts who clearly did not see the point in getting up to adjudicate the onslaught, preferring to stay on the ground in the shade and yell from their comfortable seats.

Arthur couldn't blame them. He'd never met a family for such… such noise, and excitement, and at the end of the day, they would all be pleasant to one another and pass the port.

It was unheard of.

The last four and twenty hours had been a whirlwind, and not one he could have imagined.

"Look, Lilianna," Arthur said quietly as they rounded the croquet lawn and reached the graveled terrace on the south side of the impressive house that was Stanphrey Lacey, the seat of the Duke of Cothrom, Lilianna's oldest uncle. Except that the man was now the "dowager duke," they seemed to call him. He had gone against all expectations and made his son, his heir, the next duke, before his own demise. The other brothers had taken notice, from what he'd gleaned at dinner last night, and were considering doing the same. Apparently. He'd got that right, hadn't he? The Chances were certainly like no family he had known. "When I said I would visit your family, I did not expect… this."

"May I borrow her?"

Arthur blinked. Another cousin, one whose name he had already forgotten, had appeared as if out of nowhere.

"I *said*, may I borrow her?" The dark-haired woman raised an eyebrow as he spoke. "Is he always this slow?"

"Often," Lilianna said with a giggle.

Instinctively, Arthur pulled his future wife to his side, clasping his arm around her shoulder as though she were going to be forcibly removed from his presence.

Only then did he feel ridiculous.

What did he think was going to happen? They were here with her family. There was no possibility anyone would harm her.

Still. The idea of Lilianna leaving him to talk to someone else, even for five minutes, was not one he could countenance with joy. It had been only a week, after all, since they had come to this fresh understanding, and to lose any time with her felt like a bereavement.

Now that he had her, Arthur never wanted to let her go.

"No," he said stiffly. "No, you may not."

The cousin's eyes widened. "Why not?"

"Because we are heading inside to have an important conversation with my parents," Lilianna said smoothly.

Arthur's head jerked round. They were?

"Of course you may borrow me after that," Lilianna was saying. "But you know how it is with Papa."

The cousin rolled her eyes. "My father is exactly the same. He is most tiring. Adorable, obviously, but tiring. Good luck!" She scampered off, skirts flying as she threw herself into the melee on the croquet lawn. "I thought Gwen was winning. Why have we started again?"

A chorus of groans and shouts echoed up from behind them. Arthur turned his head to watch but was forced to straighten up as Lilianna pulled him through the open French windows and into the resplendent drawing room.

"Your parents," he said resignedly. "Right."

Arthur's hopes sank. It wasn't that he did not like the Marquess and Marchioness of Aylesbury. Given the circumstances that they found him in just a week prior, kissing their daughter fiercely in full view of the whole world, it was a miracle that they had shared a civil word with him.

An important conversation. It sounded ominous.

"So," he said bracingly as Lilianna led him into the hall and along one of the maze-like corridors that typified the place. "Your parents. Precisely what is it that we needed to discuss?"

Their wedding. Their marriage. His past conduct. The way he had hurt the woman he so loved…

Lilianna pushed open a door and did not answer. "In."

Arthur threw back his shoulders, ignoring his future wife's giggle. "Right."

He stepped into the room.

It was empty. At least, it was empty of people. It appeared to be a music room, a chaise lounge placed near a large pianoforte with a harp in one corner by a large bay window and a trio of violins carefully placed on a rack mounted on the wall. There were several bookshelves packed with what appeared to be sheet music, and a small set of comfortable-looking sofas and armchairs where it looked like performances were given.

"A… A music room," Arthur said aloud.

"Precisely," Lilianna said, closing the door behind her with a snap.

"And your parents are?"

"Far from here, I would hope," she said darkly. "My mother has been nothing but trouble since we announced the engagement. Did you know there is apparently a *wrong* way to announce an engagement?"

"Erm—"

"And a wrong way to select bridesmaids, too, which is of course the way I wanted to do it," Lilianna said with a roll of her eyes. She strode across the room and stood beside a sofa. "Aren't you coming?"

Arthur hardly knew whether he was coming or going with

this family. Did they ever do anything by halves?

"What do we need to discuss?" he asked urgently, dropping his voice in case they swiftly entered the room. "With your parents. What will we be discussing?"

Lilianna grinned as she dropped onto the sofa behind her. "Nothing."

Arthur blinked. "'Nothing'?"

It was rather like being forced to learn a new language, staying at Stanphrey Lacey. It had sounded like such a pleasant idea: a country retreat, the opportunity to escape the busyness and gossip of Bath and London, and yes, spend some time with Lilianna's family.

Her family. He had presumed, evidently wrongly, that she had meant her parents and siblings. If Arthur had known that every Chance who had any possible connection to them would also be in residence at Stanphrey Lacey, he may have brought his cousin along, even if so eminently about to become a mother. For his own protection.

"I don't understand," Arthur said slowly, lowering himself to sit beside Lilianna on the sofa. "I thought you said…"

"You dolt," Lilianna said, not for the first time, and as far as he could make out, not for the last, either. "I just wanted time alone with you! My family are… well-meaning—"

"Yes," Arthur agreed hastily.

"—and inquisitive—"

"Most definitely," he said, perhaps more heartily than he should have done. The youngest Chance cousins were only eighteen, and he'd been forced to answer a great deal of questions about himself that only the naïve could get away with.

"—and imposing," Lilianna finished with a laugh. "I want you to myself, just for ten minutes."

Arthur reached out an arm and she slid swiftly against his body, tucking her head on his shoulder. "Just ten minutes?"

"You never know with my father. He can sniff out two people attempting to hide like—well. That is not a story the family likes repeating," Lilianna said, her voice thrumming against his. "And I need you, Arthur. You. Just ten minutes with you will set me up for the week."

Pride rushed through Arthur as his hand pulled tightly around her, tugging her closer to him.

Just ten minutes.

It would not be long before they would have all the ten minutes. When they would be married, and no one would be able to get in the way of—though from what Arthur had learned about Frank in the last few days, perhaps when left with just the marquess's family, even she would find a way to intrude.

The minutes ticked by, a clock or metronome or something on the pianoforte whiling the minutes away. Arthur's pulse slowed, the coziness of having the woman he loved pressed up against him, her feet tucked up on the sofa under her skirts, taking him into a state of relaxation he had not experienced in…

He couldn't remember when.

Arthur pressed a kiss onto Lilianna's forehead. "Have I told you that I love you today?"

"Not nearly enough," came the breathy response as she chuckled against him. "But you can tell me now, if you wish."

Tilting her head up, she met his eyes with hers, and a jolt of need throbbed through Arthur's core. Trying not to be attracted to Lilianna was like attempting to tell the sun not to shine. You just didn't do it.

"You know I'm going to kiss you," Arthur muttered, "if you look at me like that."

"Why do you think I'm looking at you like this?"

She tasted of sunshine and glory and passion and need, and Arthur could have wept. Having her in his arms was like nothing else he had ever experienced. God, he felt weak whenever they were together, weak for her. He could feel the pent-up need in Lilianna exploding out as she almost *crawled* into his lap, straddling him with layers of cotton and desire pooling around him.

Arthur tried not to place his hands on her buttocks, drawing her closer. He tried not to moan in the kiss, deepening it as he nibbled on her lower lip, knowing it would always elicit a whimper of lust. He tried not to think of the growing stiffness between his legs.

He failed at all three.

"We should probably stop," Lilianna murmured, breaking the kiss only momentarily to murmur her terrible suggestion.

"I will if you will." Arthur gasped, burying his head in her breasts and wondering how on earth they were going to stop themselves from ravishing one another again before the wedding.

It had been her idea. Something to heighten their need for each other, Lilianna had said.

As though their passion *needed* any heightening.

Eventually, though, Lilianna pulled away and slipped regretfully to the side back onto the sofa. "We can't."

"Oh, we can," Arthur growled, reaching for her. *Parents be damned, cousins be damned, servants be damned—*

"We shouldn't."

He groaned. "That's a different statement."

"Both are true," Lilianna pointed out, her hair mussed in that delicious way that always made Arthur want to pull all the pins out and see the mass of locks descend past her shoulders.

Arthur sighed, glancing down only momentarily to his thighs. Well, he knew what effect all that kissing would have on him. He'd just have to hope that it would calm down before he had to step outside this room.

"Do you ever… I mean, do you ever wonder?" Lilianna asked quietly, leaning an elbow on the back of the sofa.

Arthur raised an eyebrow. "Care to be more specific? I mean yes, have I wondered anything, ever? Of course I have."

She brushed the back of her fingers across his cheek and Arthur stilled. Her presence was unlike anything he had ever experienced. Worshipful and almost constantly irritated. It made his stomach tighten and his pulse jump every time they touched.

"I meant," Lilianna said softly, "do you ever think… that we may not have found each other?"

Dread curdled in him. *Yes. Too often.* In the dead of night, when he sometimes awoke having forgotten that all was mended and they would be married within days. They had procured the special license necessary, cost be damned, and soon…

"You mean, if you had not forgiven me?" Arthur asked quietly.

"If we had not forgiven each other."

"If you hadn't invited me to stay in your empty house, and seduced me?"

Lilianna smiled. "If you hadn't continued proposing to me every five minutes."

"If you hadn't thrown yourself in my arms," he countered. True, he had put himself in just the right position to catch her, but he couldn't admit to doing *all* the chasing.

"Yes. That."

Arthur swallowed. *Yes*, he wanted to say. *Yes, it frightens me. Of all the ladies of the* ton, *of all Society I could have encountered— God, I'd gone out that night to find a wife and I had told myself that it did not matter who it was.*

How stupid I was.

"We were meant to be," he said aloud, curling his fingers around her waist, not to pull her closer, but just needing to touch her. "Meant to be."

Lilianna chuckled softly. "Despite everything."

"Perhaps *because* of everything," Arthur said with a shrug. "My cousin seems certain that you are the only woman in Christendom who would have me, anyway, so I'm afraid you're stuck with me."

Another laugh. "I like your cousin."

"Yes, she's passable, I suppose," he mused, joy fluttering in him. "I like yours. I like your brothers, too, and your sister. I like your family, all of them, despite the rabble and chaos."

"They are *not*—"

A scream interrupted their conversation, echoing around the gardens and somehow filling the house.

"How could you break my mallet?"

"Now you won't be able to cheat, you cheater!"

It was followed by a roaring chorus of defending one and attacking the other. Arthur's eyes widened. "Is that it, then? Has war been declared?"

"It appears so," Lilianna said dolefully. "I suppose I should go out there and help my aunts adjudicate."

"Yes, I suppose so."

Neither of them moved. Moving, Arthur knew, would mean leaving this little sanctuary they'd found. A moment of calm, of peace, before the next round of chaos.

"Your family *is* a rabble," Arthur said softly as a scream echoed from the direction of the croquet lawn.

"Yes, they are, rather," Lilianna agreed with a chuckle. "But don't worry. I am in no hurry to add to the rabble."

Arthur swallowed, his mouth suddenly dry.

Well, it was natural to think about, wasn't it? And his cousin was due to have her baby apparently at any moment, which was a new level of fear Arthur had not thought it possible for him to possess.

And so the mind wandered. Wandered to the potential child that could enter his life from a different quarter. A part of him, and a part of Lilianna. A child, their affection in physical form.

"You told me you wanted heirs," she said quietly.

"I do," he said. "But I can wait—forever if need be. If that's not something you want, you needn't worry. My cousin can have the next earl. I'll have you."

"I do want them," she whispered. "Children. Someday. With you."

"God, I love you," Arthur said suddenly.

Lilianna raised an eyebrow. "Where did that come from?"

"What, a man can't say he loves his betrothed?"

"Not without cause, not like that," she said with a laugh.

"What was that all about?"

Arthur could have attempted to put it into words. He could have said how he could hardly believe he had his very own Chance, a member of a family that was wild, yes, but had welcomed him with open arms. How he was dazzled by her every moment he was with her. How she made him want to be a better man, a better person. How his life would never be the same now that she was in it, and he was so happy, so painfully happy.

"Thank you," he said instead. The other words could wait. He had a whole lifetime to say them. "Thank you, for loving me."

Something shivered across Lilianna's face and she leaned forward, kissing him briefly on the lips before settling back.

"Of course," she said simply. "I don't think I could stop loving you now, even if I tried."

"Don't," Arthur said hastily.

Lilianna giggled. "I'll bear that in mind."

Epilogue

May 1, 1840

"ABSOLUTELY NOT." LILIANNA spoke as decidedly as she could manage, but that did not appear to matter.

"But—"

"I said, *absolutely not*, and I meant it," said Lilianna steadfastly, glancing at her mother for support.

Her mother shrugged. "It *is* a l-lovely idea, Lil."

"It is entirely unpractical," she pointed out, smoothing her gown with shaking fingers as the carriage rattled along. "Of all days to suggest such a thing."

"But this is a day that you will surely wish to remember for the rest of your life!" Evelyn said with wide eyes, seated opposite her in the carriage. "If anything, this is the perfect day!"

"I don't know why you are fighting with her on this," Frank said conversationally to their cousin. "You know what she's like—ouch!"

Lilianna had not intended to hit her sister quite that hard, but the London streets were cobbled and jerked the carriage about something dreadful.

Still. It had ceased the debate, at least for a few moments.

That was all she needed: a few minutes to gather her thoughts. This was, after all, an important day. Perhaps one of the most important of her life. Lilianna did not want to spend it hounded by family.

"I just think a portrait of you in this gown, your hair just so, the light exquisite at this time of year," said Evelyn with a sigh, looking wistfully out of the window. "I honestly cannot think of a good reason why you should say *no*."

Lilianna rolled her eyes. "Because I am getting married today, Evelyn—I don't have time to sit for a portrait!"

The day had finally come. Arthur had stated just yesterday that it was never going to arrive at this rate because the weeks had appeared to lengthen ahead of them, preventing them from getting closer. Lilianna had pointed out that days were always one single length, and it was his own longing that was getting in the way.

He had replied, she was almost sure. Precisely what he had said, she could not recall. She had been too busy kissing him at the time.

Her mother sighed wistfully. "And th-there's the church. You know—"

"'Your father and I got married here,'" chorused Lilianna and Frank.

Lilianna gave her sister a grin. "How many times have we heard the story?"

"About a million times," said Frank with a groan. "And, worse luck, now I will have to steel myself to hear about yours over and over again."

"I don't s-see wh-why that would be s-so arduous." Their mama smiled as the carriage slowed to a halt. "It w-was a b-beautiful d-day, and—"

"Tell me at the wedding breakfast, Aunt Florence," said Evelyn kindly as the carriage door was opened by a smiling footman. "As it appears I won't be permitted the opportunity to draw today."

"You could find another model," Lilianna pointed out as she stepped out of the carriage onto the pavement, her heart hammering.

Well, here she was. Outside the church. The church where

she would become Lilianna Nelson, Countess of Tacrnsby.

It did not feel real. It would not feel real until she saw Arthur. Only when she could be absolutely certain he was here, and the last few weeks had not been a complete figment of her imagination, could she relax.

"Skirts are most inconvenient," Frank was saying behind her. "I long for the day I can wear trousers in public."

"F-Frank!"

"Well, honestly!"

"You know," Evelyn said in a quiet voice as Lilianna stared up at the church, "I could paint *you*, Frank."

Lilianna turned to see her sister's slackened jaw.

"Me? You don't want to paint *me*."

"I want to paint someone new, that's all I know, and I am finding it almost impossible to find someone willing to sit and model for me," said her cousin with a sigh, helping Lilianna's mother out of the carriage, where the marquess accepted the waiting footman's hand. "Please, Frank, what do you say?"

Lilianna laughed again at the look of horror on her sister's face.

"Sit? Without moving, for hours and hours, without my notebook?"

"Oh, I will let you keep a notebook if it helps," said Evelyn, her eyes bright. "But you won't be able to move."

"Never," declared Frank.

Evelyn nudged her in the arm. "You are most disobliging, you know."

"Yes, I get that a lot, now I come to think about it," said Frank vaguely. "Honestly, Mama, this ribbon in my hair is most—"

"It's impossible, I give up!" their cousin said over Frank's words. "I will never find a model."

The church door was thrown open by footmen, revealing Lilianna's father, who grinned and offered her his arm. "I thought I heard Frank. Lil, you're early."

"'Early'?"

"On time, that is," her father amended, drawing her hand through the crook of his arm. "Didn't I tell you that the tradition is that the bride is always late?"

"Late? We have a schedule to keep to," said Lilianna with a smile that was braver than she felt. Now that the church door was open and she could see the congregation...

All here to see her wed. To see her marry the Earl of Taernsby, rake that he was.

Assuming he had arrived...

Lilianna gripped her father's arm. "Papa, he—he is here, isn't he?"

John Chance, Marquess of Aylesbury, grinned. "He arrived three hours ago. Something about wanting to make sure that even if you turned up ridiculously early, you would know he was determined to marry you. Load of nonsense, if you ask me."

Her gaze had been flickering across the myriad of guests as he spoke and her father's words faded into the background as her eyes finally alighted on the man she had been longing to see.

Arthur.

He was standing right at the front of the nave, wearing a smart coat and what appeared to be—oh. Forget-me-nots, in his buttonhole.

Lilianna's pulse skipped a beat and she stepped forward the instant the organ started.

Well, what is the point in waiting?

The aisle appeared to be at least three times longer than she remembered when they had met with the vicar a week ago, but eventually, she and her father reached the front.

Her papa was grinning as he stood beside Arthur. "Told you she'd be here early."

"I never doubted her," muttered Arthur with a wink for Lilianna.

After considering for a moment whether or not to be offended, Lilianna decided not to be. There was a very winning charm in her future husband's eye and this was the moment that she had longed for over the last—what, days? Weeks?

Sometimes, it felt like months. Like her whole life had been consumed by this man who had entirely surprised her and made her feel… feel special. Wanted. Loved. Cared for. In ways she had never known before.

As though he would fight the world just to stand by her side.

"Dearly beloved, we are gathered here today in the sight of God…"

Lilianna started as her father pulled her a step to the side.

"Who gives this woman?" the vicar asked.

"I do," said her Papa in a clear voice. He grinned, squeezing his daughter's hand as she was amazed to see tears in his eyes, then lifted her hand to place it on Arthur's arm.

Lilianna blinked back tears of her own. "You are ridiculous, Papa."

"Always was, always will be," he said gruffly. He turned to Arthur. "And you—if you ever hurt her, I swear to—"

"Yes, th-thank you, d-dear," said his wife swiftly, pulling him away.

Lilianna swallowed a laugh. Even at her wedding, it was her mother who was truly in charge.

Someone squeezed her hand, and this time, heat flooded her core and made her gasp. She looked up.

Arthur was looking as though he would quite like to pull her behind one of the church's large pillars and do something most disgraceful to her. But he was also looking at her like…

Like his whole world had just stepped into the church. Like he had been incomplete before her hand was resting on his arm. Like he would fight anyone, her father included, to keep her.

Lilianna could not help but laugh. "Hello."

"I said, when we first met, that I supposed we would just have to get married," Arthur said seriously under his breath as the vicar's words droned on. "And I meant it."

A shiver rippled up Lilianna's spine. "And I called you a dog and told you to unhand me at once."

"I can't tell you how glad I am that we're here."

The temptation to lean up and kiss him firmly on the mouth was overwhelming, but Lilianna was interrupted by her father agreeing to something. Before she had truly readied herself, before she could have imagined it would be that time already, they were speaking their vows.

"I, Lilianna Gwendolyn Florence Chance, take you…"

The entirety of the way through her vow, Lilianna did not take her eyes away from Arthur. Then it was his turn. There he stood, proudly declaring in a church that he would forsake all others and love her, all the days of their lives.

"In the presence of God I make this vow," Arthur said with a wink.

Lilianna resisted the urge to roll her eyes. Honestly, he was such—

There were gasps, and cries of astonishment, and laughter from her brothers and Lilianna could not think.

It was difficult to think, after all, when one's new husband had scandalized everyone in Society by pulling her into his arms right there by the altar and kissing her senseless.

For a moment, Lilianna lost herself in the kiss. Flutters were aching within her and she felt whole, right with the world standing here in Arthur's arms. Her hands crept up to his neck, fingers tangling in his hair, pulling him closer, and—

The kiss ended. She blinked up with hazy eyes and saw him smile ruefully.

"Ah," Arthur muttered. "I suppose everyone is going to be stunned?"

Lilianna glanced to her right. There sat her parents, her mother beaming and her father frowning. There was Frank, and Evelyn, her two bridesmaids: the latter sighing with happiness and the former rolling her eyes. Her brothers were there, glowering at Arthur as though he had committed a crime. The rest of the Chance family sat behind them, their faces alternating between shock, hilarity, confusion, and disbelief. The only friendly face missing was Olive, who was confined to her birthing bed, the baby likely days away.

"*Stunned* is one word for it," Lilianna said, pulling herself regretfully from his arms and trying not to notice how her cheeks burned. "Ah. Vicar."

The clergyman who had married them moments ago was as red as she felt. "I-I have never—not in all my days. Not ever have I—"

"I suppose not," said Arthur cheerfully. "But then I never did things the easy way."

No, none of our journey has been easy, thought Lilianna contritely as they stood and listened to the flustered vicar attempt to give their wedding sermon. Arthur had pursued her for her childbearing and she had resisted him as she had resisted so many other gentlemen.

And he had crept under her defenses and made her love him.

Most disobligingly.

It took approximately an age for the wedding service to finish, but finally, Lilianna was slipping her hand into Arthur's, his fingers gripping hers tightly, and they were walking down the aisle to sighs and shakes of heads from their guests.

"You can't please everyone, I see," Lilianna said darkly.

"There's only one person I want to please," Arthur growled as they stepped outside the church.

"*Arthur!*"

She did not really put up much of a fight. Why bother, when she was being kissed so thoroughly by the man she loved?

The marquess shouted. "Taernsby, put her down!"

"You are not winning over my father, you know." Lilianna grinned happily.

Arthur sighed, rolling his eyes in a dramatic manner. "I married you, didn't I?"

She hit him, quite hard, on the chest.

"Ouch—Lilianna!"

"Well, that's what you get," she said cheerfully as their guests started to pour out of the church, chattering away. The gossip of their kiss in the church—in church!—would have circulated the whole of Society… what, by lunchtime tomorrow?

"Come here," Arthur said quietly.

For a moment, she thought he was going to attempt another kiss. Not that she would have been averse to that, necessarily.

Instead, Arthur pulled her around the church, away from the happy chattering guests. His fingers were warm on hers, the growing spring sunshine only adding to the fire within her.

He was hers. And she was his.

"Look, I have to tell you something," said Arthur as they halted on the opposite side of the church to the open door.

And Lilianna's heart broke.

Oh, it was so unfair. Why did this have to happen—and on her wedding day, of all days! What could he possibly have to tell her now?

"Are you ready to hear it?" Arthur said softly, stepping so close to her, she could feel his breath on her skin.

Lilianna nodded, eyes determinedly not tearing up as she—

"I am devastatingly in love with you, Lilianna Nelson," said Arthur with a wicked smile.

Her lips parted. "You complete ass!"

He stopped her mouth with a kiss and she resisted at first, furious at him, hating how easily he had twisted her emotions.

The instinct faded as soon as it had come. There was nothing like being held in his arms, nothing like his scent, the heat of him, the ardor that poured from his lips onto hers. Lilianna clung to him, his hands swiftly moving around her waist to hold her close.

"Your face," he teased, brushing kisses down her jaw to her ear.

"Your head on a spike, that's what it would have been," Lilianna said darkly—or at least, as darkly as she could manage while being ravished in such a glorious manner.

Arthur chuckled. "You think I'd be so foolish as to try to keep a single secret from you?"

"I know how foolish you are, so don't pretend… Oh…"

It was difficult to speak. Speaking was not the sort of thing one could easily manage when one's delectable husband's hands were doing that to her buttocks.

"God, I want to get you home and peel all these layers off and—"

"We have a wedding breakfast to host," Lilianna reminded him as strongly as she could manage.

And the memory that there were several hundred people still pouring out of the church and likely as not waiting for them at her parents' home made her step back.

The growl in Arthur's throat resonated deeply within her, but she forced herself to be firm. "No—*no*, Arthur. We'll have years—years and years—to enjoy one another. Today is about celebrating with family."

Arthur's face split into a grin. "Years and years. I like the sound of that."

Lilianna returned his smile as she slipped her hand in his. "Do you think we'll ever get tired of each other?"

And he looked at her as though she were the center of the world, and perhaps she was. Perhaps the two of them together were the focal point for all life in the world, and Lilianna would not have been surprised.

"You and I?" Arthur quipped with a snort. "Not a chance in hell."

Hello! Thank you so much for reading *Not a Chance in Hell*, the sixth novel in my The Chances series. I truly hope you enjoyed it and fell in love with Arthur and Lilianna just as much as I did.

If you've read the first five books of this series (which I strongly recommend!), then you'll have seen the four uncles fall in love, as well as Lilianna's cousin Thomas. I had always wanted to write a series of brothers, but I could never 'meet' the characters who were quite right. After waiting years to meet them myself, I have had a lot of fun writing the four Chance brothers—and now we're diving into their children. Make sure you go back and read them!

If you're desperate to read the happily ever afters of Lilianna's siblings, then you'll want to look out for Book 11, *Take a Chance on You* (Samuel's story); Book 18, *Why Take the Chance?* (Benjamin's story); and Book 19, *A Calculated Chance* (Frank's story). Our next Chance adventure is going to jump to a different branch of the Chance family…

Being an author can be a lonely business, but knowing that there are readers from all over the world who are going to adore my stories makes it all worthwhile. Thank you for your support, and I hope you love reading more of my books!

Happy reading,
Emily

About Emily E K Murdoch

If you love falling in love, then you've come to the right place.

I am a historian and writer and have a varied career to date: from examining medieval manuscripts to designing museum exhibitions, to working as a researcher for the BBC to working for the National Trust.

My books range from England 1050 to Texas 1848, and I can't wait for you to fall in love with my heroes and heroines!

Follow me on twitter and instagram @emilyekmurdoch, find me on facebook at facebook.com/theemilyekmurdoch, and read my blog at www.emilyekmurdoch.com.